"Just make me your wife."

"And will that be enough for you?"

"I come from a long line of women who know how to make do."

Rod had made a vow to keep her happy. To put her first. They both knew the ground rules, after all, he reminded himself as he drew Nancy into his arms, covered her mouth—warm and giving—with his. And he remembered, as he had every night since the night this baby had been conceived, every curve of her slender body, her responsiveness, her eagerness to please as well as to be pleased. And he wanted her—more than he should, more than he'd thought he could ever want a woman.

More than he would ever dare let on.

But afterward, he wondered if it had been just sex. Because if this was just sex, why did he feel as if someone had ripped a hole the size of a football field in the center of his chest?

Dear Reader,

Once again Intimate Moments is offering you six exciting and
romantic reading choices, starting with *Rogue's Reform* by
perennial reader favorite Marilyn Pappano. This latest title in
her popular HEARTBREAK CANYON miniseries features a
hero who'd spent his life courting trouble—until he found
himself courting the lovely woman carrying his child after
one night of unforgettable passion.

Award-winner Kathleen Creighton goes back INTO THE
HEARTLAND with *The Cowboy's Hidden Agenda,* a
compelling tale of secret identity and kidnapping—
and an irresistible hero by the name of Johnny Bronco.
Carla Cassidy's *In a Heartbeat* will have you smiling
through tears. In other words, it provides a perfect emotional
experience. In *Anything for Her Marriage,* Karen Templeton
proves why readers look forward to her books, telling a tale
of a pregnant bride, a marriage of convenience and love that
knows no limits. With *Every Little Thing* Linda Winstead Jones
makes a return to the line, offering a romantic and suspenseful
pairing of opposites. Finally, welcome Linda Castillo, who
debuts with *Remember the Night.* You'll certainly remember
her and be looking forward to her return.

Enjoy—and come back next month for still more of the best
and most exciting romantic reading around, available every
month only in Silhouette Intimate Moments.

Yours,

Leslie J. Wainger
Executive Senior Editor

Please address questions and book requests to:
Silhouette Reader Service
U.S.: 3010 Walden Ave., P.O. Box 1325, Buffalo, NY 14269
Canadian: P.O. Box 609, Fort Erie, Ont. L2A 5X3

ANYTHING FOR HER MARRIAGE

KAREN TEMPLETON

Published by Silhouette Books

America's Publisher of Contemporary Romance

To Jack, as always, who encouraged me to write full-time long
before I sold my first book; and to our boys, who I have no
doubt will continue to provide plenty of fodder for my stories
for years to come.

Acknowledgment

Thanks to Kathy McCormick, M.D., who helped me sort out
the medical what-ifs. Blame me, not her, for any goofs that
resulted from blending fact and fiction.

SILHOUETTE BOOKS

ISBN 0-373-27076-3

ANYTHING FOR HER MARRIAGE

Copyright © 2000 by Karen Templeton-Berger

This edition published by arrangement with Harlequin Books S.A.

Visit Silhouette at www.eHarlequin.com

Printed in U.S.A.

Books by Karen Templeton

Silhouette Intimate Moments

Anything for His Children #978
Anything for Her Marriage #1006

Silhouette Yours Truly

*Wedding Daze
*Wedding Belle
*Wedding? Impossible!

*Weddings, Inc.

KAREN TEMPLETON's

extensive background in the theater and the arts, combined with a lifelong affinity for love stories, led naturally and inevitably to her writing romances. Growing up in Baltimore, she studied art, ballet and drama, and wanted nothing more than to someday strut her stuff in a Broadway show. However, although she was accepted into North Carolina School of the Arts as a drama major, halfway through she switched to costume design, in which she received her B.F.A. degree longer ago than she cares to admit.

A twelve-year stint living in New York City provided a wide variety of work experiences, as well as her husband, Jack, and the first two of her five sons.

Between sons two and three, the family moved to New Mexico, where Karen established a thriving in-home mail-order crafts business that she gave up almost the instant the family bought their first computer and she discovered the magic of erasing mistakes without Wite-Out. Now writing romances full-time, she says she's finally found an outlet for all that theatrical training—she gets to write, produce, design, cast and play all the parts!

IT'S OUR 20ᵗʰ ANNIVERSARY!
We'll be celebrating all year,
Continuing with these fabulous titles,
On sale in May 2000.

Chapter 1

"I'm not asking you to marry the man, Nance." The blonde popped yet another miniature quiche into her mouth. "Just talk to him."

Nancy stifled a sigh. Just think—she could be home, curled up with the cats, watching Dick Clark and stuffing her face with Ben and Jerry's Cherry Garcia ice cream. Instead, she was hiding out in her best friend's kitchen, guzzling white wine and aching to ditch her shoes. Two hundred bucks, and the things hurt like hell.

"And say what, exactly?"

"Well, how should I know?" Elizabeth Sanford rearranged the hors d'oeuvres on the dish in front of her with one hand, the other rubbing the bulge underneath her emerald velvet maternity tunic. "But we've got to do *something*. Did you get a good look at him? Lord. He looks as if his dog just died."

Oh, yeah. She'd looked. There he'd sat in one corner of the burgundy leather sofa, all alone and all in black. Rod Braden. Gorgeous, wealthy, brooding. A man she'd secretly lusted after off and on for nearly four years, ever since the day she and Elizabeth had met him when they were both working for the same Realty agency in Detroit. Stayed out of the way for nearly two years while he and Elizabeth quasi-dated, a relationship that died a quick, painless death once Elizabeth met the man who became her husband. With Elizabeth safely out of the picture, Nancy even sort of made a play for Rod, only to quickly realize that goal had "lost cause" written all over it.

Not being the beating-her-head-against-a-brick-wall type, however, she'd shrugged it off, and life went on. Since then, Rod had been in and out of a second marriage, then suddenly moved to Spruce Lake, Michigan, setting up permanent housekeeping in the old mansion Elizabeth had sold him—with a straight face, no less—as a summer home some time back. And Nancy had even shrugged that off, too, figuring what did Rod Braden's life have to do with her?

Then she walked in an hour ago, caught him staring all sad and lonely like that into the fire, and the thought came, "It's the dawn of a new millennium—do you know where your libido is?" Followed closely by, "Oh, hell."

Two glasses of wine later, she was still waiting for the booze buzz to override the sexual whatever-it-was buzz so she could join this party and act like something resembling a normal person. Or better yet, pass out. Her right little toe already had.

"Well?" Elizabeth said, shoving another tidbit into her mouth.

When the going gets tough, the tough change the subject. "You know, if you don't stop eating like that, you're gonna weigh five hundred pounds."

"Hah! You're just jealous because I have boobs now and you don't."

Nancy smirked. Not that she'd turn down an extra cup size, should anyone offer, but mammary inadequacy was the least of her problems.

"And you're not wriggling your way out of this." Squinting, Elizabeth nodded at the low-necked, high-hemmed, velvet scrap of a dress Nancy had picked up cheap because it was the only size three left. "If nothing else, that outfit alone'll jump-start his heart. Shoot, *my* eyes bugged out when you walked in tonight. You rent those legs, what?"

Elizabeth's husband, Guy, burst into the kitchen, a pair of empty platters in his hand, a diamond stud glinting in his ear. He glanced at the plate in front of his wife. Sighed. "Uh, honey—isn't the idea to *fill* the plate?"

She looked down, gasped at the four lonely goodies left on it. Guy chuckled, then kissed Elizabeth on top of her upswept hair. "I knew there was a reason we bought twice as much food as we thought we needed," he said, then replenished the plates, giving Elizabeth a wink and a grin as he backed through the swinging door to the living room, balancing all three plates in his hands.

Nancy tried, really tried, to ignore the needles of envy that pricked her heart, and her conscience. She'd had no idea, when she'd relocated to Spruce Lake a couple months ago to take Elizabeth's place at Millennium Realty, the small agency Elizabeth ran with her mother and Guy, just how much her friend's bliss would point out the pathetic emptiness of her own life. Not that she wasn't thrilled for Elizabeth, but seeing her and Guy together twisted a knife in her lonely, underused heart. Oh, sure, intellectually, she knew a woman didn't *need* a husband and children. But the fact was, there were times Nancy envied Elizabeth so much it hurt.

"Hey!" Elizabeth duck-walked from behind the counter, grabbed Nancy by the wrist. "If you're gonna go gloomy on me, you can go do it somewhere else." She pushed open the door, shoved Nancy out into the living room. "Now go ye forth and schmooze."

Nancy turned to find herself face-to-face with a gently swinging kitchen door.

"And don't even think about coming back in here!"

Nancy sighed. Life was much better when *she'd* been the pushy one.

She finished off the wine, setting her glass on somebody's

abandoned paper plate on top of the piano, then smoothed sweaty palms down the front of her dress. Where, she wondered through the muzzies, had the twenty-plus years gone since Stanley Cohen's bar-mitzvah dance, when Debby Liebowitz double-dared her to ask Norman Sklar to dance? To this day, though, she had no idea if she had or not. Funny, the way the mind blots out traumatic memories. She tugged discreetly at her underwire bra, which she could have sworn was growing teeth.

"You still there?" she heard from behind the door.

"Bite me," she whispered in reply, and was rewarded with an evil giggle. She told herself it was boredom keeping her there. Her social life since moving here was not what one would call rip-roaring. Of course, one reason she'd left Detroit was to get away from a singles scene that, from the perspective of a burned-out thirty-four-year-old, had grown very tired. Like a fool, she'd naively thought the camaraderie of small-town living, of being close to Elizabeth and her new family— Guy had three young children already—would help ease the constant ache of being alone.

Wrong. Think *Pleasantville* on steroids. Which meant Nancy felt more a fish out of water than ever. And her mother, bless the dear thing, clearly thought aliens had sucked out her daughter's brain. Who moved someplace where who knew what kind of men lived? As it was, Belle Shapiro had yet to forgive Nancy for letting one husband slip through her fingers, never mind that the creep considered himself exempt from mundane concepts like…oh, fidelity?

"But," Belle had conceded eventually, "maybe this is for the best. If you never have children, you won't know the heartache of having a thirty-something unmarried daughter throw her life away. No, it's true—I wouldn't wish such pain on anybody, least of all my own daughter."

And the woman wondered why Nancy only called once a week.

But back to the here and now, where she was bored and pleasantly snockered and, okay, ravenous for male attention.

She watched as, seemingly oblivious to the chatter of two dozen other guests in the room, Rod leaned forward, his elbows on his knees. His long, graceful fingers absently hugged a wineglass as he communed with the fire, which acutely defined the sharp angle of his brow, the clefted chin, and a mouth worth bronzing. His lips were fuller than usual for a man, yet not the least bit effeminate. His eyes and hair were nearly the same color, neither brown nor gold, but something in-between, the cut-and-styled-one-strand-at-a-time hair liberally threaded with gray at the temples.

She took another swig of the wine.

He started when Cora Jenkins, the agency's office manager, laid a hand on his shoulder, her teeth strikingly white against her dark skin as she smiled, then apparently introduced her date to Rod. He seemed to shake himself, but immediately offered a hand and a smile to the distinguished gray-haired man, as well as a few words spoken in a low voice that, even at this distance and tangled in the threads of other conversations, threatened to turn Nancy inside out. Still.

She twined one wayward curl around her finger, her brow furrowed. Two things thirty-plus women weren't supposed to get: zits and crushes.

Uh-huh.

Like she really needed this pair-of-tortured-souls-adrift-in-the-night routine. A pair of tortured souls who had absolutely nothing in common, who probably couldn't sustain a conversation for more than twenty minutes without tripping over some major issue. The man was the epitome of upper-crust conservatism, while Nancy was…not. He probably didn't even like cats.

Oh, come on. This had nothing to do with cats or backgrounds or anything else. The fact was, polite or not, he'd blown her off. More than once. So—excuse me?—whence came this urge to wrap her arms around the man and tell him everything was going to be okay?

The wine, the heat, the sensuous mingling of perfumes, food aromas, laughter, all fed a gentle whirring in her head that

quickly burned a tingling path along her skin…and somehow
propelled her across the room to stand in front of someone far
too perfect for the likes of her. Women like Nancy just didn't
hook up with fair-haired, racquet-club-raised Golden Boys.
Women like her—

He looked up, and the hurt and loneliness and disappointment in those golden eyes yanked her soul up by its bootstraps.

Women like her had no business fantasizing about a relationship with a man like Rod Braden. Then again, she never
saw a man who looked more like he could use a little kindness
right now. A little feminine…understanding.

Come to Mama, she thought, and got all warm and fluttery
inside.

Rod smelled her perfume before he saw her, briefly wondered how—or why—he'd picked out her scent among the
dozen or more in the room. He'd apparently startled her: her
mouth was open, as if she'd been about to say something.
Instead, she lifted a hand to her lips and dissolved into laughter.

He thought she might be just this side of drunk, but when
she cleared her throat and looked directly at him again, her
deep brown eyes were clear and sparkling, even if her face
was flushed.

"That's not fair," she said, obviously tamping down a new
round of giggles. "I was trying to come up with some wick-
edly clever line, and you screwed me up." She sucked in a
deep breath. To quell nerves? "So. How're you doing?"

Loaded question. He took another sip of wine, considering
how to answer, even more seriously considering why things
that had been comatose not ten seconds before were stirring
now. That voice of hers probably had something to do with
it—low, sensuous, and far too rich to come out of a body so
slender that she probably didn't dare venture outside on blus-
tery days. He smiled. He couldn't help it, any more than he
ever could help the braided feelings of terror and attraction
Nancy Shapiro's presence sparked, had always done from the

first time they met, right before he'd starting dating Elizabeth. Her natural ebullience, the way her emotions crackled around her like summer lightning, at once exhilarated and appalled him. Wasn't that he didn't like her. He did. More than she knew, more than he'd ever before admitted to himself. But she was too lively, too witty, too bright, too…much. This was a woman, he suspected, who threw things during a fight, who slammed doors and burst into copious tears and got in a person's face, demanding immediate and honest answers.

Living with someone like Nancy would be an invitation to a coronary. He'd always preferred cool, together blondes— soft-spoken, genteel women who never raised their voices. That both his ex-wives and any number of also-rans, including the woman in whose house he now sat, were cool, soft-spoken blondes…well, perhaps he really wasn't in the mood to ponder such things too hard this evening.

Any more than he was in the mood to ponder why Nancy Shapiro had such an unsettling effect on him. Why he wanted to see if he could span that deceptively fragile waist with his hands, if she kissed as irrepressibly as she laughed. Which made *no* sense, since Rod didn't want to touch or kiss Nancy or get close enough to do either anytime before the *next* millennium. He wanted peace, not passion. To be left alone to nurse the wounds left from this last marital debacle in a nice, cozy cocoon of self-pity, maybe to have a chance to salvage what was left of his tattered relationship with his children, who had spent the holidays skiing in Aspen with their mother and her latest boyfriend.

So why was he here?

And why was Nancy frowning down at him like that?

He realized her hands, tipped with long, glossy nails nearly the same burgundy as that bit of a dress she wore, were planted on her hips. Or where her hips would be, if she had any. Humor sizzled in those molasses eyes as she said, "Didn't your mother ever tell you it's rude to stare at people?"

Despite his rotten mood, he grinned again, surprised to realize his cheeks actually ached a bit from the effort. The firelight sent streaks of molten amber through her curls; his fingers itched even as need warmed his belly.

"The way you have your hair fixed tonight," he heard himself say, "it's very flattering. Really shows off your eyes. Did you know—" he hurtled into the compliment with the recklessness of a kid on a sled after a foot-high snowfall "—in this light, they're nearly black?" He shook his head. "Extraordinary."

Extraordinary was right. What the hell was that all about? Something trembled, deep inside him, as he took a sip of the same glass of wine he'd been nursing for nearly an hour, watched those eyes grow huge with astonishment. Her hand went to her mouth again, and she turned away for a moment. He couldn't tell in the firelight, but he thought she might be blushing. Then she laughed again, softly this time, before twisting around to plop down beside him.

No! She wasn't supposed to...

He wasn't supposed to let her....

So why'd you give her the compliment, lamebrain?

Good question.

Now her perfume tendrilled through his bloodstream, the sweet-spicy scent threatening to dissolve what little common sense he had left. And somehow, they fell into a natural, easy conversation, about nothing, really. Elizabeth and Guy, the weather, the party, if he knew the couple standing next to Maureen Louden, Elizabeth's mother. Nancy was one of those touchy types, her hand often landing on his sleeve as they talked. Not that he minded. She got him to laugh, several times. And he enjoyed the sound of her laughter, too.

He was enjoying *her.*

She bent over to adjust the ankle strap on one of her black silk high heels; her back was flawlessly clear underneath a pair of crisscrossed spaghetti straps, her fragile-looking spine smooth as a string of pearls. Her boisterous hair teased her shoulders, teased his libido even more.

How many times in the past had he pretended not to notice her interest? How many times had he told himself *he* wasn't interested? Yet, here he was, lonely and horny and in no position even to think what he was thinking about this lovely, lively woman who was all wrong for him, even as her very presence threatened to cause a major testosterone explosion. Hell, even if she *had been* his type, it was probably a pretty safe bet she was looking for a husband. Whereas he was definitely not in the market for a wife. At this point, he doubted he could even deal with a mistress. Not that he'd ever had one before, but...

Oh, never mind. This train of thought led nowhere he had any desire to visit, thank-you-very-much.

"Aunt Nancy? Where's Mama?"

From nowhere, a pajama-clad urchin with dusty-blond hair appeared in front of them. Guy's youngest, he figured. A brief pang of bittersweet longing to have his children back as babies, to see if he could do better this time, mingled with a profound sense of relief at not having to. Hannah was sixteen, Schuyler thirteen going on forty. Rod hadn't been much better at fathering than husbanding. One day, maybe he'd figure out where he'd gone wrong.

But not tonight. Tonight he had about all he could handle convincing himself he didn't want to take Nancy Shapiro to bed, to bury his face in all that hair, to seek, in those delicate, graceful arms, a few hours' surcease from being a major screwup.

"Hey, sweetie," Nancy crooned to the child, who scrambled up into her lap, pushing up the already short dress to danger level. Unconcerned, she propped her feet on the edge of the coffee table, allowing Rod a ringside view of her legs—thin but surprisingly shapely, and sexy as hell in sheer black stockings that glittered whenever she moved. When he tore his eyes away from her gams, however, he noticed the expression on her face as she cuddled the little boy.

He tore his eyes away from *that* much more quickly.

"Mama's in the kitchen, honey," he heard her say, and the I-want-one-of-these tremor in her voice was unmistakable. "You want me to get her?"

"C'n you take me to pee?" he said. "The bafroom's all dark."

There went the laugh. "I think we can handle that."

He felt them get up, watched as Nancy carried the child out of the room. For a skinny woman, she had the cutest fanny he'd ever seen.

A few minutes later, she returned, sans child, but didn't sit. Instead, she stood in front of him, twisting a silver ring on her right index finger, as if trying to get up the nerve to say something. Someone turned up the music; people raised their voices accordingly, and she rolled her eyes. Then she grinned, and leaned over, close enough for him to feel her breath on his cheek, see the slight swell of breasts peeking above the low sweep of the dress's neckline that by rights should be too small to arouse anyone. She smelled...edible.

"I, for one, am not in the mood to watch everybody else get kissed at midnight," she said. "So whaddya say we get out of here, go get a cup of coffee?"

He looked at her as if she'd suggested they go skinny-dipping in the lake a few blocks away. "I don't think—"

But she shook her head, sending that riot of hair into a tizzy. "Forget thinking. It's New Year's Eve, and who said we have to suffer everyone else's happiness?"

She had a point. She also had the greatest mouth in the world. Generous. Spellbinding.

And she had a point.

Nodding, he pulled himself off the sofa, retrieved their coats from the den, then ushered Nancy outside without even saying goodbye to their hosts.

Nancy gasped in the glacial blast that mugged them the instant they hit the porch. The light snow needling their cheeks was nothing, but damn it was cold. Underneath her black velvet swing coat, she couldn't stop shivering.

Not just because she was cold, though.

"At the risk of sounding tacky," Rod said next to her, his

breath nearly opaque in front of his face, "my place or yours?"

She tried to laugh, but the sound froze before she could get it out. "I'm too snockered to d-drive," she chattered, "b-but I live just on the other s-side of the lake. If we go there—th-that is, if you t-take me there—I can walk b-back over here tomorrow and p-pick up my c-c-car."

He nodded—she was beginning to see a pattern here—then led her to his car, a gleaming silver luxury model sedan that had been the focus of a huge media blitz last year. *His* media blitz, she figured, when he was still head of marketing for Star Motors. Before he let her in, however, he shrugged off his topcoat—made, no doubt, from wool plucked from the underside of some hardy beastie that grazed on grasses found only on the most remote mountain range in the world—and slipped it around her shoulders.

She wanted to crawl inside this coat and live here for the rest of her life. Well, actually, she wanted to crawl inside his car first, because the coat didn't cover her feet, which had turned instantly into two-hundred-dollar popsicles.

They got in. Then they sat there. His car smelled of fine leather and his cologne and some indefinable rich smell she could easily get used to. Nancy had no idea what Rod was thinking, but she was thinking... Actually, she was shivering too hard to think, but *ohmigod* was in there somewhere.

She'd just invited Rod Braden for coffee. And he'd accepted. Somehow, she squelched the laugh threatening to blow her cool. She also remembered she *had* worked up the chutzpah to ask Norman Sklar to dance that night all those years ago. And that *he'd* accepted. She hadn't felt like this since that night—apprehensive, excited and damned smug.

If a tad perplexed. Rod hadn't said anything, or even started the car. Confined in a small space with him, he seemed...

She sighed inwardly. You know you're in trouble when you can't remember the last time you had sex. Hell, she only vaguely remembered who she'd last had sex *with*. Not that her list of partners would impress anyone, but what a pitiful comment on her thirty-four years that—if she was generous, mind—the best she could muster were two *forgettables* and one *adequate*. And let's not go into which one of those had been her husband for five years.

The buzz alone from two feet away was already more exciting than any of her actual experiences. She wasn't sure whether that was more of a comment on Rod or her, but she decided analyzing it would serve no viable purpose.

She jumped when Rod cleared his throat. "Where's your place?"

"Oh. Right." She gave him directions; the three-minute drive passed in silence. But now she noticed a sharpness to the buzzing that put her on guard, made her wonder if she'd edged closer to losing it than she'd realized. Had she misinterpreted politeness as actual interest? Wouldn't be the first time, God knew. By the time he pulled up in front of her lakefront bungalow, she decided she'd let her imagination run away with her. From her.

"Look," she said on a sigh, "I'm sorry. I don't know why I asked you to leave with me. I guess the wine impaired my reason more than I'd thought, but it's obvious you'd really prefer to be alone, so if you want to back out, it's okay—"

"Nancy," he said softly, and she turned, chiding herself for getting off on just the way he said her plain vanilla name. She'd left her porch light on so she wouldn't kill herself trying to come in later; the feeble light illuminated features that, before tonight, she'd only seen radiate grace and confidence. "If I hadn't wanted to come with you—with *you*—I wouldn't have. God knows, I didn't want to be at that party, but I don't really want to be alone, either." His lips tilted into a sad smile. "Done that enough this past little while to last a lifetime."

Her heart had become stuck somewhere at the base of her neck and was now pounding uncomfortably. She shifted, looked out at the puny snowflakes twirling in his headlights, which he'd yet to turn off. "Yeah. I know how that goes." She shuddered in the cold, swung open the door. "Well, come on, then. The inaugural meeting of the Spruce Lake Lonely

Hearts Club is about to begin.'' She hesitated, leaned back into the car. "Um, I have cats."

Rod chuckled. "There's a cure for that, you know." She rolled her eyes. "How many are we talking about?"

"Seven."

He just stared at her, then said, "Just don't ask me to clean out their boxes."

"Not a problem."

They got out of the car, icy pellets pricking their faces as they walked up to her door. Her smooth leather soles skidded on the filmy layer of snow underfoot; Rod caught her before she fell, keeping his hand on her elbow the rest of the way. Underneath his coat, she shivered, imagining what it would be like to cuddle against that solid chest.

Naked.

She pushed the thought away, then sighed when it came right back like an eager dog with a stick in its mouth.

All these years, she'd entertained fantasies of what it would be like to have Rod Braden do more than smile politely at her, imagined being alone with him, receiving his undivided attention. Well, she didn't have to imagine *that* any longer. So, um, how far did she dare push her luck?

Oh, come on. Since when did she rely on luck to accomplish anything? If you want something, you go after it. Okay, so maybe that philosophy had more than its share of holes, but it sure as hell beat waiting around for life to fall into your lap. Maybe tonight wasn't her only shot at upping the ante with Rod Braden. But maybe it was. Why heap more regrets on the already towering pile she'd accumulated over the years?

She took a very…deep…breath.

"And another thing—'' she fumbled for her key in her Judith Lieberesque purse, managed to get it in the door ''—I haven't quite decided yet whether or not to seduce you."

Talk about your stunned silences.

"Well," she said to the doorknob, since someone had to say something and apparently the honor had fallen to her, "I don't hear retreating footsteps, so I guess that's a good sign."

What she heard was a short, startled laugh. "Are you always this forthright?"

Still staring at the doorknob, she nodded. Then his hands were on her shoulders, turning her to him, the look in his eyes...*oy.*

Something told her she wasn't the only person standing here who went after what they wanted.

Chapter 2

Considering they were standing outside in the dead of a Michigan winter, his mouth should have been cold. It wasn't. It was warm and soft and scrumptious. Crème brûlée scrumptious. The thought began to pick at Nancy's wine-and-lust sodden brain that this was one of those kisses that could easily lead to Other Things. Okay, so she'd been the one to bring up Other Things to begin with, but still. This might turn out to be a pretty memorable New Year's, after all.

It had been a long time since anyone had paid this much attention to her mouth, other than her dentist, and he definitely did not count. Rod's kisses—somewhere along the way, she realized they'd shifted into plural—were as tender and magical as moonlight. And had zipped past *adequate* some time ago.

Nice, she thought, letting one hand stray up to that what-a-waste-on-a-man hair. It was soft. Glorious. Like the kisses, which just kept a-comin'…and then were suddenly over. Her heart knocking against her ribs, she licked her lips, expecting him to pull back. Instead, he tucked her underneath his chin, against his chest. Just…held her. Like she mattered.

She refused to faint.

"I'm sorry," he said, and she couldn't help the laugh.

"What? That wasn't your best effort?"

This was where he was supposed to laugh, too. He didn't. And that brought her head up to see into his eyes. "You're right," he said in a voice as soft as the kiss they'd just shared. "I'm not exactly the world's happiest human being tonight. I'm also not exactly the most principled."

Brows went up. Brows went down. "Meaning?"

"Meaning, men like me aren't supposed to spend all evening wondering how a woman kisses."

Somehow, she managed to stay cool. "And this is supposed to upset me?"

That got a smile. And a whisper of a caress along her jaw. "Doesn't a woman expect a man to be interested in her mind, not her lips?"

She backed up. An inch, maybe. "And you're from what planet? Besides, it's kinda hard to be interested in my mind when you haven't yet had a chance to get to know it. My lips, on the other hand…" Nancy cocked her head, frowning. "Just how were they, anyway?"

He ran his thumb across the lower one, the black leather of his glove smooth, erotic. She quivered. "Five-star," he said, and she grinned.

"So…does this mean—?"

His own mouth tweaked into a smile at that. "It means you have great lips, that I wanted to kiss you and I'm damn glad I did. And I'd like that cup of coffee now, if you don't mind, before I freeze my butt off."

She pulled away, not sure what to think. "And we're just going to go inside my house and have coffee and act all normal after a kiss like that and I basically announced I'd like to jump your bones?"

"Sounds like a plan to me."

Shaking her head, she finally unlocked her front door. "Sounds *nuts* to me." But since the alternative was sending Rod back out into the cold, wretched night, she figured she'd play the hand dealt her. At least she'd gotten a little necking out of the deal. And a hug. God, she'd forgotten how good hugs felt.

She flipped the switch by the door, illuminating the pair of hand-painted lamps on either side of the sofa. A chorus of meows greeted her as a motley group of animal-shelter refugees stalked, scampered and minced over to give her what-for for leaving them.

"If I'd realized I was having company, I'd've stuck name tags on 'em," she said, checking the thermostat just as the heat clicked on, anyway. When she turned, Rod was holding Bruiser, a gray-and-black long-furred behemoth with a serious attitude problem, whose motorboat purr she could hear across the room. The cat wore a goony expression not unlike Elizabeth's for Guy.

"Man, you work fast." She folded her arms, stared at the animal, who was giving her this *Nanny-nanny-boo-boo* look. "This is surreal. Bruiser hates everybody. He even flinches whenever *I* try to touch him, and I saved his tush."

The cat bumped Rod's jaw and upped the volume on the purring. "Maybe," Rod said, his mouth doing something wonderful and sexy and would you believe she was now envying her own *cat?* "Maybe he lets me hold him because I don't come on too strong. You know…I gave him a chance to come to me?"

She narrowed her eyes at him. "Meaning?"

But all he'd do was grin at her. Just like the damn cat.

Reckless. That was the only word for it. It was also a word Rod never, ever applied to himself.

Until tonight.

A single glass of wine and Nancy's perfume couldn't possibly account for how being with this woman made him feel. Yet there it was. And here he was, having just shared a purely need-driven series of kisses the likes of which he hadn't experienced since he and Cindy Lawrence had grappled in the back seat of her father's Caddy when he was fifteen. Strike that. Hot though they may have been, the kisses of a pair of hormone-crazed teens had nothing on what he and Nancy had just shared. The woman just gave a whole new slant to the concept of "good things in small packages."

He was, he realized, completely mesmerized. Fascinated. Her exuberance, her cards-on-the-table attitude had infected him, drugged him, invigorated him.

Still, thanks to Elizabeth, Rod knew enough of Nancy's situation to realize the woman wasn't quite as carefree as she seemed. She, too, bore the scars of a failed marriage, of a succession of relationships that never panned out. Her gregariousness could very well be a cover for vulnerability—and that meant risk.

A risk he wasn't at all sure he dared take, was even less sure he wanted to avoid. In any case, where was the harm in sharing coffee and cat fur, perhaps easing each others' loneliness for a couple of hours?

"Nice place," he said, letting down the now-bored cat. He scanned the joyfully cluttered room as the pride of felines gave him the cautious once-over from their assorted perches. The air was slightly damp, heavy with steam heat, redolent of old house and coffee and her perfume. But not, he noted with profound relief, of cat box. "You decorate it yourself?"

She shucked off both coats—a startlingly seductive move— laying them carefully over a lushly purple velvet sofa in the middle of the room. The glance she tossed in his direction confirmed his suspicions: that, for all her bravado, her self-confidence had taken one too many hits this past little while. "Very funny."

"No, really. It's great." And it was. Perhaps more secure than the woman herself, the room thumbed its nose at the world. It glittered and glowed and reached out and said, "Come to Mama." He'd never even been in a place like this, let alone lived in one. His was a world in which designers ruled, paying lip service to clients who wanted to believe the big bucks they shelled out for "their" look counted for something. The result, therefore, of every place he'd ever lived was tasteful perfection, all show and no soul.

Not here. Nothing matched, everything was off-balance, yet somehow, it worked. Jewel-toned pillows and a crocheted throw fought for position on the sofa, which was flanked by a couple of upholstered chairs, sitting at odd angles atop a thick-piled Turkish rug. What looked to be someone's turn-of-the-century black iron gate stood guard in one corner, in front of a pair of rich velvet draperies. White shelves, crowded with books in all sizes and shapes, many toppled onto their sides, as well as a herd of early-American folk-art animals, fit themselves in wherever they could find space among various little tables and side chairs, some of which were hand-painted in offbeat colors and patterns. Magazines and books lay everywhere there was a surface, many opened to whatever page she'd been on when something else caught her attention. Wedged between the bookcases and draperies was an eclectic collection of high-quality artwork—primitive landscapes next to delicate floral watercolors next to bold, contemporary abstracts. But all by itself, centered on one otherwise bare wall, was a three-foot high, extraordinarily fine, oil of a nude peering over her shoulder at the observer, one hand braced on her hip.

A nude with wild, curly hair just this side of auburn, eyes the color of rich ground coffee peering out from underneath dark, audaciously arched brows. And a smile calculated to make a man regret he was only looking at a painting.

Behind him, Nancy laughed. "Yeah, it's me. My ex-husband did it, right after we were married."

He turned to look at her. She stood by the doorway to the kitchen, her arms linked over her middle. She'd lost weight since she'd had the portrait done, he realized with a start, noticing that her skin was stretched tissue-thin across delicate, elegant features. Not that she looked ill, just…fragile.

Fragile was not good. Fragile brought out protective instincts he'd just as soon stayed buried. "Am I allowed to say this is very good?"

Another laugh. "His artistic abilities were never in question. Last I heard, some of his paintings were easily commanding six figures. Marriage, however..." The sentence drifted off. "Okay, coffee," she said instead, then disappeared into the kitchen. For several seconds, while he surveyed other pieces in her collection, he heard cupboard doors being batted about, the refrigerator door opening, then shutting. One of the cats, a small calico, sidled over so she could ignore him. Nancy returned to the doorway, clutching two metallic-embossed bags in her hands. Backlight from the kitchen haloed her curls. "Regular or decaf?"

Something unfamiliar and frightening surged through him. He wanted to touch her. Kiss her again. Forget everything he'd ever learned about being a gentleman. He also wanted to hold her close, wipe away the hint of worry visible in the faint crease between her brows.

Not his place, he told himself. Not now, not ever.

He should leave. Soon.

He shoved his hands in his pockets, his desire to the back of his brain. "Regular," he said, which got a lifted brow and an appreciative grin.

She disappeared again. This time, he followed, into a snow-white room with red-checked curtains at the windows, cobalt-blue countertops. Glass-paned cabinets revealed Blue Willow plates, a dozen all-purpose goblets, boxes of heavily sweetened cereals, crackers, cookies. He frowned. Lord—what kind of garbage was she putting in her system? She opened the freezer for a second—shaking her head, as if she'd made a mistake—and he caught a glimpse of neatly stacked microwave dinners.

With an annoyed sigh, he resumed his perusal of the kitchen, old and charming and broken-in. In spite of its flaws, something about the little house said "complete," that the woman who lived here knew who she was, what pleased her, and anyone who didn't like it could go jump in a lake. A challenge and a reassurance, Rod decided. And dangerous, because he felt immediately comfortable here. With her.

"Damn."

His gaze shifted to Nancy, struggling to pry a coffee filter from the stack. He freed his hands from his pockets, held one out to her. "Here. Let me." He half expected a feminist, "Forget it, I can do this myself" response. Instead, she practically smacked him with the package.

"Be my guest. Brain's okay, but the coordination sucks...thanks," she muttered when he handed her back both package and extricated filter. She flipped her hair over her shoulder; it didn't stay. He watched the interplay of muscles underneath crossed straps as she filled the carafe with water. Thought of that painting. Told himself forty-one-year-old men didn't get hard *that* easily.

A large ginger cat jumped up on the counter; she pushed it down again. Ah. Safe topic, guaranteed to keep the hormones in check. Sure, he liked cats as well as the next person, might even consider having one, in the right mood. *One.* Living in a zoo was something else again. "Aren't seven cats a bit...much?"

She clicked on the coffeemaker, laughed. "You're more diplomatic than my mother was about it. But since nothing I do is right in her eyes, anyway, I don't put a whole lotta stock in her opinion." He heard pain in that statement, possibly unacknowledged, and felt an unexpected twinge of empathy.

Nancy shifted to lean heavily on the edge of the counter, bending over to remove her shoes, which she carried out of the room. Again, he followed, until he realized she was headed toward her bedroom. "I'll be right back, but I just cannot deal with this torture instrument—" she pointed in the general direction of her bosom "—a second longer." She disappeared into the room, leaving her door open a crack. "Anyway, about the cats," she called from the other side. "See, I couldn't have any in my apartment. So I figured, when I moved here—" a groan of undisguised relief drifted from behind the door "—I'd get me a cat. *One* cat, maybe a cute little kitten, you know?"

Clad in an oversized red sweatshirt, gray leggings and thick socks, she padded back out into the living room, pulling her hair back into one of those funny long clips. Had she given up on the seduction idea, or was she wearing a black lace teddy underneath her outfit?

Curious woman.

She crossed the room, rubbing at a spot high on her rib cage. "So, anyway," she said, stopping at the kitchen door, one hand on the frame, "I get to the pound—there's a small one, right outside town—and they had these six grown cats. No kittens. And I realized, since there didn't seem to be a run on the place, the ones I didn't take would be…" She lowered her voice. "You know."

Rod leaned back against the arm of the sofa. "So you took them all."

"What else could I do?"

What a gal. "So where'd the seventh come from?"

"Wouldn't you know—a stray wandered up onto my porch the day after I brought these guys home. It was either take him in, or send him to *that place*." She shrugged. "Um, coffee's ready. You want it in here or out there?"

Impulsive. Kindhearted. Crazy. Oh, yeah…he definitely needed to leave as soon as possible. "Kitchen's fine," he said.

Her smile shot straight to his groin.

Did he have any idea how nervous she was? How close she was to making a fool of herself? He had to hear it in her nonstop prattling—she could hear her mother saying, "For God's sake, Nancy, give it a rest!"—see it in her incessant movement. Distractedly, she pulled a pair of crockery mugs from the cupboard.

Why can't you do anything right, Nancy? Why can't you be like Mark?

No. Her brother wouldn't lower himself to a cheap seduction, that was for sure. But then, having married the Jewel of Scarlet River, New Jersey, the summer after he got his master's degree in Computer Engineering—a *real* degree—and then in due course presented his parents with two adorable grandchildren, her brother probably didn't find himself in the position of being sex-deprived on a regular basis. Not if Shelby Garver was anything like Nancy remembered, at least. Her mouth quirked up into a half smile. Her mother should only know.

"Nancy?"

Rod's voice brought her back to the land of the somewhat-living. "Sorry. Lost in thought."

Instead of sitting, he took the mugs from her hands, set them down, poured the coffee. A small, insignificant thing. But since no one had done anything for her since she was about five, she was fascinated to discover how much the gesture pleased her.

"Sugar?" he asked.

"And milk, yes," she said, reveling in letting him serve her. He fixed the coffee, handed her a mug. He took his black, she noticed. She also noticed the crease in his brow as he regarded her over the first sip.

He set down the mug, linked his arms over his chest. "You look like someone who needs to talk."

She nearly laughed. Oh, yeah, right…like he was going to relate to being the child who always screwed up, no matter how hard you tried. So she shook her head. "Not about that. Besides…" She moved over to the table, took a seat. "It's my house. I get to grill *you.*"

One side of his mouth hitched north. "Oh, really?" He scraped back the other chair, dropped down into it. Somewhere along the way, he'd removed his jacket. Now she was faced with a mind-boggling array of torso muscles encased in soft, luxurious, black-as-sin cashmere. *Hoo, boy.* "You're pretty sure of yourself," he said, his voice rumbling through her senses like a lazy freight train.

She wasn't sure of anything. But she smiled, took a swallow of coffee. "I'm a salesperson, remember?"

"Damn good one, too, from what Elizabeth tells me."

The first flicker of pride she'd felt in ages warmed her blood. "I used to be."

"Used to be?"

"It was easier in Detroit, I guess. I'm starting over out here. And I was doing a lot of commercial stuff. Now it's mostly residential, which yields less return for time invested." Then she laughed, slapped the table. "Hey! You shifted the conversation to me when I wasn't looking—"

His hands shot up, as did both corners of his mouth. "Oh, no. You did that to yourself."

"Piffle. You knew exactly what you were doing!" Laughing, she leaned forward, pointing at him. "Let's get one thing straight—I'm the manipulative one here, got that?"

Rod leaned back in his chair, arms crossed over his chest again. He wasn't frowning, exactly, but he sure wasn't smiling, either.

"And why is that?" he asked softly. "Why do you feel you have to force things to go the way you want them to?"

Her own laughter died as the old, chronic hurt twisted her heart. "Because," she said on a deep breath, daring to meet his gaze, "single women have to take care of themselves. And since the world at large ain't too keen on giving its women what they need, forcing things to go our way is generally our only option."

He didn't seem to take offense. "Survival instinct?"

"Maybe."

He surprised her by reaching across the table, capturing her hand in his. "Platinum butterfly," he said, lifting her fingers to his lips. Just as soon as she collected a few brain cells, she was going to ask him what he meant. He beat her to it. "Durable, exquisite, delicate, all at once." He let go of her hand, leaned back again. "Quite a combination."

The calico cat jumped out of her way when she shot up from the table, not knowing where she was going.

"I really must be out of practice," Rod said behind her. "What did I say?"

Arms folded across her stomach, she paced the tiny kitchen, the cat mewing in sympathetic confusion at her feet. "I'm not sure. It's just that..." She blew out a stream of air, then faced him, twisting a strand of hair around her finger. Stupid, the way she felt dizzy like this. "Oh, man…this is going to sound corny, but no one's ever called me *exquisite* before."

Rod frowned. "I've seen that painting, Nancy."

It took a moment. "Oh…yeah, well, to hear Stan tell it, my main allure was being free and available. Of course, I didn't know that at the time." No. At the time, she was thrilled that someone of Stanley Metzger's talent thought her interesting enough to paint. There'd been times when she wondered if he'd married her just so he wouldn't have to pay a model. But since he'd only painted her once, and she had the painting…

She looked up at Rod, unprepared for the mixture of compassion and apprehension in his eyes, even less prepared to deal with either of them. The wine-induced buoyancy had fizzled out some time ago, she realized, rudely dumping her into a vat of self-pity. At the moment, every mistake she'd ever made seemed to be screaming, "Hey! Remember me?" Or maybe that was her mother's voice.

Nancy faced her fogged kitchen window, absently stroking the ginger tom, and decided she was too tired and too fed up with life in general to worry about making an impression on this man. On any man. "Call me superficial, but until ten seconds ago, I didn't know how much it mattered to have someone, *anyone,* consider me…attractive. To care enough about me to at least…*lie*…"

Out of nowhere, tears bit at her eyes. She took a deep breath, trying to control them, only to fall apart when Rod took her into his arms.

"I don't lie," he said quietly, and she let 'er rip.

She had no idea how long they stood there, how long she cried. But when she was done, rather than feeling better, she felt like an idiot. She pulled away, grabbing a paper towel from the rack to blow her nose and wipe her eyes.

"Just what you needed tonight, I bet," she said between swipes. "Coffee with a maudlin drunk."

He'd followed her, only to hesitate—she could see the questions in his eyes, wondering how much to do or say, how far

to wade in—before lifting a hand to her face. Kindness winning out over caution, she thought. With one thumb, he wiped
away a tear. "You're not drunk," he said gently. "And hardly
maudlin. My guess is, someone's been trying too hard. Trying
to be what she thinks she's supposed to be, not what she wants
to be."

Realization sliced through her, threatening new tears, even
as she wondered how this man she barely knew could hone
in on things she hadn't even admitted to herself. "Maybe so,"
was all she said, then sniffed.

"I know so. Better than you might imagine." Her eyes shot
to his, waiting for the explanation, but apparently none was
forthcoming. Instead, he traced one escaped strand of hair with
his fingertip, frowning. "Were you serious about no one ever
telling you you're pretty?"

A raw, wretched laugh stumbled from her throat. "Oh,
yeah."

"Not even your parents?"

"Now there's a laugh." She swiped at her nose with her
hand. "You're looking at someone who lived her childhood
in a perpetually awkward stage. I was too skinny, too short,
my hair was hopeless, and my teeth were in braces longer than
any other kid I knew. There's a video of me taken at my
brother's sixteenth birthday. I was twelve, and for some reason
insisted on wearing this light green dress. I looked like a praying mantis in a fright wig. A *male* praying mantis, no less."

His low chuckle made her shiver. "Trust me. I do not think
of insects when I look at you. And unless your ex-husband
embellished, the woman in that portrait has nothing to feel
inferior about."

That stopped her. "Really?" she said, realizing at that moment just how much she craved approval, *real* approval. Part
of her was ticked as hell that she did want it, but the other
part really didn't give a damn anymore.

Again, she saw a qualm or two skip across his features, the
indecision in his eyes. "Really," he said, stepping closer.
"Nancy, you're lovely." His fingertips grazed her temple as

his eyes traveled slowly, luxuriously, over her features. "No, you're not typical," he said with a smile, which got a weak laugh, "but that's why I can't take my eyes off you. Not that I'd dream of embarrassing you by cataloguing your attributes…"

"No, no, please. I'll take the risk."

He chuckled, the sound warm and lovely and, in a way, lov*ing*. "Okay. You've got amazing eyes, first of all, the way they're deep set like that, the way your brows and cheekbones set them off." He knuckled her chin. "Great jawline, fantastic chin, a nose the gods would envy."

She had to laugh. "Yeah, well, considering how much it cost, a little deity-envy is the least it should get. Go on."

"We've already covered your mouth…" His eyes dropped to that particular feature, and she thought how much she'd like him to cover it once more. With his. Then his attention shifted again, this time to her hair. "And this—" he fingered one strand "—is magnificent."

"You sure you don't mean 'wild'?"

"Wild is good," he said, and smiled for her.

And suddenly she saw it. Her reflection in his eyes. Not of her face, but her need, glittering like molten gold. Still, from what little she knew of Rod, this wasn't someone prone to acting on impulse, of giving in to something, just because. Sure he'd kissed her—and damn well, too—but he'd also made it pretty clear he was only expecting coffee. If she was smart, she'd take the hint.

If she was determined, she'd take advantage.

"You *do* want me, don't you?"

He laughed, a little. "I guess…yeah."

"You…guess?" Teasing.

After a heart-stopping moment, his lips met hers. Softly. Sweetly. But when he lifted them, he was frowning. "The guessing part isn't about how much I want to take you to bed. It's about whether or not it's right."

That made sense. Too much, unfortunately. Not that a little thing like scruples was going to stop her. She looped her hands around his neck, no easy feat since he was more than a foot taller than she. "And here I didn't think you liked me."

His smile was gentle. His hands skimmed her arms, raising a flock of goose bumps. "Let's see…you were wearing a sweater that came down past your hips. Black, with huge red flowers embroidered all over it. A long black skirt. And these little flat shoes that made you look like a ballet dancer." He touched her hair. "It was raining that day, and your hair was all fluffed out like chocolate cotton candy." His gaze touched hers. "And you smelled like my grandmother's bedroom, of sandalwood and roses."

Her heart was hammering so hard she thought her ribs would crack. She remembered the day, and the rain, and her annoyance with her impossibly frizzed hair. "You remember what I was wearing the day we met?"

He nodded. "And each time we saw each other after that, believe it or not." Once again, he touched her cheek, and sparks skittered all the way to her toes. "Believe me…I like you, Nancy. Always have. Always been attracted to you, too. Doesn't mean I think we're right for each other."

Her insides had turned to water. She licked her lips. "You're probably right. But that doesn't necessarily preclude our going to bed with each other, either. Not if we both understand…."

His expression stopped her cold. A muscle ticked in his jaw, but neither smile nor frown crossed his features. *Uh-oh.* He was going to turn her down, then forever brand her as a brazen hussy too stupid to tell the difference between desire and intent. Okay, so he'd admitted wanting to go to bed with her, too. Didn't mean he intended following through on it.

Then his hands slowly began making small, gentle circles on her back, as if afraid any sudden move might make her do something crazy. But she'd already done that, hadn't she? Invited a man she'd never even dated into her bed?

She let out a soft yelp as, in a single swift and graceful movement, he framed her face in his hands, forcing her to meet his gaze once again for the millisecond before he captured her mouth. A hard kiss, this time. Demanding. Testing. Guaranteed either to send her shrieking in the opposite direction or reduce her to a greedy, needy puddle at his feet.

Well, there was some definite whimpering going on here, but shrieking? Uh, no. Then she realized her breast had somehow found its way into his hand.

"Oh, mm…you found it," she whispered between kisses.

"Uh, yeah. Pretty much right where I expected it to be."

"No, I mean…well, we're not exactly talking *Baywatch* quality here."

He backed away just enough to frown down at her, then slowly, deliciously, scraped his fingernails across the nipple, his face a study in concentration.

She shuddered, gasped, saw a star or two. He laughed, softly. "Give me a perfect half-carat diamond over a ten-carat Cubic Zirconia any day. Besides, you hear anyone complaining?"

She swallowed, shook her head.

"Good. Then no more of this I-hate-my-body business." One hand still claiming her breast, his other one slipped beneath both leggings and panties to cup her bottom. "Got that?"

She murmured something unintelligible as her nipple strained toward his palm; he tightened his grasp, skimming his thumb over the hard peak. Need shot through her like a behind-schedule express train. Oh, man—she'd forgotten how good that felt. Her mouth fell open, her eyes closed.

"Look at me," he commanded, his voice roughened. Soft.

She opened her eyes to look deep into his.

Oh.

Oh…mama.

"I don't have anything with me—"

"It's okay," she interrupted. "I can handle that part of things. And I'm…um…"

"Yeah." Was that a hint of desperation in his voice? "Me, too. Just had a complete physical a couple months ago."

One of the cats meowed behind her, making them both

jump. She tried to pull away, though she wasn't sure why. But Rod held her fast, those strong hands warm, careful, on her…everything. However, in a brief but noteworthy moment, it occurred to her he could be a lousy lover, for all she knew. Or, well, he could think she was. Frankly, this could be one helluva disappointing experience.

And once they crossed the threshold to her bedroom, that would be it. So the question was—was it better to continue dwelling in What-if? Land, where she could continue to shape and prune her fantasies to her own, admittedly impossibly high standards, or forge ahead to reality, where she ran the risk of having her dreams shattered…and common sense restored?

His soft chuckle caught her attention. "For someone I'd pegged as impetuous to a fault, you seem to think enough for a hundred people."

She smiled, a little, lifted one shoulder in a shrug. He kissed her forehead.

"You can change your mind, honey. I'll limp to the car, but I'll survive."

"Yeah, well, I'm not sure I would."

He snagged her chin in his hand, his touch sending shivers of anticipation streaking through her bloodstream. "This is a first for me, Nancy," he said, his mouth a breath from hers. "I don't do casual sex. Never have. But—"

"No!" she said, pressing her fingers to his mouth. "No buts." She drew in a breath, let it out in shaky spurts. "I'm new to this, too," she whispered, then let her forehead drop to his chest. He drew her close, his breath warm in her hair. "And I meant what I said, about this just being for…now. It's only that—" she rubbed her face against the soft wool of his sweater, discovering that his own heartbeat was as rapid-fire as hers "—it might be nice to have someone make love to me again while I still remember how."

She felt his chest expand, collapse, on a huge sigh, before he carried—yes, carried!—her into the bedroom, shutting the door on the cats.

Chapter 3

Something was batting his nose, soft but insistent, accompanied by a low rumbling and the distinctive aroma of cat breath, barely tempered by the smell of freshly brewed coffee sifting in through the open door. Rod peered out of one eye at the little calico, who grinned down, then slung her rump toward him, smacking him in the face.

He carefully, but quickly, removed her to the floor, then yanked the comforter and sheet back up over his bare shoulders, taking in the pristine simplicity of this room as compared with the living room. Ivory walls, nearly bare floors save for a couple of floral-patterned rugs, linen tab curtains over the wooden blinds. A couple of paintings, a hand-painted chest and a cheval mirror pretty much did it. The bed was the only really fancy thing in the room, its black wrought-iron headboard nearly matching the gate in the living room.

Memories of Nancy's hands, clamped to that headboard, shot through him.

A shiver raced over his skin. Cripes, it was cold. And it did not escape his attention, morning-fogged though his brain might be, that the naked, sweetly scented woman with whom he'd shared this bed last night wasn't nestled against his chest, all warm and soft. His body groused a little in regret. His brain, which was rapidly clearing, was extremely grateful.

He glanced at the clock by Nancy's bed: 7:14. The light filtering through the open blinds was weak, pale, like someone recovering from a lengthy illness. He felt much the same way—wiped out, depleted, unsure of his footing.

Petrified. Sated, yes, but petrified.

She was something else. He blew a stiff *whuh* of air through his lips, remembering how a single well-placed caress had taken her over the edge before they'd even fully undressed. He'd never known a woman to be that responsive, *could* be that responsive. Had never known a woman's cries of fulfillment could make his heart burst like that. The way she looked at him afterward....

"Bless you," her smile had said.

Minutes later, she'd taken—no, welcomed—him inside her, trembling with eagerness, a fierce need to share...comfort...succor. She was an erotic combination of madonna-lover-friend-stranger who resurrected old, forgotten fantasies while forever obliterating them as well. And he'd been just as eager, just as fierce, plunging deeply, then deeper still, until she gasped again with expectant pleasure. Her fingers were soft and smooth against his face as she rose to meet him over and over and over until it was no longer the warmth of her body enveloping him, but her very soul. The explosive power of his own release shattered him, and he cried out, his eyes shut against a haze of crimson as her sweet, exquisite convulsions ferried him back to earth.

When he'd recovered enough to look at her face, she was beaming, inordinately pleased with herself.

And for him.

He hadn't had the heart—or maybe it was the guts—to leave. Or the willpower to turn down an encore. Or three.

Now he groaned, sat up in the bed. Not that he was surprised, mind, but didn't it figure that the woman with whom he'd just had the greatest sex in his life was the one woman he didn't dare have it with again?

He wasn't a complete fool. Nancy's generosity came at a price: she fully expected to get as good as she gave. And she damn well deserved it, too. Just as he'd suspected, she withheld nothing. A fount of emotions, in all shapes, sizes and colors, she said whatever popped into her head, did whatever struck her at the moment, made love with an abandon and ingenuousness that took his breath away.

Oh, sure, she *said* this was just a one-time thing. But he saw that hope in her eyes. That need.

The sooner he stopped this, the better. This—she—would never do. Not even for a fling, contrary to his body's imploring. The risk was far too great.

Nancy Shapiro represented everything he'd learned was foolhardy from the time he was a little boy. In a way, he almost envied her, but he could never be like her, letting his emotions run riot like that. Passion was an excess, a human weakness he had to strictly control. Love inevitably, inexorably, led to pain. And anger—the flip side of love—only led to acts or words almost invariably regretted, but rarely forgiven.

There was little to be gained by giving passion its head. Hadn't he been able to hold on to his sanity through the divorce only by remaining calm and rational, by not reacting to Claire's accusations and histrionic outbursts in his lawyer's office? Had he opened the Pandora's box of resentment and betrayal and pain that tried a hundred, a thousand, times to leech past his defenses, to remind him of things best forgotten, the already tense proceedings could have easily degenerated into a dogfight. For his children's sake, he had refused to let that happen. It simply wouldn't have been right.

So maybe his life wasn't perfect. But whose was? Keeping things on an even keel was far preferable to a roller-coaster ride of emotional mayhem…and that's what a relationship with Nancy Shapiro would be. He'd known it from the beginning, and last night had only reinforced his conviction.

Keeping her in his life would be like letting someone store a ticking bomb in his garage. Even though his last earthly thought would probably be of last night, never were two people less suited for each other.

The little calico had circumnavigated the bed, jumped back up on Nancy's side, and was making sure strides back in Rod's direction. Whoever coined the term "pussyfooting" had clearly not met this cat. Before she could stake her claim, however, Rod untangled himself from the creamy sheets and stood, immediately shivering in the still chilly room.

He made a quick trip into the adjoining bathroom, then dressed, furtively, aware of Nancy's voice drifting in from another part of the house.

In a half hour, he told himself, it would be all over. But right now, he felt as if someone had taken a pumpkin scraper to his insides. He stepped from the room, dislodging Bruiser from the nest he'd made in the lining of his jacket before slipping it on, then followed the sound of Nancy's voice to the kitchen.

She was on the phone, her back to him, the extra-long cord stretched to the max across the room. A Dr. Seuss nightmare of a cat with a mane and extravagant leggings, but otherwise shorn, sat on the counter, batting at the coiled cord, while two others were exchanging mild words over whose turn it was at the food dish.

Under other circumstances, he would have laughed. The gloriously sexy creature of a few hours ago now looked like a Muppet. Not only was she dressed in a scruffy, furry robe in an amazing shade of lurid pink, her feet encased in a pair of heavy white socks, but she'd done nothing with her hair, which stood out from her head like Medusa's snakes. The fact that Rod found her disarray arousing only reinforced the treacherousness of the situation. He stood at the door, mildly aware he was eavesdropping.

"Ma... Ma!" One hand came down onto the counter, sending at least two cats fleeing for their lives. "That's not true, and you know it!"

Uh-oh.

"I was going to call you, but you always beat me to it." Normally, her New Jersey twang was soft-edged enough not to really notice it. This morning, however, it was out in full force. Frowning, she reached up to her windowsill, plucking off a dead leaf from an ivy plant. "I know it was New Year's Eve. Which is why I *wasn't home?* What? You expect me to call you from my cell phone in the middle of a party. Oh, please don't start in again about this...."

Her head dropped back; he saw her take a deep breath, then sag against the counter. "How many times we gonna go over the same ground? I moved here totally of my own free will." She covered her mouth with her hand, then let it drop. "What's in Jersey for me, Ma?... Well, I'm sorry, but I think I'm a little old to be living with my parents—"

Rod sneezed—there was enough cat fur floating in the air to make coats for a small country—and Nancy spun around. The frown on her face vanished, replaced by that incandescent smile.

Damn.

"Okay, okay..." She raised her hand, her mouth open, trying to get a word in edgewise. "Ma—I gotta go... Okay, *okay,* I promise, I'll call you later... No, I don't know when... No one's asking you to stay by the phone, Ma. Look, I really have to go...yes, I promise... Yeah, Ma. I love you and Daddy, too."

She hung up the wall phone, but didn't let go right away. Her forehead braced on her arm, she seemed to be working on getting her respiration back to normal. Funny. Rod and his father had never had fights. Not like that.

"I take it you and your mother aren't on the best of terms?"

Her laugh into her sleeve was harsh. "Let's just say her concept of maternal devotion includes the terms *manipulative* and *suffocating.*" She turned to Rod. "My ex may have had little to recommend him, but he at least got me out of Jersey and away from Belle the Wonder Maven."

She'd started to smile again, but apparently something in

his expression—stark terror, perhaps—cut it off at the pass. Her arms tucked themselves against her ribs as she jerked back to look out the window, began the nervous chatter of the night before. "I told you the snow wouldn't amount to anything. I don't think we even got an inch of fresh last night—"

"Nancy."

She bent her head slightly, the wild curls slipping forward as if to offer her comfort. "Last night was really good," she said, one hand knotting, then unknotting, on the counter. "Actually, last night was indescribable. And to think I'd been afraid—" She cut herself off, faced him again. A shaky smile warmed her lips even as confusion simmered in her eyes. "Let's not screw it up by talking, okay?" She pushed herself away from the counter, walked over to the refrigerator. "I have eggs, at least," she said, opening the door. "How do you like them? Or there's frozen waffles, I think." A cloud of frost tumbled from the freezer when she opened it and started poking among all those green boxes.

Now Rod knew why one-night stands weren't his thing. Torn between wanting to comfort her and wanting to bolt, he said, "I'm not hungry. I'm also not leaving this house until you hear what I have to say."

The door slowly swung closed. Her fingers still clamped around the handle, she said, "Isn't this backward? I mean, isn't it usually the woman who wants to talk?"

"Isn't it a little late for us to be thinking in terms of convention?"

She huffed a sigh. "Good point." Then turned. "So talk already."

He rubbed the back of his neck, looked out the window for a second, then back at her, avoiding those eyes, already littered with fragments of hope. "Okay, look—originality's not my strong suit, especially before 8:00 a.m. So—cliché number twenty-seven. Last night was very special." He stepped close enough to brush a corkscrew curl away from her face; it sproinged right back. "Like you."

The ginger tabby jumped up on the counter, *brr-upping* at her. She picked it up, cuddling it against her chest. "But?"

"But…nothing's changed. This isn't going to develop into a relationship."

Her calmness scared him, because it seemed so against her nature. She rubbed the side of her nose, not looking at him, then retucked her arm against her middle.

"It's not that I didn't know this, going in," she said, almost to herself. "Even had a list of reasons why you and I would never work." Now she tilted her head. "Unfortunately, three-quarters of those reasons no longer seem to make sense this morning. So, just because that's the kind of gal I am, I have to ask, *why?*"

He wished he was dead. "I'm sorry. I truly am. But you can't change the rules after you've played the game." Man. Talk about sounding lame. "You even said as much, that you just wanted the one night."

"And *you* said you didn't do casual sex."

"I don't. And it wasn't." Her brows rose. "Just because it was an isolated incident doesn't mean I considered it casual."

"I see. So, I'll ask again, since you still haven't answered the question—why, exactly, is this a one-time thing? I mean, we're both single, and I assume you found me at least attractive enough to do it with once. No, wait—it was four times, wasn't it?"

"Nancy, for God's sake, don't do this to yourself. This has nothing to do with you."

"Funny. I could have sworn I was in the bed, too."

He plowed one hand through his hair, a gesture of frustration he generally never allowed himself. By the time he was six, his grandparents had drummed into his head that people of their station were expected to do the right thing, to take the high road. And, thus far, despite a few personal casualties along the way, he'd succeeded in meeting those standards. Now, however, he found himself in the unenviable position of realizing that no matter what decision he made, it wasn't going to be right. That someone was going to be hurt. The stunner, though, was that *he* might be the someone, as well as Nancy.

But he did owe her the truth. "Nancy, listen to me. Please. I just can't get involved with anyone. I've been married twice, and both times I failed miserably."

"*You* failed?"

He hadn't expected the oblique defense. "My ex-wives would say so, yes."

Nancy snorted, then clutched the cat more tightly, burying her face in its fur. After a moment, she said, "Tell me something. And I'm only asking for a simple yes or no answer, not the gory details—you ever have a night like we just had with either of your wives? Or anyone, for that matter?"

She'd backed him into a corner. He pushed his way out again, convinced this was one time telling the truth would serve no purpose.

"Last night was spectacular, Nancy. But not unique."

He'd hit home, watched what he knew was a fragile ego shatter. "I see. Well...guess that puts me in my place."

"Honey—" desperate, now "—I'd think you'd be the last person to consider basing a relationship on sex."

"And if that's all that was," she retorted, "we wouldn't be having this conversation. Or I wouldn't be, at least. I've had *sex,* Rod. Maybe not as much as some women my age, but enough to know that what we had last night went so far beyond the physical that I can't even remember exactly what happened."

To hear his thoughts echoed nearly did him in. But to admit he felt the same way would only undermine his resolve to save her from far worse pain down the road. "Then you were the only one." He crossed his arms, cringing at the hurt in those deep, dark eyes. But he dug himself in deeper, hoping like hell he'd come out on the other side in more or less one piece. "I remember every detail, plain as day. And there were some great details, granted. But what you're talking about, if I understand you, is not something I'll ever experience."

Not again in this lifetime, at least.

''And how do you know that? You think, because you've never felt that way—and, by the way, neither had I before last night—you never will? Or can? So we're not on the same rung of the ladder, yet. That's not unusual, you know. I mean, given time—''

''Nancy! *I can't love you.*'' He'd practically bellowed the words, then immediately pulled back, reclaimed control. ''Or anyone. I don't want to get married again, don't want more children—''

''Whoa, wait a minute—who's talking about having children?''

''No one has to, honey. I saw the look on your face when you held Guy's little boy on your lap, the way you baby these damn cats—''

''Leave the cats out of this.''

''Tell me you don't want babies of your own, Nancy.''

He could see the tremors racking her from where he stood. After a long moment, she looked away.

''Yeah. That's what I thought. Honey, I've got my hands full with the two kids I've got. And I'm past forty. The last thing I want is to start all over again. I simply can't give you what you want. And deserve.''

''Oh? And what is that?''

By now, a veritable ravine had worked its way between her brows. He tried to take her hand; she snatched it away. ''You need to be worshipped,'' he said gently. ''To be the center of some guy's universe, and a mommy to an adoring batch of children.'' He pressed one hand to his chest. ''You've glommed on to the wrong guy, sweetheart. I'm incredibly attracted to you, yes. And, yes, it appears we're sexually compatible. But I can't love you. Cliché number thirty-two—you're better off without me.''

Nancy turned her gaze to the window, her fingers continually stroking the cat's fur. For several seconds, she didn't speak. ''Well,'' she let out at last, ''if you get to be honest, so do I.'' She faced him, a damn-the-torpedoes look in her eyes. ''I've fantasized about having you in my bed for a long,

long time, Rod Braden. Not that I ever thought it would happen. But whaddya know? It did.'' Her lips curved in a little smile. "And boy, you really know how to make those fantasies seem pale by comparison.''

She dropped the cat, faced him, her arms folded across her chest. "Okay, so I'm ticked you're being so...whatever it is you're being. But you know what? One night was more than I had two nights ago, more than I ever thought I'd have. It was a whole lot of fun, and for sure I wouldn't mind a repeat performance sometime before I die. But since you just pulled the plug, I guess that's that. However, I have not 'glommed' on to you. Once you walk out that door, that's it. I won't call you, or bug you or insinuate myself into your life. I'd've been more than happy to give this thing its head, see where it went...'' She shrugged again. "But I'm not Lady Liberty. I don't do torches. You're right—if you can't see and appreciate what we had, then I *am* better off without you.''

Surely there was something else to say, another cliché that would magically salve the wounds he'd just inflicted. Her eyes told him otherwise, however. Just as they told him he needed to get his sorry hide out of there, and fast.

With a nod, he left the kitchen, disentangling his coat from hers from where she'd left them on the sofa, before letting himself out into the bitterly cold morning.

Rod told himself he'd taken three hours out of his life to keep this doctor's appointment more from his long-standing friendship with Arlen James, who'd been a family friend for as long as Rod could remember, than because of any serious concerns about his health. After all, he ate well, exercised, had never smoked, and hadn't even consumed any alcohol since that glass of wine at the Sanfords' party more than a week ago. Discipline and moderation had always been his by-words. Besides, losing control was not his idea of fun.

Neither was having a wretched blood pressure cuff cut off his circulation. At least this time Arlen's grunt wasn't accompanied by a pair of dipped, wiry gray brows. Not quite as dipped, anyway. "Good," the doctor said with a nod, wratching open the cuff. "It's down. Country air must be doing you some good."

"Well, that should make you happy." With a halfhearted smile, Rod rolled down his sleeve. "It's been a calm week or so." Notwithstanding his inability to eradicate Nancy's face from his thoughts, the feel of her against his skin, the scent of her, still in his nostrils. "Of course, there's no guarantee it'll stay that way." He reinserted the cuff link in place, snapped it locked. "I've got the kids every weekend this month."

Arlen hitched his trousers up at the knees and dropped into the chair behind the metal desk in the examining room. The swivel chair creaked as he scooted it closer to the desk, the sound abnormally loud in the artificial silence made possible by triple-glazing and an impressive address. "Been sleeping well?"

Rod hesitated just long enough to make the doctor glance up at him. "Well enough."

"Work going okay?"

He shrugged. "Keeps me off the streets."

Arlen stared at him for a moment, adjusted his wire-rimmed glasses, then abruptly rose. White coat flapping around his long thighs, he gestured toward the door leading out to his office. "Come out here. I want to talk to you."

"Actually, I've got an appointment in forty-five minutes—"

A smile. "This won't take long."

Rod's stomach clenched unpleasantly as he slipped his jacket back on, tweaked each cuff. "Sounds menacing," he said, trying for upbeat.

Arlen paused at the door, then chuckled, carving a pair of gullies on either side of his mouth. "Oh, hell, Rod, I'm sorry. No dire news, nothing like that," he threw over his shoulder as he strode out of the room, clearly expecting Rod to follow. "Sit." He nodded at the mushroom-colored upholstered arm-

chair that sat in front of an ornate mahogany desk, settling his
lanky frame into the black leather chair behind it.

Rod sat, crossing his ankle at his knee, cautiously regarding
the tanned, white-haired man in front of him, trying to cal-
culate his age these days. He had to be easily seventy-five, yet
looked no more than sixty. Arlen's ties to Rod's family went
back further than Rod's memory, that was for sure. And after
his grandparents' deaths, he remembered many times when
Arlen and Molly James's presence in his life had been the
only thing that seemed to make sense in a world that by rights
should have been downright idyllic. After Rod's parents
moved to Bloomfield Hills when he was ten, however, Rod
had begun to sense an uneasiness between Arlen and his father
he didn't understand for some time, about things they hadn't
discussed for nearly twenty years, by mutual consent. Things
that were behind him now. And he had no desire to resurrect
ghosts.

The uneasiness humming in his veins at the moment, however, made him wonder if Arlen wasn't about to. "Why do I
feel like a kid who's been called into the principal's office?"

Arlen's thin, sharply defined lips pulled up into a placating
smile as he leaned forward, lacing together the consummate
doctor's hands. "I don't know if this makes me old-fashioned
or cutting-edge, but I'm not the kind of physician who treats
the symptoms without addressing the cause. Yes, your blood
pressure's down, but not where it should be for a man in your
condition." He took a deep breath. "You're stressed, Rod.
And no, I don't mean by the divorce, or the kids, or the new
business, though they haven't helped. This has been building
up for years."

And there they were. The ghosts. Some of them, at least.
Well, two didn't necessarily have to play this game.

His hands tented in front of him, Rod tapped one index
finger on his lips, trying not to feel like a trapped animal.
"Meaning?" he asked quietly.

"Meaning…I've been keeping track of your life since you
were, what? Five or six, something like that. And I'd hoped,

for your sake, after you got out of Claire's clutches—well, I've never made it a secret what I think of her, although you got two great kids out of the deal—you'd finally get your head on straight. Work through some things. Apparently, I was wrong.''

Rod lowered his hands to his lap. Remained silent. The last thing he needed was a lecture, but Arlen was one of the few people in the world to whom he'd extend that privilege.

''I'd hoped,'' Arlen continued, ''that at least, you'd learn your lesson with Claire, make a better choice the second time. Instead, I'm wondering why you married Myrna to begin with.''

Admitting he'd often wondered the same thing would probably serve no useful purpose. Myrna had been perfect, on the surface—beautiful, monied, even-keeled, an ideal way to keep predators at bay without putting himself on the line. ''I thought it would work,'' was all he said. ''But she…couldn't deal with the kids, which I should have realized.''

The doctor made a move that was half nod, half shrug, then scratched behind one ear. ''Be that as it may. But then there's your work. Here I think you've taken some steps to get out of the rat race, but far as I can tell, all you've done is switch mazes. Now why is that, Rod?'' Heavy brows formed a V behind his glasses. ''Wasn't it just a year ago you sat at my table and admitted how bored you'd grown with Star, how you were actually relieved when they decided to—what's that term they used? Ah, yes—make your position redundant. Even I know you don't need the money. If you still wanted to work, you could have done anything at all. Yet here you are, doing virtually the same thing you've been doing for fifteen years. Maybe I'm missing something here, but that sure as hell makes no sense to me.''

Rod shifted in his chair, caught himself. ''Marketing's what I do.''

''What you do, huh? Not…what you *love?*''

A beat, then: ''You don't have to love something to be good at it.''

"Fine. Then come on board with the foundation, put your skills to good use for something you actually believe in. Something close to your heart."

"They get my money, Arlen," he said quietly. "That's enough."

The ghosts hovered on the edges of the conversation, taunting. After a moment, Arlen let out a sigh. "Dammit, Rod. For years, I watched you bust your butt to please your father—"

"I don't want to talk about this, Arlen—"

"Then we won't. But growing up in that house…" He shook his head, his mouth taut with disgust. "That you turned out as well as you did is a testament to the human spirit." He hooked Rod's gaze in his own, obviously expecting a reply. When there was none, he rose from his chair, circled around to ease one hip up on the front edge of his desk. "Your parents have been gone for twenty years, Rod. You don't have to play it safe anymore, you know."

Rod stood, slipping his hands in his pant pockets. Breezy. Nonchalant. Far more shaken than he dared let on. "I really do need to be going—"

Arlen stood as well. Eye to eye, he thrust one finger in Rod's face. "You don't want to talk, I can't make you. But let me tell you something—keep up this pretense of everything being fine, ignoring the fact that you're one of the most miserable bastards I've ever met, and you're headed straight to cardiovascular hell. You have no *life*, Rod." He backed up a millimeter, crossed his arms. Grinned. "For that matter, when's the last time you had sex?"

Shards of tension shot up the back of his neck, as Nancy's laughter and tenderness and sweet, lush scent slammed into his consciousness. "None of your business."

Arlen grinned more widely, misinterpreting. "That's what I thought. Well, here's a news flash, son—unless you want to shrivel up into something putrid and unrecognizable, you need female companionship from time to time." He pointed that damned finger at him again. "In your case, more than from time to time. And next time, I suggest you try marrying a woman you love.''

That got a hollow laugh. ''Oh, no. Not after—''

''Screwing up twice already? So what? Took me four trips to the altar to work the bugs out. But work out they did.'' His eyes narrowed. ''Might for you, too, if you stopped trying to choose the kind of woman you think you're *supposed* to marry and pick one you *want* to marry.''

''No such woman exists, Arlen,'' he said mildly, ignoring the hair bristling on the back of his neck, ''because I'm not getting married again. And if you value our friendship, you'll kindly remove that nose of yours from my business.''

He turned to leave, but Arlen grabbed him before he'd gone three feet. Concern simmered in those blue eyes, concern Rod had seen many times before. ''You don't have to listen to me, but that doesn't mean I'm going to keep my mouth shut. Not this time. Not like I did before.''

''Your concern is duly noted,'' Rod said through the ghosts. Through the ever-present pain. ''But I'm fine, Arlen. Really. Everything's under control, okay?''

Out in the hall, the polished steel elevator doors shushed open as he heard from ten feet away, ''And who the hell d'you think you're kidding?''

Without answering, Rod stepped inside the elevator, let the doors close.

Chapter 4

Nancy knew it was crazy to still be ruminating about her whatever-it-was with Rod after nearly three weeks. You'd think, with all the practice she'd had at getting over men, this would have been a piece of cake.

Work, she told herself, forcing bleary eyes back to the Sheldons' contract. Selling one house and buying another concurrently was always a pain. Now that they'd gotten a decent offer on their old one, she had to find them new living space as quickly as possible. God, she was tired....

Okay, girl—listen up: One cup of coffee and one night of hot sex do not a relationship make, got it? Except *that* one night of sex put the dribs and drabs of her previous experiences to shame. Maybe Rod wasn't burned into her soul or anything romantic and profound like that, but he sure was burned into her body. *Yowsa*—she twirled her string of garnet beads around one finger—a *week* with the man would probably hold her for the next forty years.

Again, she stared at the paperwork in front of her, grabbing a handful of hair and tugging at it, as if trying to let more air into her brain. He'd done her a kindness, she told herself. Man had more baggage than an airline.

Her stomach growled, as if she needed reminding. What was with this, anyway? She'd been hungrier than a bear all this week—

"Oooh, don't we look serious this morning."

Nancy looked up, forced the muscles between her brows to relax, then waved Guy into her office while she filled in three more lines in the contract. Elizabeth's husband plopped himself in the gray upholstered chair in front of her desk, munching onion rings from a cardboard container.

She glanced up, chuckled. Salivated at the onion rings. "Mmm…nice tie."

Brilliant blue eyes sparkled in the clear winter light pouring from the shadeless window behind her, thanks to a truckers' strike that had delayed delivery of the miniblinds for Millennium Realty's new offices. Guy plucked the tie, festooned with Mickey Mouses, off his plaid-shirted chest, and grinned. "Yeah, it's great, isn't it?" He let it drop, held out the onion rings. "Kids gave it to me. Want one?"

She started. Oh. An onion ring. Not a kid. She gratefully accepted, then flipped the page, fighting a slight wave of dizziness. "Didn't figure Elizabeth had. So," she said as she munched, "what's up?"

Her peripheral vision caught the nervous shift in the chair before he laced his hands over his stomach, almost immediately lifting one to scratch behind a gold-studded ear. He wore his hair shorter than when Nancy had first met him, longish in back but neatly layered on top and front. On Guy, it worked. "Actually, I—we—need a favor. See, Elizabeth's been a little cranky lately—"

"Our Elizabeth?" Nancy said in mock amazement, sparing him a smile as she wrote. "Cranky?"

"Well, that's the kindest word I can think of at the moment. In any case, I got tickets to the Detroit Symphony concert tonight, aaand…" his face scrunched up into a please-don't-hit-me grimace "I wondered if you could sit?"

Nancy leaned back in her chair, her arms crossed over her velour tunic. "It's Saturday, Guy. What if I had plans?"

His face fell. "Do you?"

She sighed. "I wish. Yeah, I suppose I can sit tonight—"

"And I've made reservations to spend the night someplace fancy, expensive and childless," he added in a rush.

Look at that face, wouldja? No wonder he had Elizabeth eating out of his hand. "Anybody ever tell you you're devious?"

"Most of my clients, actually, but let's not go there."

She laughed. "Fine. I can spend the night, no problem. But I assume I was second choice?" Elizabeth's mother was besotted with her new step-grandchildren, ready to baby-sit at a moment's notice.

Guy got up, peered out the office door, then came back, leaning over Nancy's desk. "Maureen backed out on us," he whispered. "Hugh asked her to go away for the weekend."

Nancy's brows shot up. "Really?" For several months, Nancy's widowed mother had been dating Hugh Farentino, the developer of the planned community that had been primarily responsible for the agency's sudden boom in business. "You think things are getting serious, then?"

"Let's just say Elizabeth and I are taking bets on whether we have a baby or a wedding first."

Nancy fixed a smile to her face, refusing to let this good news get to her. It really did seem at times as if she was the only woman in the world destined to remain single.

"Hey, baby!" Cora Jenkins swept into the office, her bright purple cape in full sail, plunked a white bag reeking of something gloriously greasy on Nancy's desk, then turned to Guy. "There you are," she said to Guy. "The Reinharts are here, honey. Said you were supposed to show them houses this afternoon. Whoa, Nancy—you okay?"

She'd stood to walk to her file, found herself clutching the open drawer to keep from losing her balance. The dizziness passed in a second, but she looked up to find two pairs of eyes trained on her like bird dogs.

"What? Yeah, I'm fine." She straightened up, brushed a curl off her cheek.

Guy tossed the empty onion-ring container in her garbage can. "There's that nasty flu going around," he said to whoever was listening as he made his way to the door. "All three kids had it last week. My mom even came down to help out, otherwise Elizabeth might have gotten it, too."

Nancy smiled at the love in Guy's voice. She didn't know all the details of why his first marriage had failed, but Elizabeth had confided that Guy sometimes still had to fend off vestiges of guilt about his wife's walking out on him and their three children when the youngest was barely six months old.

His first wife had been one clueless woman, that was for sure.

"It's not the flu," she reassured him, her gaze lighting on the bag on her desk. "Oh, Cora—please, please, please tell me some of that's for me!"

"It's all for you, baby," Cora said as Guy left.

"Oh, bless you!" Nancy tore into the bag. "How'd you know I wasn't going to get lunch today?"

"You still weren't back from your morning appointment when I left, and I know you've got that one o'clock. Lucky guess."

Groaning in sweet anticipation, Nancy attacked the turkey club before she'd even gotten the wrapping completely off. "I don't know 'ut's wrong wi' me," she forced out around the bite, then swallowed. "I used to be able to skip lunch all the time without any problem."

"Which probably accounts for why you weigh less than a good-size chicken."

Nancy swatted at her, crammed a French fry into her mouth. "It's weird, though—the past few days, I've been eating constantly."

A big grin split Cora's face. "And at the rate you're going, that's going to be gone before the grease has had a chance to set on the fries. Lord, I can't remember the last time I saw anyone eat like that." A laugh thundered from her chest.

"Save when Elizabeth got pregnant and didn't know it for two weeks. Oh, there's the phone—"

Nancy never saw Cora leave.

Dizziness. Exhaustion. Ravenousness. Oh, no no no no no...

Oh, *hell*.

The sandwich abandoned, she frantically pawed backward through her calendar, only to realize—duh!—it didn't go past January 1. But surely it wasn't that late, she thought as she lugged her shoulder bag up onto her desk, hauled out her checkbook and the handy-dandy calendar inside it. Okay, okay...God, they could probably hear her heartbeat in Toronto. There it was. December 17, which made her due on the...she counted forward...fourteenth.

Which was five days ago.

But...but...she'd used a diaphragm. And the stuff. That should have been fine, right? It had always been fine before....

Barely two minutes later, she burst into her house, racing to the bathroom without even removing her down coat. Her heart thudded against her chest as she yanked open the vanity drawer, rummaged through the contents. She found the spermicide first, flipped it over to read the expiration date. See? See? February, it said. February... She looked closer, squinting.

Nineteen-something.

Uh-oh.

Unable to shake the feeling that life as she knew it was about to end, she plucked the diaphragm case out of the drawer, her hands shaking so hard it took three tries before she could unsnap it. She snatched the rubber cylinder from its little plastic bed, then waded through a sea of cats to the living room, where the southern exposure-lit windows were brightest. The animals writhed around her feet as she held the diaphragm up to the light, having to clamp one hand on her wrist to stop the trembling. "Oh, dear God," she whispered, as the sunlight clearly defined, like a microcosmic constellation, a series of tiny holes in the rubber.

Her mother would have a field day with this one.

* * *

Arms tightly twisted together over her suede jacket, Hannah Braden hunched in the passenger seat of her mother's Cadillac, as far away from Claire's overpowering perfume—and her cigarette smoke—as possible. Outside her window, which she wished she could open without freezing to death, tree after boring tree whipped past, a charcoal blur against an overcast sky. She'd forgotten to bring her Walkman, which meant she'd been subjugated for the past hour to that New Age crap her mother loved. If she'd been younger, she would have been sorely tempted to cry. Or pitch a fit. But over the past several years, the edges of her emotions had worn down. Oh, yeah, she was seriously pissed off. She just no longer had the energy or enthusiasm to act on it.

All she'd wanted was to spend the weekend with one of her girlfriends, like any normal kid, you know? They'd planned on going to one of the malls tomorrow, seeing a movie, just hanging out. But *noooo. She* had to spend the weekend out in the boonies with her father, because that's what children of split parents did, bounced back and forth between Mommy and Daddy like good little Ping-Pong balls. At least when Dad still lived in Bloomfield Hills she'd been able to see her friends at some point during the weekends she and Schuy stayed with him. Now that he'd moved permanently into that mausoleum, however, every weekend she spent with her father was a weekend of being consigned to oblivion. And what really ticked her off was that neither of her parents seemed to care that they were seriously screwing up her life.

"I hope my picking you up early was okay," her mother said over Yanni or somebody, flicking ashes in the tray suspended from the dash. "But Rafe and I are going out this evening, so I have to be back in town by six at the latest."

Hannah shrugged, removing her velvet headband, pushing it back into place. A still-glowing ash floated up from the tray, barely missed putting a hole in her sleeve. God. At least Myrna hadn't smoked.

"My chemistry teacher wasn't thrilled about it," she said, picking up the thread of the pseudoconversation. Her voice sounded as flat as the leaden sky outside. "We were in the middle of a crucial lab."

"Oh, well—" more ashes into the tray "—I'm sure you can make it up."

Right. At the expense of missing basketball practice. But then, Claire had never thought that a high priority, either.

The seat shifted behind her as Schuyler leaned forward, sticking his face between the bucket seats, then popped a bubble right in Hannah's ear.

"For God's sake, Schuy—cut it out! *Ewww*—why do you have to chew that watermelon stuff? It's disgusting!"

Schuy grinned, then popped another bubble.

Slugging him would be too kind. Besides, he was nearly as big as she was now. Kinda took the joy out of it, knowing he could hurt her back. In any case, they were through the iron gates leading to the mansion. The place was huge. And amazingly ugly. Why her father had bought the thing to begin with, she had no idea. A "vacation" home, he'd said. Yeah, right. For the Addams family, maybe.

Claire navigated the car into the circular driveway, cut the engine as she stubbed out her cigarette. Apprehension sizzled through Hannah's veins, as it always did at these changings of the guard. When they'd all still lived together, it had been much easier to gauge their moods, although her father was generally so even-tempered, it was hard to actually describe what he had as "moods" at all. Still, she always felt uneasy, almost like a stranger, during these transitions. Especially with Dad, since his mental state was so much trickier to figure out than her mother's. Actually, now that Hannah and Schuy were older, their mother paid little attention to them. Which was just fine with Hannah, since she and Claire had never exactly been bosom buddies to begin with. In any case, it was pretty clear that her mother's catching herself another husband had taken precedence over nurturing her children, and the procession of potential candidates zooming in and out of their lives was positively dizzying. Doctors, lawyers, business moguls, software developers, even a professional race-car driver. Hannah didn't even bother to look up when the doorbell rang anymore, let alone leave her room.

Not that her relationship with her father was much better. It wasn't strained, exactly, as much as...she couldn't quite find the word. Foggy, she supposed. Like a fuzzy photograph. Maybe it was that he tried too hard, you know? The typical divorced - dad - gotta - spend - quality - time - with - my - screwed - up - kids syndrome. Neither she nor Schuy could make a move without his being *right there.* Yet despite all her father's efforts to "be" their father, and though Hannah really believed he cared about them— he called nearly every day, even when he was traveling—there was something missing.

So her mother didn't have much use for her children in her life, and her father didn't seem to know what to do with them at all. Just your typical dysfunctional all-American family, that was them.

Dad was standing on the steps, in cords and a heavy off-white turtleneck sweater, the bitter wind ruffling his thick hair. Still pretty good-looking, she supposed, for someone his age. He was smiling, but he looked...tired.

And far older than he'd looked the last time she'd seen him.

She wasn't prepared for the worry that stepped up her heart-rate. He'd said it was just as well Star had let him go, that the freelance work suited him much better. He'd said he and Myrna had parted by mutual agreement, that the marriage had simply been a mistake. And Hannah *knew* Dad and Mom didn't belong together. *Sheesh.* How had they ever hooked up to begin with, was what she'd like to know. Still, it seemed the more things changed—supposedly for the better, to hear her parents—the more unhappy everybody was.

God. They were all, like, totally screwed up.

Every time Rod saw the kids, it was a shock. Spawned from tall stock—Claire was only a few inches shorter than he—they grew faster than crabgrass after a rainy spring. Good Lord!

Hannah was what? Five-ten already? And even though she'd put that height to full advantage playing basketball, she still often wore a defensive expression, as if daring anyone to point out what she clearly regarded as her freakish size. He caught that look now, as she climbed out of the car, jerking a hank of long, pale blond hair behind one ear.

Or maybe her size had little to do with it.

Schuy bounded up the drive, a marionette in baggy jeans, a navy hooded sweatshirt underneath a ski jacket, and one of those knit caps the kids called a "beanie" pulled down past his eyebrows. Braces glinting in the dull light, his brainy, geeky son gave him a hug, then disappeared into the house and presumably into the kitchen. Claire minced along behind, grimacing as her heels sank into the gravel driveway, puddled in places from the last snow. Leave it to his ex to coordinate her outfit to the gray day, from the fox jacket over matching wool slacks to the ridiculously high heels. She'd pulled her still-blond hair back into a slick, neat chignon at the nape of her neck, accentuating features as classic as ever. But in the stark daylight, her makeup looked desperate, her salon tan sprayed on. She'd been a beautiful woman once. Could still have been, had she not fallen victim to vanity and self-indulgence. He thought, briefly, of how much Myrna had been like Claire fifteen years ago.

Of how little like either of them Nancy was. How predictable and safe he'd thought them, Claire and Myrna, how unpredictable Nancy was, even including the bizarre times she picked to pop up in his thoughts. Well, there you have it, he thought for the thousandth time. If he couldn't manage a relationship with "predictable and safe," clearly he'd made the right decision about Nancy, who was anything but.

Then why couldn't he get the woman out of his mind? Why did he continue to see Nancy's generous smile, those bottomless my-soul-is-yours-for-the-taking eyes, superimposed on the face of every woman he met?

"For God's sake, Rod," Claire barked, slamming him back

to earth. "When are you going to get this driveway properly paved?"

He shrugged, thinking that Claire probably wouldn't be amused to know the thought of having made love to her—willingly—now vaguely repulsed him. "I like the sound of gravel crunching underfoot," he said mildly, slipping one hand into his pocket. "Reminds me of my grandparents' driveway, when I was a kid."

Before Claire could comment, Rod changed the subject. "Any trouble getting them out early?"

"What?" She navigated the granite stairs, careful not to touch the carved stone railing which would hardly be clean, now would it? At the top, she extracted a silver cigarette case from her leather purse. "Oh. No, none. They weren't doing anything important, anyway."

"I see. I'm hocking my soul to send them to one of the best private schools in the country, and you're telling me they're not doing anything important?"

"Oh, for heaven's sake, Rod—you know what I mean." She clicked open the case; he took it from her, shut it, slipped it back into her purse.

"You want to slowly kill yourself, fine. But not in my house."

Glaring at him, she fished the case back out of her purse, quickly pulled out a cigarette and lighter, lighting it before he could say anything else. "Then I won't come into your precious house," she said on a stream of smoke. "I can't stay but two seconds, anyway."

"Hot date?" Rod said, tamping down the disgust that rose in his throat every time he had to deal with this woman these days. Had she always been this self-absorbed? Or had he simply been unwilling to notice at the beginning, when the convenience of taking the stunning, socially prominent blonde as his wife eighteen years before quashed any discernment he might have had? No, no…he'd liked Claire at first, had enjoyed her company, both in bed and out of it. He had to acknowledge the possibility that he was responsible at least in part, for the negative changes in his ex-wife's personality. It can't be easy living with a man, sharing your life and your body, knowing he doesn't love you.

"Wouldn't you like to know?" she said, and the wisp of sympathy he'd tried to feel for her vanished. She turned, taking a quick drag on her cigarette and spewing out the smoke on a vicious hiss as her gaze lit on her daughter coming up the drive, a bag dangling from each hand. "For heaven's sake, Hannah—stop slouching. Just because you're tall doesn't mean you have to look deformed, you know. What boy is *ever* going to look at you as long as you walk like that?"

Echoes, faint but barbed, pricked Rod's consciousness. "Claire, that's enough." Rod descended the stairs, took his daughter's bags from her. She met his eyes with resigned annoyance. No, more than that. Disappointment. Realization knifed through him that maybe he'd never loved any woman, but he'd never for a moment doubted the love he felt for his children.

Powerless though the pain in his child's eyes might make him feel.

"How's it going?" he said, leaning over to kiss the top of her head. She shrugged, nodded, as if to say, *Okay, but that's all you're getting from me.* Another echo, this one louder, more insistent, chilled the blood in his veins.

She hitched her shoulder bag up higher, regarding the house with obvious distaste. A cloud blanked out the sun for a minute, flattening the light, making her look too pale. Stressed. Kids shouldn't looked stressed, he thought.

He wished she was a baby again, or even a little girl of five or six. Small enough and innocent enough to cuddle in her daddy's lap and believe that he could make everything better. He hadn't, though, had he? Somehow, despite his best intentions, he'd made everything worse. And there was no going back. Hannah was nearly grown up, and he'd blown it.

Financially, his children had never lacked, just as he never had—for food or shelter or the best schooling, clothes, sports equipment and medical attention money could buy. But one look at his daughter's face, and he knew her life was as empty as his had been. For different reasons, yes, but emptiness is emptiness. The cause is immaterial.

The difference was, though, *he* felt guilty about it.

For another minute or so, he and Claire exchanged the minimum of words necessary to dispense-receive information about the children they'd created, then she glanced at her watch, gasped and took off like the White Rabbit from *Alice in Wonderland*. Five seconds later she was gone in a spray of soggy gravel.

"Yeah. Goodbye to you, too, Mother," Hannah said softly beside him. He slipped one arm around her shoulder, aching for a connection he had no idea how to forge. Wasn't even sure she wanted, judging from her set mouth.

"Interpersonal relationships were never your mother's strong suit."

His daughter glared at him, then pulled away and started up the steps. And he thought, *What the hell did I do now?* Shivering in the frigid breeze whipping off the lake, Rod hurried a bit to catch up to her. "That new Brad Pitt movie is playing at the Quadraplex in the mall—I thought we could go see it tomorrow."

"Already saw it," she said, then turned around, her expression...blank. "Besides, I've got like three major tests next week, so I pretty much planned to spend the weekend studying, if that's okay."

"Oh, uh, sure." He smiled, but it never got farther than his lips.

You know, for someone who'd spent his entire life trying to do everything right, he sure had a lousy track record.

After her last appointment, Nancy hightailed it to Elizabeth's as fast as her little MG would take her. One hand on the wheel, she speared the other shakily through her mop and reined in the hysteria looming large on the horizon. Okay...so the diaphragm was defective and the goop had expired and she'd had sex during Prime Time. Lots of women had sex then, unprotected. That didn't mean they got pregnant. Maybe she was just more tense than usual. That often delays things. Right?

"Yeah, and maybe Elvis isn't really dead," she muttered, the MG's brakes squealing as she pulled too quickly into Elizabeth's driveway. The white-paneled front door flew open; Micah and Jake bounded out of the house and down the wooden steps, and she felt what little blood she had left drain from her face.

This is what lacy diaphragms produced, four, six years down the road.

"Aunt Nancy!" they screamed, hurtling themselves at her the second she'd opened the car door. Her heart twisted like a wrung washcloth in her chest as she buried her face in sweet-icky little-boy scent. Four-year-old Micah planted a noisy, suspiciously sticky kiss on her cheek, before taking off after his brother back up the porch steps. When he hit the top, he turned, giggling. "We got a ham'ther, Aunt Nancy! An' it lives in our room an' everything!"

They disappeared past their mother, standing in the doorway. Her moonlight-colored hair had that wind-tunnel look about it as she more or less clutched a peach satin wrapper over her protruding belly. A storm of emotions whipped through Nancy. Anxiety. Excitement. Hopefulness. Stark, raving terror. And still envy. Elizabeth would not be raising *her* child alone.

Everything suddenly seemed too bright, too *there,* even as— and this made no sense—nothing felt real at all. Like a dream.

"The boys insisted it was your car," Elizabeth was saying, "but I said, no, can't be, Nancy isn't due for another hour…oh, *shoot.*" She twisted around to shout back into the house, "Micah James Sanford! Did you mess with my clock again?"

Having reached the doorway, Nancy managed a weak laugh. "No, no, honey—I'm early." She took a deep breath. "I—"

"Mama? C'n I take the ham'ther out of his cage?"

Instant concern sparking in her green eyes, Elizabeth tore

her gaze away from Nancy to palm the riot of blond curls at her hip. "Uh, no, baby, I told you—he has to sleep during the day. If you take him out to play now, he'll be cranky. Like I get when you come into the bedroom too early on Sunday mornings." She looked back at Nancy, her mouth open.

"But Mama—"

Elizabeth let out a sigh. "Sorry," she said to Nancy, squeezing her shoulder. "Hold that thought." Then to her stepson, "Micah, sweetie, I said no." Before he could protest again, Elizabeth awkwardly lowered herself to her knees and looked the little boy straight in the eye, clearly ignoring the trembling lower lip that presaged one of his outbursts. "I know how much you want to play with him, honey, but not until after dinner. Then Aunt Nancy'll help you put him in his roly ball so he can run around downstairs, okay?"

Micah knotted his arms at his chest, glowering to beat the band, then stomped off, kicking a plastic truck out of his way.

"Micah—" Elizabeth warned.

"You're mean," the child hurled back. Elizabeth looked up at Nancy, shrugged.

"Charming, isn't he?" She swiped her tangled hair off her face, then held out a hand so Nancy could haul her to her feet. Nancy knew how much Elizabeth, with virtually no previous experience with children, had been concerned about taking on Guy's brood. She also knew no one could have done a better job than Elizabeth was doing. And told her so. She also told her she did *not* handle rodents.

Elizabeth had already turned toward the stairs, shuffling the occasional stuffed toy or truck out of her way as she walked. Waddled. A faint streak of what Nancy guessed was red crayon meandered along the wainscoting leading to the back of the house; a peek into the living room revealed what looked like the aftermath of an explosion at a toy store. Hard to believe this was a woman who had lived, pre-Guy, with a white sofa and a crystal collection and who actually cleaned out the insides of her kitchen cabinets at least twice a year. Was that a cobweb up in that corner?

"Oh, don't be such a wuss," Elizabeth said, swatting one hand, the other one grasping the wooden banister as she started up the stairs. "If you can deal with those mangy cats of yours, you can handle a cute little hamster."

Nancy laughed. "Okay, who are you and what did you do with Elizabeth?"

"Yeah, yeah," she said, her ascent slowing the closer she got to the top of the stairs. "At least it's not a rat. I drew the line at anything I'd call the exterminator to get rid of. This little thing's pure Disney." She stopped to catch her breath, two steps from the top. "And Ashli's spending the night with a friend, and she's the only one of the kids I trust not to drop, strangle, or loose the thing."

Nancy started to point out that the thing would probably survive staying in its cage for one night, then realized that maybe handling hamsters was something she'd have to do sooner or later, anyway, which reminded her that she had more pressing worries, just at the moment.

They'd reached the master bedroom—at last, a large, dormer-ceilinged room wrested from two smaller ones, with yellow walls and white trim, a lace-canopied cherrywood four-poster bed and an assortment of pastel hooked rugs. Once again lost in her own thoughts, Nancy was only vaguely aware that her friend had been prattling about something having to do with Micah. Then, with a weary, but contented, sigh, Elizabeth sank onto the bench in front of her vanity, which was littered with lipsticks, perfume bottles, a plastic dinosaur and several matchbox cars, and studied Nancy for a moment. The beginnings of a late-winter sunset hazed the room in an iridescent apricot light, turning the dust motes into softly spinning glitter. Safely tucked behind a wooden grill, the old-fashioned radiator clunked, clanked, then hissed on as Nancy lowered herself onto the edge of the floral duvet-covered bed, swallowing down the panic. She traced the outline of a stain of some sort. Chocolate milk was her guess.

"So talk to me," Elizabeth said, efficiently corralling her hair into a French braid. "Micah would only growl at me all day today. Communicating in a known human language is a major thrill at this point.'' The braid finished, she picked up a mascara wand before glancing at Nancy in the mirror. Instantly, she pivoted in the chair. ''What?''

Okay, she had to say this. To someone. Maybe saying it would either make it seem more real or make it go away, like confronting the monster in a nightmare. ''Here's a tip for you. Never trust a diaphragm that's three years old.''

It took a few seconds. Then, eyes wide: ''Nance! Ohmigod! You're preg—?''

''Mama!'' Both women whipped around to the pair of deadly serious children crowded into the bedroom doorway. ''Micah won't listen to me when I tell him to stop messing with Einstein!'' Right on cue, an enormous gray dog that looked like a cross between an Irish wolfhound and a briar patch slithered between the two children, then lumbered over to Elizabeth, collapsing with a huge, put-upon sigh at her feet.

''Jake, honey—Nancy and I really need to talk right now. Alone. So could you and Micah *please*—?''

''But Micah keeps poking his fingers in Einstein's face!''

''Einstein's plenty big enough and smart enough to leave if Micah's bothering him, Jake,'' she said. ''That's why your daddy named him Einstein. I suppose.'' She stood, ushering her sons out the bedroom door. ''Isn't 'Reading Rainbow' on now?''

Micah tilted his head up. ''I'm hungry.'' Elizabeth tossed an apologetic look in Nancy's direction.

Nancy shooed her out of the room. ''Go. Be a mommy. I'll be here.''

After Elizabeth and the boys left, Nancy slowly lay back on the bed, her hand spreading across her tummy. Kids didn't start out like that, she reminded herself. Not to mention the fact that this could be a false alarm. Please, God, let this be a false alarm.

The shudder of disappointment took her completely by surprise.

''Okay, they're set at least for the next ten minutes,'' Elizabeth said as she swept back into the room. She sank back on the vanity stool, one hand on her chest, lowering her voice to conspiratorial depths. ''You think you're *pregnant?*''

''I don't know.'' The words rushed out, stumbling over the fear. ''I mean, I'm a little late—''

''Define *a little*.''

''Five days?''

Elizabeth's brow crumpled. Not good.

''So I thought maybe I'd miscalculated when my last period was, but when I got home, I checked my calendar there, and…I hadn't.'' She paused, tears brimming. ''And I'm never late. Ever.''

''Oh, honey…'' It took a couple of heaves, but Elizabeth managed to push herself off the bench and over to the bed, where she sat down, heavily, which made Nancy slide in her direction. ''Whose is it?''

Nancy blinked, skootched away. One fat tear escaped, lazily tracked down her cheek. ''I can't believe you're asking this.''

Brows lowered. Thinking. Brows shot up. Revelation. *''Rod?''*

''What? You thought maybe I had a selection?''

For the first time since Nancy had known her, Elizabeth was speechless. Her mouth was open, yes, but nada was coming out of it.

''In fact,'' Nancy filled in, ''this is partly your fault.''

A beringed hand slapped a recently blossomed bosom. *''My* fault?''

''Well, yeah, since you were so hot to get us together.''

''Cripes, Nance, there's together and then there's *together*. Besides, how on earth was I to know you'd do the deed with an antique diaphragm? And aren't you supposed to use some stuff with it?''

''Well, hey, honey, guess what? That wasn't exactly farm-fresh, either. Parted like the Red Sea, waved those overachieving little sperm right on through.''

''That overachieving sperm.''

''Huh?''

"Technicality. Only one sperm got through, you know."

"Something tells me it—or is it 'he'?—had company. Where are you going?" she said to Elizabeth's back as it vanished into the adjacent bathroom. A cabinet door creaked open, slammed, then Elizabeth reappeared, holding out a pink-and-white box.

"Pregnancy test," she announced. "I have a few extras." At Nancy's raised brows, she said, "I wanted to be sure, so I bought...several. Guy assured me when the third one was positive it was probably a pretty good bet I was pregnant, so I had these left over."

Nancy regarded the box as if it might blow up in her face. Elizabeth rattled it, making Nancy jump.

"You gonna find out now, or wait until the head pops out?"

"Isn't it too early to tell?"

But Elizabeth shook her head. "These new ones are real sensitive. Three days, that's all you need." She grabbed Nancy's hand, plopped the box into it. "And they only take a minute."

Nancy looked at the box, then up at Elizabeth, who sighed. "You're only gonna make yourself ill wondering," she said gently.

Two minutes later, Nancy emerged from Elizabeth's bathroom, paler and wiser. Elizabeth, now dressed in a tunic and leggings, took one look at Nancy's face, then swept her as far into her arms as her unborn child would allow.

"Damn," she said into Nancy's hair, then held her at arm's length. "What are you going to do?"

A shrill, maniacal laugh shot out of Nancy's throat. "I don't even know what to *think,* and the woman asks me if I know what I'm going to *do.*"

Elizabeth gave a worried little huff, then sat back in front of her mirror. "When are you going to tell Rod?" she asked softly as she clipped on one, then the other, oversize pearl earring from the dish in front of her.

Nancy dropped to the bed again, clutching one of the testers for support. "I was thinking somewhere around the kid's thirty-fifth birthday."

"No, I'm serious."

"You think I'm not?"

Elizabeth twisted around, sort of, one arm braced along the top of the chair. "Nancy. You can't keep this from him."

"Elizabeth. You weren't there when the man said, point-blank, no room for discussion, he did not want any more children."

Narrowed eyes met hers. "Then perhaps he should have thought of that before you two fooled around. Or used something himself."

A flush sped up Nancy's neck, firing her cheeks. "I, um, kind of forced the issue."

"Uh-huh. Like you expect me to believe you tied the man up and had your wicked way with him, what?" Elizabeth shook her head. "Birth-control failure happens. More often than people like to admit. You *have* to tell him, Nance. At least give him the opportunity to decide what role he wants in his child's life."

She didn't want to think about any of this. Wasn't ready to. Knew she had no choice. She jumped up from the bed and walked over to the window, watching the last rays slant across the pockmarked white yard. An off-kilter snowman listed over by the fence; back by an old grape arbor, a swing set patiently waited for spring. And up in the sprawling oak tree in the center of the yard, Guy had started building a tree house that was going to be *Architectural Digest*-worthy by the time he was finished with it. He and Elizabeth had had their challenges, and they'd be the first to admit the first few months of their marriage had had some rocky moments, what with Elizabeth trying to adjust to suddenly being a mother and Guy's almost suffocating attempts to ensure his new wife's happiness. It wasn't a perfect marriage. Of course, this wasn't "The Donna Reed Show," either, she thought with a smile. But their commitment to each other, to their family, had never been in question. And their new child would be born into a home full of love and confidence and joy.

A home with two parents.

What sort of beginning, what sort of future, could Nancy offer this child spawned of a single night of loneliness-induced lust? Yes, she'd wanted to be a mother for as long as she could remember. But not like this. Not alone. Not by a father who had already spurned it. Her eyes stung. How could she have been so *stupid?*

"I'm not exactly in the same position as you, Elizabeth," she said quietly, knuckling a frost-feather from the window-pane.

"So what're you going to do?" came the surprisingly crisp reply. Nancy turned around to be singed by the fire in Elizabeth's eyes. "Leave town? Give the baby up for adoption?"

"Oh, for God's sake, Elizabeth!" Nancy cried, fisting her hand against the window. "I don't know, okay? Things just don't fall neatly into place for me like they always have for you." The tears came, copious and hot, and she just gave in to them. "So just back off for a minute and give me a chance to figure out what the hell I'm supposed to do!"

"Mama? Why's Aunt Nancy crying?"

Nancy spun around to the window again, frantically scrubbing at her face, as she heard Elizabeth lead Jake back out of the bedroom with whispered assurances. A minute later, she felt her friend's arm slip around her shoulders. "I'm sorry, honey," she said, rubbing Nancy's arm. "Motherhood has made me just a bit on the pushy side, I guess. But may I remind you how much I fought this, fought falling in love with Guy? I was so damn sure I knew what was best for me, that I'd be no good at being a mother, that I couldn't love Guy as much as he needed to be loved. Less than two years ago, none of this was on my agenda."

"Is there a point, Elizabeth?"

"Yeah, somewhere in here. Come here." She guided Nancy back over to the bed, settling them both on the edge. "Rod's a good man. I may not have been able to love him, but I know integrity when I see it, and the man's got more than a dozen ordinary men. His reaction might surprise you. Yes, yes, I know what he *said*. But I cannot believe that Rod Braden would ever turn his back on his own child. Or on the woman carrying that child.''

''It was a one-night stand, Elizabeth…why are you shaking your head?''

''Because this doesn't add up. I know both of you, remember? Not once in all the time we dated did Rod ever suggest taking me to bed—''

''I told you. I initiated it.''

''And I happen to know other women who came on to him that he turned down.'' Once again, her brow puckered. ''That's no womanizer, honey. I don't pretend to know what's going on in his head, but I'd stake my life that whatever happened between you means far more than he's admitting.'' She took a breath, as if to say something else, then seemed to change her mind, instead giving Nancy's shoulder a squeeze. ''Tell him, honey. Keeping this a secret isn't going to do anyone any good, believe me.''

''Hey, you two—'' Guy's warm, mellow voice in the doorway made them both jump. He looked from his wife to Nancy, his customary grin dying as he quickly figured out who was having the crisis. He cleared his throat, jerked his thumb toward the door. ''I take it I should leave?''

Beside her, Elizabeth let out a sigh. ''You know, I'm not all that sure Nancy's up for baby-sitting tonight. Maybe we should cancel.''

Nancy protested before she'd even gotten a good look at Guy's horrified do-you-have-any-idea-how-much-these-tickets-cost? expression. ''No way!'' she said, forcing a smile. ''I'm fine. Really. Besides, I've already rented a movie, and I'd planned on ordering pizza. Who wants to watch *A Bug's Life* and eat pizza alone?''

''But you're—'' Elizabeth started.

''Fine,'' Nancy finished, snagging those green eyes in hers.

''Really.'' She caught Guy's what-the-hell? gaze, tossed him a scrap of reassurance, too. ''Really.''

''Welllll...'' Genuine concern dragged out the word. ''If you're absolutely sure...''

Nancy stood, dragging Elizabeth up with her, scanning the blonde's swollen figure. Her stomach lurched, thudded, lurched again. ''Positive. You two go on, get out of here.''

A half hour later, she watched Jake and Micah each dispense no less than a dozen hugs and kisses to their parents before the couple could get out the door, saw Guy slip a protective arm around Elizabeth's waist to guide her down the stairs.

And her heart bled.

Chapter 5

Nancy sat in her car the following Sunday, staring up at Rod's house, questioning his sanity. She'd never actually seen the place, not close up, although she'd heard about it plenty from Elizabeth. Some self-made business tycoon type had built the monstrosity back in the fifties, both to show off his new-found wealth and to appease his Spruce Lake-born-and-bred wife, who refused to move to one of the posher Detroit suburbs.

She shook her head. The place might be the most expensive property in town, but it was also the tackiest. The only thing missing was gargoyles. Now, in another part of Michigan, the ivy-covered stone structure would have fit right in. But in unpretentious Spruce Lake, it just looked bizarre. And it certainly did not look like Rod Braden.

And she was certainly doing a great job of procrastinating, wasn't she?

Her stomach took a slow, nauseated turn. Elizabeth was right—this wasn't something she could keep from him. She'd spent the rest of the weekend holed up in her little house, thinking. Planning. Praying. Elizabeth suggested taking things one step at a time, rather than trying to figure out everything all at once. And this time, Nancy didn't find her friend's obsession with order a pain in the can. Especially since she wasn't exactly coming up with any hot ideas herself.

Of one thing, however, she was absolutely certain: she was going to keep this baby. Some people would say she was crazy, others would say she had guts, and her mother probably wouldn't say anything, because she'd never speak to her again. But she'd wanted a baby of her own since she was old enough to know where they came from. Of course, the plan had been to get married first. Which she'd done, actually. Except picking a self-centered jerk who was already fixed when they got married—and who hadn't bothered to dispense this tidbit of information beforehand—had kinda screwed up her plans. And after the divorce, when no other potential candidate seemed to be forthcoming, she'd briefly considered using a sperm donor, having a baby on her own. But it never seemed right, somehow. Especially whenever she thought of how she'd tell her mother.

Oh, well.

In any case, that part of the decision was made. No way was she giving up something she'd yearned for all her adult life. While she wasn't exactly rolling in dough, she did okay, and Elizabeth had steered her toward some excellent investment opportunities over the years. If she kept things simple, she could even stay home with the child for six months, maybe even a year, without having to go back to work....

She laughed softly to herself, shaking her head. So much for "one step at a time." The way she was going, she'd have the kid's college picked out before she was four weeks pregnant. That, she could handle. Sleepless nights and breastfeeding and terrible twos and broken appendages and teenage angst, she could handle.

Telling Rod Braden they'd made a baby that night...

Oy.

She took a deep breath or two, got out of the car. Walked up the driveway. Then the steps.

Rang the bell.

Seconds later, a slender teenage girl more than a head taller than she answered the front door. Why it hadn't occurred to her that Rod's kids might be there this weekend, she didn't know, but they obviously were. And the one standing in front of her was wearing a we-don't-want-any expression Nancy had used a time or two herself over the years.

Smile, honey, she told herself. *You're carrying this child's brother or sister.*

Nancy smiled. "Hi, I'm Nancy Shapiro. You must be Rod's daughter?"

This babe wasn't giving an inch. She shifted, her arms pretzling over her rib cage. "Maybe," she said. "You know my father?"

Good one. "I sure do. If he's in, I'd really like to see him—"

"Hannah?" came the deep voice from inside the house. "Who is it, honey?"

Hannah—nice name—turned back inside the house, muttering about "some lady who wants to see you." Nancy bristled, wondering why it was certain people seemed to think having money and position excused them from learning basic social skills. A second later, Rod appeared in the doorway, sinfully gorgeous in coffee-brown corduroy pants and a loden turtleneck sweater. Surprise leapt from his eyes.

"Nancy!" A smile flickered, faded, then finally held. "Please…come in. I was just fixing lunch for the kids. There's plenty if you'd like to join us…."

After his daughter's borderline rudeness, his immediate hospitality, despite his obvious confusion, knocked Nancy off-balance. For a moment. Come to think of it, he was acting exactly as she'd expect him to. But sharing a private meal with him and his children, being social…uh, no. That, she wasn't up to.

''No, no,'' she said quickly, backing up. ''I should have called first. I'm sorry. I'll…maybe I could come back?''

Rod frowned, then said quietly to his daughter, ''Honey, would you mind checking the pasta, see if it's done yet?'' He waited a moment, as if to be sure Hannah was out of earshot, then said, ''Nancy, if you're trying to play casual here, it isn't working. Is something wrong?''

Like she was going to tell him out here. ''Not…necessarily. I just…need to talk to you. But this obviously isn't a good time….''

''No, no…it's fine. Please—'' he waved her inside the marble-floored entry ''—come in. You look frozen half to death. There's a fire in the den.'' He led her past the curving staircase, a moldy-looking living room to the right and on into a marginally less moldy-looking room with a resolutely cheerful fire popping in the stone fireplace. ''I'll, uh, just get the kids started…'' He started away. Turned back. Nervous. Suspicious? ''Can I get you anything? A cup of tea?''

She gave a weak laugh. ''You must have been an innkeeper in a previous life,'' she quipped, then shook her head. ''No, nothing, thank you. I'm not staying.''

Rod nodded, then left her to the comfort of the warm, cherrywood-paneled room. She knew he'd bought much of the furniture the old man had chosen to leave behind when he moved to his Arizona condo; the well-worn leather furniture, the threadbare Oriental rug, must have been part of the deal. A quick glance revealed large, light ivory rectangles set in dishwater-gray walls where she assumed pictures of some sort had once hung. A pair of floor-to-ceiling mullioned windows looked out over the expansive backyard, though ''yard'' seemed a pathetic term to describe the veritable forest of evergreens and winter-bare deciduous trees visible from where she stood. Before she realized what she was doing, she visualized how the room would look with freshly painted walls, maybe a handsome striped wallpaper, brightly upholstered furniture, a new rug. Like Charlie Brown's pitiful little Christmas tree, it wasn't a bad house, really. Just needed some love.

Chastising herself, she sidled closer to the inviting fire, rubbing her hands together—she saw no point in even removing her coat, figuring she wanted to be ready to escape at a moment's notice.

"There." Rod said, striding into the room. "I'm all yours." She cringed at his choice of words, her stomach crashing to her knees. In spite of the fire and three layers of clothing, she couldn't get warm. Trepidation and soul-deep coldness combined to set her insides trembling so badly she wasn't sure she could speak.

Rod was instantly beside her, a strong hand supporting her elbow. "Are you ill? What is it, for God's sake!"

"I'm not ill, Rod." Her eyes burned, but she felt reasonably sure she could get through this dry-eyed. "I'm pregnant."

Predictably, every drop of color drained from his face, until he was about the same color as the dingy walls. His hand fell from her arm as he took a small but nonetheless visible step back. "But it's…it's only been what? Three weeks? Isn't that too early to know for sure?"

While she could hardly blame him for the frantic, thready hope underscoring his words, give the man ten points for not questioning whether it was his baby. "I'm only a week late, true." She hauled in a breath. "But I never am. So I took a test—they have ones now that can tell even after only a couple days—and…it was positive. As was the second one I took, just to be sure."

Horror sparked from those golden eyes for a second or two before he walked over to one of the windows, massaging the back of his neck. When he spoke next, however, he might have been asking her what brand of tissue she preferred. "I thought you said you were using something." His sudden calmness after just having been blindsided struck her as odd, if not downright scary.

"I was. A diaphragm. It was, um, defective."

"Aren't you supposed to check those things periodically?" Still calm. Too calm. "Make sure they're okay?"

"Last time I checked, it *was* okay." Her heartbeat pounded in her ears as she prayed he wouldn't ask the next question.

"Which was when?"

Oh, hell. She rammed her hands in her pockets, ran into an old ticket stub, pulled them out again. "A year and a half ago," she mumbled.

Rod returned his gaze to the window, expressionless save for the hand fisting, unfisting, at his side. "You know I don't want another child," he said at last, his voice flat but brittle.

"Yeah. I got that message loud and clear."

He turned back to her, his mouth taut from the effort of keeping his emotions under check. Here she was, experiencing arguably the worst moment of her life, worrying about the way Rod was holding it all in. Go figure. "Yet you told me."

She crossed her arms. Or tried to. The coat was too bulky. And now she was beginning to overheat. "I almost didn't," she said, which got a pair of raised brows. "But since I intend to keep the baby, and since I'm not going anywhere, I figured you'd put two and two together pretty quickly. And I figured I'd rather get this over with now."

He frowned. "Get what over with?"

"Having you tell me it's completely my decision whether or not I have this baby, but since I was the one using the defective diaphragm and since you're the one who doesn't want kids, this is my problem to work out, so thanks for telling you but I'm on my own."

She waited, sure the explosion was imminent now. He had to be furious. *Had* to be. Yet he just stood there, obviously angry, obviously unwilling to let it out. The frown deepened, but that was all. "Why do you assume I'm going to tell you you're on your own?"

"Uh…lucky guess?"

A heavy sigh pushed through his lips. "I'll be honest with you, Nancy. Right this minute, I haven't the slightest idea what to think. Or do."

"Yelling might be an option."

His brows lifted. "And what good would that do?"

"Oh, I don't know…maybe make you feel better? Cripes, Rod—I just told you I screwed up, got myself pregnant, and you're just…just *standing* there—"

Gold eyes pinned hers. "Got *yourself* pregnant?"

"Oh, hell—you know what I mean."

His whisper was fierce. Controlled. "I know there were two of us in the bed that night. And while I'm not happy about this, yelling or losing control hardly puts me in the right frame of mind in which to make a decision that'll be best for everybody."

Something zipped up her spine that felt suspiciously like pique. "*You* have to make a decision?"

One hand came up, another sigh spilling from his lungs. "I didn't mean that the way it sounded. Of course, we'll work this out together. But I'm not going to turn you out on your own, nor will I abandon a child I helped to create, no matter what the circumstances of its conception."

She wasn't sure she was hearing correctly, what with hammering heartbeats and the crackle of the fire and her emotions going haywire inside her head. "You mean…you don't expect me to terminate the pregnancy?"

For the first time, something genuine flared in his eyes: *appalled* was her guess. "You don't solve a problem by pretending it never happened," he said. "You own up to it. Deal with it. Make the best of it, if that's possible. But you don't take the most expedient route just to save your backside."

Pride stirred in her heart, mixed with not a little amazement. Granted, this child hadn't been conceived in love, but out of a momentary lapse of good judgment on the part of two people old enough and smart enough to know better. And granted, whatever choices they made about the hows and whos and whens of raising this baby weren't going to be easy. But right at this moment, Nancy could only hope this child had inherited a tenth of his or her father's integrity.

Before now she hadn't been able to put into words what had attracted her to Rod from the very beginning, when he shook her hand on the day Elizabeth introduced them, nearly four years ago. He'd looked her directly in the eye and smiled, and something had tingled right up her arm, straight to her heart. All this time, she'd thought it was lust. Now she knew she'd actually been bowled over by something fine and rare and precious. Something that, despite the impending appearance of this child, she also now knew would never be hers. She'd had glimpses—that first meeting, their one night together, a moment ago—and she would have this most excellent man's child.

But that would be all she'd ever get, make no mistake. For whatever reasons, Rod Braden had locked up his heart safe and sound inside a shell of icy determination to do what was "best." At one time, Nancy might have been willing to try melting that shell, to see what glorious things might come from letting their hearts blend. That time had passed, however, despite the now ironic circumstances that would, in effect, bind them for the rest of their lives. Now she had only enough energy for herself, and for the child just beginning to take root under her heart.

She realized that, with his declaration, Rod had shown all there was of him to see—a good, stalwart man, willing to take responsibility for his actions. A lot, actually, considering. But not enough for Nancy. And so she plucked the seeds from her heart that she might have been willing to let blossom, once upon a time, and mentally squashed them.

Admiration for the man was one thing. Lust, even, she could understand. But having this baby on her own was nothing compared to how stupid she'd be to let herself fall in love with Rod Braden.

Rod couldn't tell what she was thinking, which unnerved him. Nancy Shapiro wore her emotions the way she wore her clothes, and with just as much variety and unpredictability. Now her expression, though calm, was masked, as if she had decided he was no longer worthy of being privy to her thoughts. Ten minutes ago, he'd had no idea how much that would bother him.

Part of him wanted to touch her, to reassure her. Another part, however, the part that knew better—and where, pray tell, had that part been three weeks ago?—cautioned against making any moves which might be misconstrued as affectionate. Baby or no baby, an emotional involvement was out of the question. Took guts, her telling him like this, knowing how he felt about…things. He was also acutely aware that telling him was *all* she'd done. She'd informed him, period. She'd made no demands, had leveled no accusations, hadn't pleaded for aid in any way. Still, there was a lot to discuss, to sort out. But not with the children still here.

"Look—I'm supposed to drive the kids back to town early this evening, but I'm free after seven. Why don't we have dinner, talk things over then?"

Her face, more fragile-looking than ever, cracked a thin smile. "So I had to get pregnant to get you to ask me to dinner, huh? Wow, mister, you sure do strike a hard bargain."

"Nancy—"

"Joke, Rod. You know, when someone says something and it strikes you funny, and then you go 'ha, ha'?"

"Sorry. I guess I don't have much of a sense of humor when it comes to things like…this."

She took in a deep breath, let it slowly out. "Then I suggest you work on that, bud, because I'm not sure how we're going to get through this, otherwise." Before he could say another word, she was out of the room, headed down the hall toward the front door, her sneakered footsteps soundless against the thick pile of the Persian runner topping the marble. He caught up with her, amazed at how quickly someone so small could cover ground, and opened the door.

"Don't dress up. I'll pick you up at seven-thirty."

Her brows lifted. "That wasn't even a question."

"It wasn't meant to be."

Her coat was already buttoned; she'd caught her hair in the collar, couldn't tell where to pull it free. He did it for her, quickly, ignoring the impulse to let his fingers savor the soft curls for a moment, to inhale her scent. She nodded her thanks, her eyes wary, distrustful, then yanked on her driving gloves. "Well. This is shaping up to be an interesting next couple of decades, wouldn't you say?" She skipped down the steps, toward her car. A gust of wind caught her hair, whipping it into her face as she opened her car door and got in.

She was nearly out of the driveway before he realized she still hadn't actually agreed to have dinner with him.

Both Rod's hair and the shoulders of his navy car coat were flocked with snow when Nancy opened the door to him at 7:33. It had been snowing in earnest for some time, in fact, enough to make her wonder if they should be driving.

Rod shrugged, the snow rapidly melting in the warmth of her little house. "We're not going far," he assured her. "Besides, I've been driving in Michigan snows since I was sixteen. As long as I can see past the hood ornament, we're fine." He seemed to hesitate, as if making a decision, then squatted down, calling a couple of the cats to him. Bruiser trotted over first, followed by the shaved Persian.

"She's beginning to look more like a cat," Rod observed, stroking the poor thing's head.

"She's beginning to look more like something that originated on this planet," Nancy corrected, slipping into her coat. She angled her head, frowning slightly. "The baby is one thing, but nobody said you have to kiss up to my cats."

He lifted his eyes to her, but said nothing. Then he stood, refastening the toggles on his own coat. "Ready?" God, he looked ill. Determined, but ill.

"Rod, listen. We don't have to talk about this right now. I mean, we've got more than eight months—"

A weary smile spanned his features. "I finally invite you to dinner, and you're turning me down?"

She thought about that. Among other things. Then, with a protracted sigh, she followed him out the door to the Range Rover. What he used when he was slumming, she supposed. Ten minutes later, they pulled up into Rod's driveway. As opposed to a restaurant parking lot. "I should have known I wouldn't get an actual dinner out of this," she muttered.

He just grinned. A real grin, disarming and charming and...

Oh, no, you don't. So the man smiled. Big deal. Please note the sadness lurking in his eyes, the tension radiating from every pore of his body.

She flinched when her door swung open. "You, my dear," Rod said as he helped her out of the car, "are about to eat your words. As it were." He took hold of her elbow so she wouldn't slip on the icy walk. "Unless I'm mistaken, your eating habits are for the birds."

Even in the frigid air, she could smell him. And God knows she could feel him. The strength of his touch zipped straight to places she should have ignored three weeks ago. If she didn't watch out, she was going to start feeling extremely sorry for herself. Then she realized he was dissing her eating habits, figured she should at least make *some* show of taking umbrage. "And how would you know that?"

"I've been in your kitchen. I've even seen inside your refrigerator. You're a walking toxic dump, Nancy Shapiro. And if you're going to serve as an incubator for...my child, I fully intend to make sure you eat properly."

If he thought he was disguising the uneasiness in his voice, he was extremely mistaken. Still, she yanked her arm from his hand, throwing herself off balance so that he had to catch her again before she landed on her assets. "Excuse me, but a keeper I don't need. I'll admit my eating habits haven't been exactly wonderful, but I'm hardly going to put my unborn child in jeopardy."

"Good." He unlocked the front door. The house, dimly lit now, was even more ghastly at night. She barely suppressed a shudder. "Then I take it you'll have no trouble with what I've prepared."

"Which is?"

At Rod's direction, she shucked off her coat and gloves, then tucked her arms against her sweatered middle as she walked into the living room.

"Fish, veggies, potatoes. Nothing fancy."

Huh. Visions of battered fillets, coleslaw, fries popped into her head. Her stomach did a little "yes!" number. Then she frowned, scanning the lumpy, colorless furniture and tattered damask drapes in the room. No less than five lamps valiantly glowed on various tables, to no avail. "Rod, I hate to say this, but this is one butt-ugly house."

His laugh was soft, but at least genuine, behind her. "*Nouveau gauche* isn't to your taste, I take it?"

She smiled in spite of herself as she looked around. "You have someone come in to clean?"

"What would be the point? At least, not until it's fixed up. You know why I bought it?"

Nancy turned to him. "To be closer to Elizabeth, would be my guess."

His brows rose at her clearly unexpected answer. "Point to you," he said with a slight nod.

"So why didn't you dump the place when things…?"

Oops. Cripes, lady, be a little insensitive, why not?

"Because, oddly enough," he replied in a way-too-calm voice, "I like it. I like Spruce Lake. Both the house and the town remind me of where my grandparents lived. Place needs a lot of work, I know, but we're getting there."

What the place needed was dynamite, but she thought better of mentioning it. Rod hung up her coat in a hall closet, turned back to her. "Cider?" he said, and she jumped a foot.

"Where?"

"What? Oh, uh…in the kitchen?"

They frowned at each other for several seconds.

"Oh!" she said, erupting into laughter, not because any of this was funny, but because the strain was suddenly too much. "*Cider.* I thought you said *spider.* Yes, that would be great, thanks," she said, and then promptly burst into tears.

Oh, God, this man had a great chest, she thought as, sobbing like a complete idiot, she found herself sitting on one of the least lumpy pieces of furniture, carefully wrapped in his arms. And wouldn't it be nice, she thought some more, if she could just stay here and pretend he was comforting her because, well, he actually felt something for her besides guilt and/or responsibility?

She straightened up, dug around in the pocket of her baggy jeans for a tissue, then honked. "Sorry," she said on a sniff. "Hormones." She looked up in Rod's face and nearly cringed. Oh, yeah. Guilt with all the trimmings.

Now she swallowed at the unexpected touch of his fingers to her cheek. "You didn't get into this situation alone," he said, quietly, "and you're not going to get through it alone, either." Then he stood, took her by the hand, and led her into the kitchen.

This was getting very weird.

The kitchen, he'd already redone, judging from the airy, open design, the pickled cabinets, the gleaming silvery-gray granite countertops. The walls were a surprising and luscious shade of tomato-red, the floor a pale gray tile. An enormous wrought-iron rack hung from the ceiling, from which dangled an array of pots and pans to put Williams-Sonoma to shame. The kitchen opened onto a vast family room with a stone fireplace on one end, pine paneling, and an assortment of comfortably upholstered furniture in reds and beiges and forest-greens. Charming, cozy, unpretentious. She wandered out into the family room, slipping off her Nikes to let her wool-socked feet ooh and ahh in the thick carpeting, then returned to the kitchen, sliding up onto a red leather bar stool.

"You like?" Rod said, handing her the cider.

"Very much. As you may have guessed from my place, I tend to think of red as a neutral. I love it."

His broad smile warmed her far more than she dared let it. Then he turned to the stove, checking the various pots simmering and bubbling on the stove, then back to her. "I want to take things slowly. With the house," he added. "Do it my way, for a change." A frown creased his brow, then he let out a short sigh. "Okay, I'll admit when I realized I'd over-estimated my powers of persuasion with Elizabeth, I regretted buying the place. But putting it right back on the market would have announced my idiocy to the world, so I kept it.''

She took a sip of the cider, wondering if it was safe to venture back into the conversation. ''It wasn't your fault, you know. Elizabeth's calling it off.''

''I know that now. Hell, I knew it then. I thought she was someone she wasn't, that's all.''

She nodded, and the mug slipped, hitting the counter with a thud and spilling the contents over her hand. She winced, jumping when Rod appeared with a damp dish towel, wrapping it around her hand.

''Here,'' he said gently. ''Let me look at it.''

''It was just a bit hot, is all,'' she said, laughing. Trying to, anyway. ''I'll live.''

''If you're sure…''

She grabbed the cloth from him, wiped up the spilled cider, then handed it back, wondering how she was ever going to carry through on her resolve if he didn't stop being so bloody nice all the time, didn't stop touching her. ''You thought about marrying Elizabeth, didn't you?''

Her boldness clearly surprised him. ''I considered it, yes.''

''Even though you weren't in love with her?''

He took a moment, then said, ''I thought we'd be good together.''

''Uh-huh.'' She leaned forward, her elbow on the counter, her chin in her hand. ''You know what I think? I think you cared about her more than you let on. Maybe you didn't love her, exactly, but I'm guessing you weren't any too thrilled when she broke it off.''

That got another startled look, followed by a hollow—and telling—laugh.

''So why'd you let her believe it didn't really matter, when she called it quits?''

''Wasn't that for the best?''

Nancy stared into her mug for a moment. ''Sacrificing your own feelings to make someone else happy, you mean?''

He visibly stiffened, straightening up and walking back to

the stove. "I told you—I didn't feel that way about her. Certainly nothing like what she clearly feels for her husband. I think we're ready," he announced, pulling something out of the oven. "We'll just eat in here, if that's okay with you. If you think the living room's awful, you should see the dining room."

Uh-oh. Mother had said take one *tiny* step forward, not one *giant* step.

She slid off the stool, then crossed to the table set booth-style in one corner. Rod was moving swiftly, efficiently, and silently. Annoyed, she caught his arm before he could return to the stove.

"Look. I don't know how much time we're actually going to spend together because of all this, but if we don't at least learn how to have a conversation without fear of stepping on each others' toes, it's going to be a very trying twenty or so years. I'll be the first to admit, diplomacy isn't my strong suit. I open my mouth, and the truth just kinda falls out. So. You got unresolved issues about Elizabeth or anyone else, fine. None of my business. You don't want to talk about it, I don't want or need to know. If I inadvertently step into forbidden territory, tell me to back off, or shut up, whatever—I can take it. But just say *something*. This strong, silent number is for the birds."

He glared at her for a long, tense moment, causing her to wonder if she'd actually get dinner after all. At least it was a step up from icy reserve, however, so she figured she'd be grateful for small favors. Just as she was about to pinch him to be sure he was still breathing, he nodded so suddenly she blinked.

"Point taken." He crossed to the refrigerator, nodding toward the built-in granite table. "Please, sit," he said quietly, pouring milk into two cut crystal goblets, which he then carried to the table, simply set with woven red placemats, white candles in pewter candlesticks, and unadorned white plates that probably didn't come from any discount store. Betcha that wasn't stainless flatware, either.

She sat, watching him cautiously as he filled two plates and brought them to the table as well. His face was a mask, save for that tight jaw, but stress radiated from him like sound waves.

Nancy sighed, rubbing one temple. "I came on too strong, huh?"

Rod had been about to sit across from her; he hesitated on the way down, glanced at her, then sat, shaking his head. "No. No, I was just thinking about what you said, in the light of what I'm about to suggest."

"Oh?" she said, taking a bite of what turned out to be the best fish she'd ever tasted outside some place where the waiters' tips could probably fund a small country. "And what is that?" She took another bite, then sampled the asparagus, hoping she could manage not to scarf it down like some junkyard dog. What *had* he done to these potatoes...?

He shook his head again. "Food first. And conversation. Like a date."

She nearly choked. "A date?"

"How's your salmon?" he asked, ignoring her.

She blinked. Swallowed. "Oh! Uh, fabulous. It's all fabulous." Her mind was still working on the "date" comment, but her mouth and stomach were quite content to discuss the food. "You're a helluva better cook than I am."

That actually got a laugh. "I learned to cook when I was in college. Junk food never held much appeal."

Did he have any idea how his eyes crinkled at the corners when he laughed? Wow. Nancy forked in another bite of fish. "This is serious restaurant-quality stuff, here, you know?"

Rod wouldn't look at her. She took a sip of her milk, her eyes narrowed.

"What did I say?"

"Nothing. It's just..." Wistful smile. "I toyed with the idea of having my own restaurant, at one time."

"Get outta here! So, why didn't you?"

His mouth tightened. "It just never worked out, that's all. More potatoes?"

She thrust out her plate. She also got the hint. "Ah," she said as Rod returned to the stove, refilled her plate. "This one of those forbidden areas?"

He returned, set her plate down in front of her, then sat. "Let's just say it's not something I think about anymore, that's all."

Like a puny fast-food hamburger, the truth was in there, somewhere. But nowhere near the surface, she guessed. They ate in silence for the next few minutes, then she said, stubbornly, "Seems a shame, though. Giving up on the restaurant idea, I mean." Realizing she was lusting after the single asparagus spear still on Rod's plate, she looked up. "You ever regret not doing it?"

He leaned back in the booth, holding his milk as elegantly as a wineglass. "Following a dream isn't always an option. In my case, there were other people to consider...." He suddenly leaned forward, his gaze intent, as if trying to pass along a secret without getting caught. "I'm not like you. I can't just do whatever I want to, whenever the mood strikes. And that's not meant to be a criticism, so please don't take it that way. There are times..."

He stared hard at the glass, his mouth set, then looked back up at her. "Sometimes I wished I *had* taken some chances. Maybe things would be different if I had. But I have to believe I made the best decisions I could, at the time, decisions that were best for everyone." His shoulders hitched, dropped. "Everyone makes sacrifices, Nancy. It's just part of life. And thinking about things I can't change is a waste of energy."

She took a swallow of her milk, suddenly and acutely aware that Rod had just opened up to her in a way she figured he rarely did. Not completely, perhaps, but it was a start. She wasn't sure whether to be flattered or freaked, although freaked was winning out. "Something tells me you've made more sacrifices than most men in your position would have," she said to her glass, skimming one finger along the rim, then lifted her eyes to his. "And why are you telling me all this, anyway?"

He shifted, stood up. Began to clear the table. "There's homemade raspberry sorbet for dessert," he said, carrying the dishes to the sink.

He'd evaded her question. Prickles of dread raised the hair on Nancy's arms. She rose as well, crossed to the sink. "Rod?" She laid one hand on his arm, rock-hard beneath her touch.

"My previous two wives," he said softly, "both complained that I never really talked to them. I figured, this time around, maybe I should think about improving on that."

The prickles turned to jabs. "This time…around?"

"Now…" Refusing to meet her gaze, let alone her question, Rod pulled a pair of already filled dessert dishes from the freezer, handed one to her, along with a slender silver spoon. "How about we have dessert in front of the fire?"

His long legs ferried him into the family room within seconds. Nancy trotted along behind, contemplating whopping him on the head with the spoon to get his attention. He set down his dish on an end table next to a very comfy-looking plaid couch, then crouched to poke at the fire.

"Excuse me for being repetitious," she said to his back, "but *this* time around?"

Dusting off his hands, he rose, turned to her, his expression a curious mixture of hope, fear and resignation. He slipped his hands into his pockets, cleared his throat. "There's really only one solution to this that makes any sense."

"This?"

He nodded toward her abdomen.

"Oh. Right. And what's that?"

Like an afterthought, a smile flashed across his face. "Marriage."

Chapter 6

Nancy collapsed onto the sofa with a little gasp, her spoon flying out of her hand to land neatly between the cushions. "As in, to each other?"

"You sound surprised."

The spoon duly retrieved, she now clutched it to her paltry bosom. "Surprised, hell," she finally got out. "Try *flabbergasted.*"

His smile put out of its misery, he sat beside her, poking at his own sorbet. "It really is the only reasonable solution."

"Wait, wait, wait...was I hallucinating, or did you not tell me, in no uncertain terms, that you were not, repeat *not,* the least bit interested in getting married again? Not to mention the fact that you said you didn't want another kid. Then there are a few other minor details, like the kids you've already got. My cats. My furniture." She stuffed a huge spoonful of sorbet into her mouth, her taste buds bursting into the "Hallelujah Chorus." "And, last but certainly not least—hello?—*we don't love each other.* Far as I can tell, the only thing we know we have in common is great sex." She jabbed the spoon toward the dish. "And a mutual appreciation for your culinary talents. Not a whole lot to base a marriage on. Call me weird, but I'm not real big on living a lie."

He sighed, ran his hand through his hair. It fell neatly back into place. Figured. "I was afraid you wouldn't take this well."

If there'd been a wall handy, she would have beaten her head against it. "Then why'd you even bring it up?"

He set his dish on the coffee table and stood, rubbing the back of his neck. "Because I'm not the type who breeds illegitimate children and then just goes about my business," he said, his rigid control at painful odds with his words. "Because I already have two children who look at me as if I just crawled out from underneath a rock, to whom I have no intention of giving any more ammunition. What am I telling them about responsibility if I let you have this baby on your own?"

"Whoa, hold on a minute—" She clunked the empty dish on the coffee table in front of her. "Correct me if I'm wrong, but that's quite a leap from responsibility to marriage! The out-of-wedlock stigma went out some time ago."

"Not for me, it didn't." He crossed his arms, his mouth set. "Maybe I wouldn't win the Ward Cleaver Award for Faultless Fathering, but I'm still the only example they have. And I want them to know if you play, you pay."

Nancy called her wits back from where they'd scattered about the room, got up, and walked over to this man who'd fathered a child by mistake and now was willing to spend the rest of his life paying for it. Okay, so was she, but she'd always wanted a child. She wanted *this* child. He didn't.

Nor was she all that hot on the idea of serving as his penance.

"Rod?" She watched and waited as he took in several deep breaths, then pivoted to face her. "Do you really want to marry me?"

"This is what's best for everybody. Perfect, no. I'll admit that. But best."

God. Did the guy have this tattooed on his forehead, or what? "I see. And, by any chance, have you bothered including yourself in that equation?"

The change in his expression was barely perceptible—a slight enlarging of his pupils, a flick of his brows. "What I want isn't the issue here."

"Well, it is for me. Frankly, I'd rather my child grew up in a stable, loving home with one parent, than with two parents who got married only because one of them decided they 'had' to."

"Nancy, think how much I can offer him. Or her."

"Hey, hey—maybe I'm not rolling in it, unlike some people I could mention, but I'm hardly indigent! I could even stay home with the baby for a while. I don't *need* your money. Or your name."

He crossed his arms. "And what's your mother going to say about this?"

There went the wind right out of the old sails. "Wow," she said after a moment. "Talk about targeting the customer's weak spot."

The corners of his mouth tilted, just slightly. "You took that course, too, I take it?"

"*Bubeleh,* I *wrote* that course. In any case, my mother will live," she finally said, but without a whole lot of enthusiasm. "It's not like I'm sixteen."

"So it won't hurt her as much because you're older and supposedly wiser?"

Nancy's spun around, walked away, spun back around, her arms knotted over her middle. "You're wasted in marketing, Braden. You should be a lawyer."

"My father did that, thank you. That was as close as I wanted to get."

O-o-o-oh, did we hear bitterness in that remark? But right now she had other, more pressing, issues to address, like hanging on to her independence, so wondering about Rod Braden's past would have to wait. Even if that past might affect her future far more than she would have thought, oh, say ten minutes ago.

So she scraped out one more thing from the bottom of the bag. "It's early yet. Maybe we should wait."

"Until what? You're showing?"

"Well, no. But at least until the first trimester's past—"

"No."

"That's it? Just *no?*"

"Yes."

She rolled her eyes. "Then, I assume this is going to be one of those temporary arrangements? You know, where the two people get married for a year or something, then divorce and go on their merry ways—"

"No."

She looked at him. "*Another* no?"

"Damn straight. I don't make conditional commitments, Nancy." She watched as he approached her, hands in pockets, something actually close to a scowl on his face. Now, the last thing she expected, especially concerning the circumstances, was a prickle of sexual awareness from some undefined spot way down deep. But that scowl...wow. There was something about a determined, gut-wrenchingly handsome, basically good—if misguided—man, wearing a face like that just...wow.

She had to think about this. So she kind of folded herself up sideways into the sofa corner, her feet on the cushions, and pushed her heart, among other things, back down where it belonged. Rod sat by her feet, knees apart, hands entwined, looking out over the room. "We've both been married before," he began. "And divorced. In my case, I wasn't in love with either of my wives." He glanced at her. "Were you in love with your husband?"

"Do I get more points for a *yes* or *no* answer?"

He shook his head, smiled. "Just answer the question."

"Then...yeah. I loved the jerk. Right up until the day I found out he was cheating on me."

"Well, there you go. Maybe we both started from different

standpoints, but the results were the same, right?'' He went on before she could answer. ''You've been disappointed in love, I'm not looking for it, which means neither of us is going to base this marriage on anything but practical issues.''

''Excuse me—'' One finger went up. ''Perhaps this might be a good time to reiterate that, from my viewpoint, not being in love with each other is a very practical reason *not* to get married. Not to mention *your kids*...why are you shaking your head?''

''Because you're wrong.''

''Well, thank you for giving my viewpoint such thorough consideration.''

She started to get up, to leave, but Rod pulled her back down onto the sofa. ''No, wait...hear me out.'' He let out like the hundredth sigh of the evening, looking so miserable, and so intent, Nancy almost felt sorry for him. To her surprise, he leaned back against the sofa and brought her right foot up onto his knees, whereupon he began gently stroking her instep. Not sexually—exactly—just...friendly-like.

''Okay, look. As far as the kids go, they're with their mother most of the time, and they're nearly grown. I really don't think the stepmother issue *is* an issue. Besides which, they're bound to like you—yes, they are—and I really think, when all's said and done, you and I could be pretty good friends.'' He patted her foot. ''See, Claire and I never really liked each other, I decided. We were hot for each other, and thought we needed each other in some shallow, social way, but that was about it. Then there was that second fiasco. Myrna. I'm still not sure what she and I had, but it sure wasn't friendship. She was on the rebound, and I was...'' He let the sentence die out on its own. ''Anyway,'' he said with renewed energy, ''since we've got this baby coming, and since I think we probably get along better than I ever did with either of my wives—''

''There's no way this would work, Rod,'' Nancy said.

''You want to think about it?''

She leaned forward. "Did I hear correctly? Did *you?* I. Don't. Want. To. Marry. You."

He smiled. A pretty good one, too, showing teeth and everything. "You're letting your emotions talk for you, Nance. From a practical standpoint, you'll realize this marriage has just as good a chance of working as any. But I'm not going to coerce you." Then his fingers moved, very slowly, *verrrry* steadily, up underneath her pant leg, not doing anything, really, except tracing tiny little circles here and there and basically making her throat go dry.

The fire popped and crackled a few feet away, waiting for someone to say something.

She heard "I'll think about it" come out of her mouth.

So much for resolve.

Nancy slipped her feet out from underneath his hands, ignoring their little moans of disappointment as she resheathed them in her sneakers. She got up, walked back through the house, retrieved her coat from the hall closet and was halfway down the steps before she realized her car wasn't in the driveway.

The snow had stopped, leaving the air crisp, the moon suspended like an opal in the blue-black sky. The fresh snow glittered in its bath of gentle, silvery light. It was all fresh and new and untouched, like the child growing inside her.

Rod's child.

She twisted herself around to find him leaning against the doorjamb, his arms crossed, one of those half smiles tilting his lips. "Kind of a cold night for a walk, don't you think?"

Befuddled. That's what she was, what Rod Braden made her. He liked her, but would never love her. He wanted to marry her, for all sorts of altruistic motives that only he understood, but he would never love her. And unless her hormones were in major wishful-thinking mode, he wanted to make love to her again. But he would never love her.

He was offering everything he had to give—his protection, his name, his money, his presence in his child's life, a house that needed serious help. Quite possibly his body. In short, everything but his heart.

While she'd been standing there, doing all this pointless thinking, Rod had put on his coat and was now headed toward her. When he reached her, he surprised her—again—by leaning down and kissing her. Nothing earth-shattering, no tongue action or anything, just this nice, sweet, safe, warm kiss that she knew was more than a lot of women would ever have. More than she'd ever had up to this point, that was for damn sure. Oh, but this wasn't fair. At all.

Pride was one thing. Blatant stupidity, something else entirely. Unfortunately, only time would tell in which camp her instant decision would fall.

"Okay. As much as it pains me to say this—" she hauled in a breath "—you're right." The moon was bright enough for her to see his brows lift. "My mother would never let me hear the end of it if I turned you down."

"Smart girl," he said, then kissed her again, with a little more oomph this time. But when he lifted his head, the deep sadness in his eyes made her ill.

"Rod! What on earth are you doing here? It's nearly ten o'clock."

"The kids still awake, Claire?"

"Well, yes, I suppose…" Suspicion flickering in her pale blue eyes, Claire stepped aside to let Rod into the Bloomfield Hills condo in which she'd been living since their divorce. Quite the showplace, thanks to a healthy infusion of Rod's money, complete with marble floors, walls sponged to look like weathered stone, and outrageously expensive minimalist furniture that hurt to sit on.

Deep rose fingernails tugged at the hem of the baby-blue cashmere twinset that matched her eyes. "Is everything okay?" This late at night, her voice seemed even lower than usual.

"Everything's fine." Well, not exactly. But as fine as it was going to get. "I just need to speak with them, that's all."

"You could've called."

"Well, I didn't."

After a brittle moment, Claire turned and led him back into the apartment, her girdled bottom motionless inside beige wool slacks.

He didn't even react to the man seated on the three-thousand-dollar torture device she called a sofa. Balding, paunchy and reeking of slightly greasy money, whoever this was probably had no idea he was just one of a series to Rod's easily bored ex-wife. He stood when Rod entered, a good four inches shorter than Claire, unimpressive in khakis and a long-sleeved black polo shirt.

Claire briskly introduced them—Rafe something-or-other—then left Rod to find the kids on his own. Which he did, in Hannah's bedroom, both of them watching a video and stuffing their faces with microwave popcorn.

"Dad?" Hannah rolled over, her brows tightly drawn together. "What gives? We just saw you—"

"You mind pausing that for a minute?" Rod asked, slipping off his coat and hanging it on the back of Hannah's desk chair. "I've got some news."

Hannah simply stared at her father, for a moment too stunned to speak. "You're getting married *again?* In two *weeks?* Why?"

He wouldn't look directly at her, which made her nervous. She glanced over to meet Schuyler's puzzled expression, shook her head—*I don't get it, either.* Most of the time, her younger brother was a major pain, but they were in this one together. Whatever it was.

"You guys are really going to like Nancy," her father said, as if they wouldn't realize he'd said the exact same thing about Myrna, less than a year ago.

"*Like* her? Jeez, Dad—you didn't even give us a chance to *meet* her. And now we're supposed to be all excited that you're marrying the woman? God! Didn't you learn anything the last time?"

Not once could she remember her father ever raising his voice to her. Or his hand. Neither Rod nor Claire believed in corporal punishment, which meant spankings simply never happened. But, right now, the look on her father's face made Hannah cringe.

"While I appreciate this is a shock, Hannah—and Schuy— I will not have you question my judgment. Or my reasons. Nancy is nothing like Myrna, which should afford both of you some reassurance, at least. So, yes, to answer your question, Hannah—I did learn from the last go-round."

Hannah flipped back around, stabbing the play button to resume the video. She felt torn up inside, furious that neither of her parents seemed to give a damn what either she or Schuy might think about the various significant others—or, in her mother's case, *in*significant others—who seemed to flit in and out of their lives with increasing regularity.

"Well," Schuy said behind her, "at least she's got a cool car."

Hannah snorted and turned up the volume, only to glower when Rod took the remote from her and paused the video once again. She buried her face in her arms, refusing to look at him, to listen to him, to let another parent lie to her again about how everything was going to be fine when they kept changing the rules like every three minutes.

"We thought we'd come into town tomorrow, take you both out to dinner. How's that sound?"

"Do whatever you want," she said into her arms, her breath hot and sticky against her skin. "You will, anyway."

She flinched from the touch of his hand on her hair, even as all she really wanted was to bury herself in his arms. Her mother had never been the cuddly type. But she remembered snuggling with Dad, when she was little. Then her parents divorced and her father got all…what? Not cold, exactly, as much as he just seemed to be buried inside himself. She'd always thought it kind of neat the way he never got angry, never yelled. But as she got older, she often wondered if he never got upset because he really didn't care.

Well, she wasn't like that, and right now, she was mad as hell.

Enough to not let her father see just how mad she was.

"Does Mom know?" she heard Schuy ask.

"She will in a minute. I wanted to tell you guys first."

That surprised her. Hannah propped her chin on her arms, so she could breathe, if nothing else. "Why?"

"Because you're my kids," Dad said simply, as if that somehow explained everything. "Well, it's getting late—"

She rolled over, suddenly curious. "Does this mean you're moving back?"

He shook his head. "No. I'm happy working from Spruce Lake. Nancy's job is there, too."

"But that house is like, *so* ugly."

Already at the door, her father smiled at that. "Then maybe you and Nancy can fix it up. She's already got several ideas."

I'm sure she does, Hannah thought, and punched the remote again.

"It's a school night," she heard behind her. "Don't stay up too late."

Her door clicked shut; Schuyler crashed down on his stomach beside her, reached for the popcorn. "Maybe it won't be so bad," he said, munching. Hannah blew through her lips. "No, really. After all, it's not like we have to live with them or anything, right? I mean, we're still gonna be here, and Mom is like the Queen of Permissiveness." He flopped onto his back, his hands behind his head. "So let Dad have his little midlife crisis, Han. Wanna bet he gets tired of this one, too? If you ask me, it's just not worth getting your drawers in a twist about."

"I guess," she said listlessly, halfheartedly taking a pull from her soda can. "I just wish…"

"What?"

She looked at her brother. For a dork, she guessed he wasn't all bad. "I just wish they'd get their damn acts together. God, Schuy—they think *our* hormones are out of control!"

Schuyler laughed so hard he nearly choked on his popcorn.

* * *

The grandfather clock on the landing struck the last notes of midnight when Rod walked in, the silence in its wake profound and taunting as he removed his coat and stashed it in the closet.

Two weeks, that's all he had to get used to the idea of being married again. Of being married to Nancy. Who was having his baby.

He stopped, right in the middle of the hallway, and thought about that. Before, he'd been more concerned with making sure she accepted his sorry-assed proposal than about how he would actually feel if—when—she did. Yesterday, even, the thought of being married again, of being a father again…he blew out a stream of air, finally hauled himself into the family room.

Okay, let's be realistic about this. At the moment, nobody really believed this was a good idea. Even him. *Especially* him. Oh, yeah, Nancy had accepted, but she'd sat stiffly in the car when he took her home, discussing plans for the wedding with about as much enthusiasm as making arrangements for a gallbladder operation. The kids clearly thought he'd lost it— not that he blamed them, really—and Claire had just laughed.

Screwed up again, eh, boy?

He dropped onto the edge of the sofa, scrubbed a hand over his face, then stared at the dying fire, fighting back bitterness and fury and a sense of helplessness he'd thought he'd long since overcome.

Never saw a kid who could never get anything right, you know that?

He saw his father's face, alcohol-florid underneath silver hair, his eyes the pale, dirty blue of foot-thick ice, quivering with rage at a small boy who never quite knew what he'd done wrong. No one knew, no one even suspected, Rod imagined, who his father really was.

Don't say anything to make him angrier, his mother would whisper later, in his room. *Don't let him see he's gotten to you. Anger only feeds anger, gives him something to work with. Whatever you do, don't let him see you lose control.*

When he was older, when he understood more than a child should have to, her mantra changed, slightly. *Don't ever love too much,* she'd said. *Love only leaves you vulnerable. Weak. Dependent on someone outside yourself for approval. Love always hurts, in the long run, one way or the other.*

Her example, far more than her words, took root early on.

Any other kid growing up as he had would have probably shunned any suggestion of family life altogether. Leave it to Rod, however, to do exactly the opposite. He yearned for the security and peace so lacking in his childhood, a haven where people cared about, respected, appreciated each other. Since romantic, sexual love, as far as he could tell, provided the worst soil possible in which to sow the fruits of a harmonious home life, he'd pursued a series of what should have been uncomplicated relationships, based on mutual interests and backgrounds. Relationships in which passion—that two-sided coin of love and hate that had so mercilessly shattered his childhood—played no part.

Claire. Myrna. Even Elizabeth. Three times, the little boy who still wanted to believe in fairy tales saw hope in an entirely logical premise that refused to cooperate with reality. Three times, he watched that hope crumble to dust. Now the man with very grown-up needs, the man who was no longer sure what he believed in, had gotten himself tangled up with one very real, very passionate Ms. Nancy Shapiro, with her seven cats and her ingenuous smile and that take-no-garbage-from-anybody attitude which, he knew, only thinly veneered her own insecurities.

He might never forgive himself for this one.

''Between you and me, sweetheart, I'd've thought a man with this much money would have better taste.'' Belle Shapiro's voice rang out, like an off-tune trumpet, from the living room.

Cut-to-the-chase-Nelly, that was her mother. Nancy slammed the front door shut with her hip, dropped her mother's suitcases with offbeat thuds to the floor, feeling about as much like a woman on her wedding eve as a smashed cockroach.

Underneath her down coat and black wool turtleneck, she was about to melt. She tore off the coat, flinging it across a bench in the entryway, pushing up her sleeves as she joined her mother. Actually, considering, the place didn't look too bad. Since the bungalow was wall-to-wall boxes at this point, they'd decided Belle should stay here. And since Nancy hadn't been born yesterday, she—as well as a red-shirted team who'd attacked the heretofore untouched areas of the house like scrubbing bubbles—cleaned. Which, for good or ill, took her mind off things.

"How's about you think of this as a work in progress, Ma? Rod wasn't here full-time until a couple months ago, so let's not beat the man up, okay?"

Belle gave her the Look. "You should see the house your brother bought, up in Ridgewood. Did I tell you about that?"

Only about a hundred times in the past five years. Old news was not a concept with which Belle Shapiro was familiar. Nancy threw up her hands and headed for the kitchen, figuring her mother would follow. She did.

"Six bedrooms, it has, and just for the four of them, can you imagine? They promoted Mark again, did I tell you? Shelby doesn't have to work or anything, just stay home and decorate, take care of the kids. She'd head of the PTA now, did I tell you? So what is this, granite? Never cared for it myself. Too cold. God, I have such a headache—you think you could manage a cup of tea? Is it me, or is it chilly in here?"

Chilly? The way her mother's mouth was going? Not bloody likely. Nancy filled a cup with water and stuck it in the microwave, snagged a teabag from the cupboard and prayed for the grace to get through the next two days without decking her own mother. Since Belle's plane had landed an hour and forty-five minutes ago, Nancy had apologized for a) the plane's being late, b) the godawful food on the plane, c) the weather, and d) her hair, her clothes—what? she thought she was still a teenager, wearing jeans and sneakers?—her perfume, and why did Nancy insist on driving a car that made Belle feel like a sardine in a can? To top it off, Nancy realized she'd reverted to sounding like Fran Drescher with a head cold.

And just think, she'd yet to tell her mother *why* she hadn't been able to give her more notice about the wedding. Frankly, Nancy had thought a thirty-second you-may-kiss-the-bride-dealie at City Hall would more than suffice. But Elizabeth—after retrieving her jaw from her cleavage—had insisted on hosting a simple ceremony in her living room and Rod had insisted they invite her parents and his kids. You know, to throw people off the scent?

Then he'd come home with this *dress,* of all things, when she'd planned on wearing something, anything, she already had. And it was totally to die for, some 'twenties number embroidered with silk roses and dripping with antique lace, and she'd been so stunned, she could hardly breathe. She didn't have to wear it, he'd said, she could take it back if she didn't like it.

As if.

What on earth was she gonna do with this guy?

"I still can't figure out why the rush," Belle was saying, interrupting Nancy's thoughts. She looked over to catch her mother making a valiant effort to heave herself up on one of the bar stools, but her polyester pants kept sliding off the leather. Hard to imagine somebody actually *designed* something in that shade of green. "Your father'd already promised Mo the week off, so what was he supposed to do? And Mark has a seminar he couldn't get out of. So here I had to schlep all the way cross country by myself—"

"Ma, it was a two-hour flight, nonstop from Newark—"

"I mean, if you say you've known the man for...how long did you say?"

"Ma?" Nancy placed a mug of tea down in front of her mother. Belle made a so-this-is-what-you-serve-your-own-mother? face, but cautiously picked it up and took a sip.

"What?"

"I'm pregnant."

She reached out in time to keep Belle from toppling off the stool.

Her complexion now about the color of a matzo ball, Belle just blinked. "You're getting married—" she lowered her voice "—because you *have to?*"

"No, Ma. I'm getting married because, since there's this baby coming, it seemed like a reasonable thing to do. Ma...*Ma!*" She scooted around the bar and whacked her mother on the back. "*Breathe,* for God's sake!" Respiratory function reestablished, Belle turned stricken brown eyes to her daughter.

"Everything I've ever taught you, everything I've done for you, and look. Look!" she shrieked, one hand flapping at Nancy as if she was supposed to look down at herself. Although what she was supposed to see, God only knew. "First you marry that...that *artist* who couldn't keep his pants zipped, and now..."

She started wheezing again.

Nancy pushed the mug toward her. "Here. Drink your tea. When you've finished with your updated list of everything I've ever done to break your heart since Naomi Gould potty trained a month before I did and made you the scourge of Elmhurst, maybe you'll listen to me for thirty seconds."

Belle pushed her lips out and her brows down. But she drank her tea in silence, giving Nancy a minute to realign her brainwaves. She shoved her hair back from her face, then said, "Okay, so maybe we didn't exactly plan this baby. Since *I* wasn't planned—yeah, you can wipe that look off your face, you think I spent the first eighteen years of my life sleeping next door to you and Dad and never heard you talk?—since I wasn't planned, even you have to admit these things happen. Maybe not to your children, up until now, but believe it or not, the rest of the world isn't exactly losing sleep over this. Secondly, Rod, being a decent kind of guy, isn't turning his back on me or the baby. He could have, but he isn't. Thirdly, if I told you your future son-in-law's net worth, you probably *would* keel over, so I'm not gonna. Suffice it to say, however, financially, this is a good deal. A very good deal. And last, but not least by a long shot—'' she leaned closer enough to see that her mother's foundation had collected in the creases around her eyes ''—my choice—and make no mistake, this was *my* choice—was to marry Rod, or raise this baby on my own. So which would you have preferred?''

Belle drew her lips together into a tight little line, then clumsily slid off the stool, her sensible, crepe-soled shoes landing with a muffled thump on the floor. She took her mug over to the stainless-steel sink, washed it out. ''That house your brother bought in Ridgewood, it's got *cultured marble* sinks. So much nicer.''

Nancy resisted the temptation to let her head clunk onto the counter. However, the sound of voices distracted them both. Belle's brows lifted in question.

''That would be Rod. And, um, his kids.''

''*Kids?* The man's already got kids? So now you have to play stepmother to some other woman's children, no less?''

Nancy shushed her with her hands as the voices came closer. Schuyler entered first, looking like some poor soul wearing everything he owned at one time, in ragged, baggy jeans and a black hooded sweatshirt big enough to fit an extra kid inside. His glasses slipped halfway down his nose, he shifted a bulging backpack up onto one shoulder, sending wary glances first at Nancy, then her mother. Hannah followed, dressed similarly to her brother, except for the purple down vest over a Detroit Lions sweatshirt. Static fanned out her long hair around her head; Nancy could hear it crackle as the girl grabbed it with one hand, twisting it around to fall in one long sweep over her left breast. Clearly, judging from the girl's dour expression, weddings were not her thing. At least, not her father's weddings.

Nancy tried a tentative smile on the children, which wasn't returned. What were the odds Belle might have missed that little non-exchange?

Rod brought up the rear of this cheery little group, smiling as he removed his suede gloves, stomped his hiking-booted feet on the mat. ''Ah,'' he said, taking in both Nancy and Belle at once. ''You made it!'' He crossed the kitchen in a bubble of cold, damp air and aftershave to offer his hand to Nancy's mother, a broad smile forcing two sets of creases into wind-flushed cheeks. ''I trust you had a good flight, Mrs. Shapiro?''

Nothing.

Nancy glanced over, noticed Belle's mouth sagging open like a dead fish. With a sigh, Nancy clamped an arm around her mother's shoulders, gave her a quick, forceful squeeze. Kind of a verbal Heimlich maneuver.

''Nice to meet you, too, Mr. Braden,'' popped out of her mother's mouth.

Rod then introduced his kids, who shook hands with Belle only after Rod glared at them, and the next few minutes were filled with the kind of awkward, hollow, getting-acquainted chatter that, on a one-to-ten barf scale, easily ranked about a twenty-two. The agony was somewhat relieved when Rod gave Hannah and Schuyler permission to take their things to their rooms, only to zoom right back up there when he announced he needed to make a call to California before the close of the business day.

After he left, all Nancy could hear was the hiss of the radiators and her mother's way-too-thoughtful breathing. ''The kids hate you,'' Belle said at last.

''They don't know me,'' Nancy replied, choking down a faint hint of nausea.

''No wonder you didn't tell me he had kids. The way they look at you—'' She shuddered. ''But that's not as bad as the way *he* looks at you.''

''He, who?''

''Your *fiancé*,'' Belle said pointedly. ''This is a huge mistake you're making.''

The nausea was no longer a hint. Nancy sank back against the counter, feeling a clammy flush wash over her skin.

"Okay, I'll bite," she said, scraping together the nerve to meet her mother's gaze. "Why is this a huge mistake?"

The last thing she expected to see in Belle's eyes was concern. Genuine concern. For Nancy. Not for what some old biddy she met in the supermarket was going to think. "No man," she said, "should be looking at the woman he's about to marry like he's afraid of her, *bubeleh.*" Nancy could only stare at her mother as she walked over, slipped her hand into her daughter's. "Far better you should raise this child by yourself than shackle yourself to a man who doesn't love you. You remember Bitsy Herman, the woman who lived two doors down from us, before we moved to Jersey? Same thing happened to her—she got pregnant, the family pressured them to get married..." Belle sighed heavily. "Forty years, she lived with that man, never a single word of complaint out of that woman's mouth. But I overheard her maid blabbing to one of her friends in Sears linen department, how Bitsy would just sit in her living room and watch TV most of the day, plotzed out of her gourd. Turns out that husband of hers would come home and barely say two words to her. Just eat his dinner and go right back out. When they found him dead in that bimbo's bed, rumor has it Bitsy laughed for the first time since anyone could remember. It's true, I swear to God. Took her husband's insurance money, moved to Miami, hasn't touched a drop of liquor since."

"Ma—what's this got to do with me?"

"That maid of Bitsy's? Said Harold always looked at Bitsy like he was afraid of her, just like Rod looks at you. I know, I know...I'm just an old woman and what's Bitsy Herman to you?" Belle shrugged. "Just an observation. And that's all I'm gonna say on the subject, since, as you're so fond of pointing out, this is your life and what business is it of mine what you do, right? So where's the bathroom? That tea went straight through me."

Despite the ton of bricks sitting on her chest, Nancy somehow managed to point the way to the powder room under the stairs.

She thought of Rod, tending to business the day before his wedding, coolly efficient as always. She thought of Elizabeth's expression, even as she offered her home for the wedding. She thought of how Rod had bent over backward to do the Right Things since his proposal while still keeping her at arm's length, as if...

As if he was afraid to touch her. As if he'd realized, too late, what his generosity was going to cost him. Well, it wasn't too late, by gum. And baby or no baby, she was damned if she was going to be the millstone around anyone's neck.

She hauled in a deep breath, which seemed to settle her stomach a bit, then headed toward Rod's office.

Chapter 7

Rod had barely hung up the phone when Nancy burst into his office. She zoomed across the room at about Mach 3 and planted both hands on the front of his desk.

"I can't do this, Rod! Getting married just because of one night's overindulgence is *insane*. If you still want to be part of the child's life, we can work something else out, but I can't marry you!"

That's when he noticed the tears. Also that she wasn't all that steady on her pins. He whacked his thigh in his haste to get to her, grabbing a tissue from the box on his desk on the way. The second he clasped her shoulder, though, and started to wipe her cheeks, she snatched the tissue from him, jerked away. "Dammit—would you quit being so *nice* all the time?"

His hands dropped to his sides. "Would you rather I was mean to you?"

"Yes. No. Oh, crud…" She sank onto the leather armchair in front of his desk, dropping her head into her hands. "Why can't life just be easy? Or at least make sense?"

Since he didn't wish to be slugged, he fought the urge to

touch her again. An urge he'd been wrestling with for two weeks, since his body reacted to her like a missile to a homing device. They hadn't discussed sleeping arrangements after the marriage—hell, they hadn't even discussed what to do with her furniture—but he'd made her off-limits before the wedding. Until he figured things out. Or until she forced him to. Except here it was, D-Day eve, and he didn't have a clue.

Of course, if he didn't talk fast, he realized, there would be *no* D-Day. "Honey, you're just nervous. And I'm sure your hormones are beginning to do a real number—"

"My hormones have *nothing* to do with this!" she said, honking loudly into the tissue. "This is about making a far greater mistake than the one we made on New Year's. I'm no Bitsy Herman, and I think I have just enough pride left to back out of this fiasco before I end up a weepy lush whose entire life hinges on who's doing whom on 'General Hospital.'"

He thought better of remarking on her incoherence, but he still had to find something in the conversation to grab hold of before her hysteria drowned them both. "Okay…let's talk this through—"

"I don't want to talk this through! I want to call off the wedding!"

"And bring Elizabeth's wrath down around our heads? Not to mention your mother's, who I doubt will take kindly to being dragged all the way here for nothing."

"Oh, for God's sake, Rod!" She huffed a sigh, scrubbed her cheek with the heel of one hand. Sniffed. "You do realize you're the only one who seems to think this is a good idea, don't you? Elizabeth turned gray when I told her, your kids look at me like they expect lizards to spew forth from my mouth, and my mother…" She glanced away, her chin wobbling. "You *do* look at me like you're afraid of me." His heart nearly bolted out of his chest as moist eyes found his. "As if you can see your future, and there I am, like it or not, all because of a faulty diaphragm—"

He squatted in front of her, praying for the right words to

quell both their fears. She didn't give him a chance. "How can you possibly want this marriage when you don't even want the child?"

How could he not touch her? He reached up, brushed his fingers through her hair. "Even an old hardhead like me can change my mind, honey." Her eyes widened as, his knees about to give out on him, he stood again to lean back against the desk. "I do want this baby, Nancy. More than even I would have believed five weeks ago."

She glowered. But in a sweet, melting kind of way. "Nice of you to clue me in."

"Yeah, well, yeah, this knocked me for a loop at first, but now I'm actually getting excited about it. God knows, I'm going to be the oldest father at the soccer games, but...maybe this time, I won't screw it up."

A frown dipped her brows. "What do you mean?"

"I wasn't home very much when Hannah and Schuy were little. We had a nanny, so even when I wasn't working, Claire and I were out three or four times a week at this or that function. Or I'd come home, and they'd be in bed already. I was lucky if I saw them a total of two hours a week, some weeks."

"Huh. No wonder they're a mess."

"You could have taken the polite route and not pointed that out."

Her shoulders hitched, dropped.

"In any case...I figure this kid is my chance to get it right. So I want to be there. Here. As much as I can be, Nance. Not just every other weekend, or a couple of weeks during the summer. I want to hear this child's first word and see his or her first steps. I want to go to dance recitals or football games or whatever he or she wants to do, I don't care, just as long as I can be there, too. And since you're kind of a major part of the package, I want you there with me."

A shadow flickered in her eyes; she folded her hands together in her lap. "Handy, in other words."

"A lot more than handy. Necessary." She raised her eyebrows at that, but said nothing. "I've never raised a child as part of a real partnership, where each person truly respects the other.'' He lowered his head to look up into her face. ''I'd just like a shot at being a decent father, for a change. A decent…husband.''

After a moment, she got up from the chair and walked over to the window, her hands on her hips. The leaden, late-day light tinged the fringes of her hair silver, vermeiled her skin, making her seem not quite real. ''I still say you should've been a lawyer.'' Her voice was low. Weary.

''But did I convince the judge?''

Her hand settled at her throat. ''You really, truly want this baby?''

''I don't lie, Nancy. I told you that.''

Silence shimmered between them for several seconds, until, at last, she said, ''All my life—well, ever since I hit puberty, I suppose—like most good little girls in my neighborhood, I dreamed of my White Knight, of the kind of man I'd have children with.'' Still gazing out the window, she laughed softly. ''So I only got part of the dream. At my age, I guess I can't be too choosy.''

Her words sliced through him. ''And I still say we have a far better chance of making things work out this way than we would…''

''…if we were in love?'' she finished to the window.

''Yes.''

Now her hand drifted to her belly, still concave underneath her sweater, as she apparently considered their conversation.

''Nancy?''

She turned.

''I'll do whatever I can to make you happy.''

A smile ghosted around her mouth. ''Yes. I'm sure you will.''

''Then…?''

It seemed forever before she answered. ''Then…I guess it's time to transfer some cats.'' Mischief danced in her eyes. ''Think maybe the kids'd like to help?''

He let out a breath worthy of a tightrope walker who'd just

made it to the other side of Niagara Falls. "I take it…we're over that hurdle?"

She was already at the door, but turned to face him, her head tilted in that way he'd already learned meant trouble. "For the moment."

Then he frowned. "You really ready to deal with the kids?"

"Hell, no. But if I'm going to do this, it's going to be on my terms, one of which is I refuse to slither off into a corner every time Hannah and Schuy come to visit. Okay, so this isn't exactly your normal family situation, but while we're all in the same house, we're going to at least *act* like a normal family."

"And does either of us have the slightest idea what that means?"

She shrugged. "As if I'd let that stop me from trying? And one more thing…seeing as you're so hot to start fresh with this child, perhaps you ought to seriously consider repairing whatever it is you think's broken with the ones you've already got. Being the greatest dad in the world to little whoosit here's never going to make up for what you could lose with those two."

With that, she was gone.

Nothing could make a cat disappear faster, Nancy had discovered, than the distinct clanking of a cat carrier. She hauled the three slightly battered numbers she'd found at assorted yard sales out of the garage and set them, open, in the middle of the box-infested living room. She'd been too busy to haul her stuff over to Rod's before the wedding.

Okay, so she hadn't decided where to put any of it once it got there. Two grown people, expecting a baby, getting married, and no one wanted to talk sleeping arrangements. Moving into his bedroom seemed kind of presumptuous, but if she took over one of the guest rooms, she'd feel like, well, a guest.

Was this bizarre or what?

She wriggled out of her coat, threw it on top of the nearest cardboard tower, then turned to the silent teens behind her.

Their expressions hovering somewhere between disgusted and bored, they stood beside the carriers, their arms crossed.

Speaking of bizarre situations. Rod had basically ordered them to come with her, and frankly, Nancy was just as glad. She didn't have a shot in hell of getting them to open up to her as long as they had their father to sulk behind. Of course, if she was being completely honest here, had they not been Rod's children, she could have lived the rest of her life happily enough without ever saying another word to them. Sullen teenagers weren't exactly her thing.

Funny thing was, though, how much they reminded her of her cats. It was clear they were marginally curious about her, where she lived, why she was now going to be a part of their lives, however peripherally. But it was as if they'd made a pact with each other or something: first one to be nice to the Wicked Stepmother has to do the other one's chores for a month, something like that. If they even had chores, which she somehow doubted.

Fighting back another round of nausea, Nancy began calling her kitties, knowing full well they were all huddled together somewhere, snickering behind their paws, going, "Yeah, *right*. In your dreams, lady."

From the kitchen, something thonked to the floor. Of course, by the time she got there, nary a hair nor whisker could be seen.

"How many are there?" Hannah said behind her, effectively shaving five years off Nancy's life.

"Seven," she replied, once her heart slipped back down out of her throat.

Hannah slung her hair over her shoulder, then laughed. Tightly, like she wasn't supposed to. Something about the girl's features reminded Nancy of Rod. The way her brows arched, she thought, the patrician slant to her nose. And her mouth. Definitely her mouth. Wow. With her height, and that beauty…can anyone say *Vogue?* "How come so many?"

"Because I'm a sucker for sad, furry faces. As long as

they're not even remotely rodents.'' She thought of Micah and Jake's hamster and shuddered.

''Oh! There's one!''

Nancy followed Hannah's pointed finger to the top of the corner cupboard, where Ditsy, the little calico, sat with a smug grin on her face. ''Heh, heh…and you can reach her without standing on anything.''

Hannah retrieved the miffed beast, then carted her out to put her in one of the carriers. A sneeze from behind the stove led to Nancy's capturing Bruiser. Plucking assorted dust bunnies and other indecipherable nasties from his fur, she lugged him into the living room…where she found both kids astutely studying her nude portrait.

Oops.

She stuffed the cat into another carrier, calmly walked over to the wall, removed the painting, and placed it on the floor. Backward.

''Hey,'' Schuyler said, obviously impressed. ''That was, like, you, huh?''

''Oh, that was definitely me,'' she said as calmly as she could manage, wondering if viewing their stepmother's nude portrait would further warp a pair of already borderline-messed-up kids.

''Cool.'' He pushed up his glasses. ''So, how many more felines are there?''

Nancy breathed a silent sigh of relief. ''Five. And they could be anywhere.''

Schuy went off to the bedroom to hunt, while Hannah continued to stare at the back of the canvas. ''Go ahead,'' Nancy said. ''Live. It's not like I'm ashamed of it or anything. I just don't normally show it to thirteen-year-old boys.''

''Oh, our parents have always been real open about stuff like that,'' Hannah said, arranging her features into sophisticated. ''There's nothing there Schuy hasn't already seen.''

''Not of his stepmother's, he hasn't,'' Nancy muttered, and Hannah actually laughed. She tilted the painting back, craning her neck to see it again.

''Who did it?''

''An old, forgotten husband.''

Hannah looked at her, her expression unreadable. ''You were married before, too?''

Nancy nodded. Hannah seemed to consider this for a moment, then examined the painting once more. ''I think it would look really cool over the fireplace in the den—oh, look—under the table in the corner!'' The teenager snagged Schmutz, gasping when she got a good look at the shorn Persian, as Schuy loped out of the bedroom, a cat under each arm. They spent the next couple of minutes trying to stuff loose cats into carriers while keeping already captured cats from getting out. Nancy couldn't have asked for a better ice-breaker: within seconds, both kids were laughing so hard she thought they were going to wet their pants. ''And you're telling me,'' Hannah said, her cheeks flushed, ''we're supposed to get two *more* cats in there?''

''Now that you mention it—'' squatting by the carriers, Nancy took a minute to catch her breath ''—maybe I should just come back for the other two later.''

''Hey—'' Schuy held up one hand. ''My honor's at stake now. It's bag the whole lot, or forget returning to the village.''

Nancy straightened up, shaking her head. ''It's like watching William F. Buckley doing 'Wayne's World,''' she mused aloud.

''Disgusting, isn't it?'' Hannah glanced around the living room, nodding in approval. ''Neat room,'' she said, plopping on the sofa. ''Wow—imagine being able to actually *sit* on the furniture and not break your butt. Hey—you know what? This stuff would look really rad in the living room. Or maybe the den…Nancy? Hey, Nancy—whoa. You okay?''

The room had suddenly turned into one of those twirly paint things she used to see at bazaars when she was a kid. Hannah jumped up and caught her before she completely lost her balance, but not before a wave of nausea nearly overwhelmed her. She broke out in a cold, icky sweat as Hannah eased her onto the couch. Closing her eyes only seemed to make the spinning worse.

"Oh, God," came slow, the-light-has-dawned words. "Are you *pregnant?*"

So much for waiting a few weeks and then surprising the kids with the news. Nancy opened her eyes, carefully, regarding her almost-stepdaughter with a mixture of caution and, she realized, relief. "How'd you guess?"

Hannah sighed, then sat down again, her long legs stretched out awkwardly in front of her, her arms just sort of "there" at her sides. "Some girl at school got kn—got pregnant last year, but she decided to keep going to school, you know? Anyway, she was barfing like every three minutes. It got real old."

Nancy managed a wan smile. "Think how *she* must have felt."

Hannah grunted, then shook her heard. "She was only fifteen. God. I mean, she was like, so not ready to be a mother."

"I got news for you, honey. Sometimes, you're not sure you're ready at thirty-four." She rested her head on the back of the sofa, closed her eyes again.

"You gonna barf?"

"Not unless you keep bringing up—pardon the pun—the subject."

"Oh." Silence. Then, "You want some water or something?"

"Actually, there's some Coke in the fridge. Maybe that'll help. And get yourself some, too, if you want."

She felt the sofa shift as Hannah got up. "Nah, I'm not into that sugary stuff anymore," she said from the kitchen. The refrigerator door opened. "Guess you already emptied the refrigerator, huh? There's like *no* food in here." Nancy decided no comment was safest. "Anyway—" she heard the *whfft* of the soda bottle being opened, then the *snuk-snuk-snuk* as Hannah presumably poured it into something "—I only drink juices or mineral water, stuff like that." Since the voice was getting closer, Nancy decided to open her eyes. "That's how old you are? Thirty-four?"

"Every bit of it," she said, taking the glass of soda with a nod of thanks. Hannah crashed down beside her, apologizing when Nancy winced. "Sorry." Then she clammed up. Nancy ventured a glance in her direction.

"What?"

"Well, it's just…" She shifted, crossing her legs up under her. "I mean, I thought grown-ups were supposed to be smarter than that."

"As in, smart enough not to get pregnant if we don't want to."

"Well, yeah."

Nancy sighed, then patted Hannah's knee. "Well, take it from the old, wise woman who is now a whole lot wiser than she was five weeks ago—birth control doesn't always work. Which is why, unless you're really prepared to deal with the consequences, they ain't kidding when they say the only safe sex is no sex."

They both fell silent when Schuyler shuffled out of the bedroom with a black-and-white kitty in tow, then shoved her into the cage with the calico and the Persian. "Which one's left?"

Nancy mentally ticked off the ones they had. "An orange tiger named Pita."

"As in bread?" he asked.

"As in Pain in the…Butt."

Grinning, Schuyler shuffled off to the bathroom.

"Do you and Dad at least love each other?" Hannah asked suddenly.

Nancy leaned her head back again, suppressing a moan. *Oh, God, please…not now.* "I'm not going to lie to you," she said at last, figuring it was just as well she couldn't see the girl's face. "Believe it or not, sometimes even adults get carried away with the moment, which is what happened here."

"You at least *like* my father?"

Nancy opened one eye, glanced over at Hannah, who seemed more interested than grossed out. "I don't go to bed with men I don't like, Hannah.'' At the blush that swept up the girl's neck, she added, ''And I don't go to bed with every man I *do* like, either, in case you're wondering.''

''But you don't love Dad,'' she repeated, as if trying to make the wrong puzzle piece fit into the slot. And Nancy heard the edge to her words, wondered what was coming.

Her eyes stung. How could she tell this child that we can't always let our feelings blossom, no matter how much we might want them to? That sometimes, keeping our hearts to ourselves is the only way to survive? ''I already told you, honey. No, I don't.''

She started when the teenager leapt off the sofa, her hands knotted at her sides. ''So, you marry him for his money, or what? Deliberately get pregnant, then play on his sense of responsibility, knowing he'd offer to do the right thing?''

For several seconds, Nancy wasn't sure she could feel her heart beating. While she stared at the furious teenager, trying to beat down the nausea and catch her breath at the same time, Schuyler entered the room, the ginger tom in his arms. He bent down to put the cat in the carrier, his gaze darting between his sister and Nancy. ''Han,'' he said quietly, straightening up, but she cut him off.

''And don't you go taking her side, Schuy!''

The kid's calm demeanor crumbled like fake glass. ''I'm not taking sides, Hannah! I'm sick to death of taking sides!'' One slender hand swept through his shaggy hair as his long legs closed the space between him and his sister in three strides. Nancy's heart twinged at the way the boy awkwardly stroked his sister's arm, trying to soothe. ''We both want the same thing, Han. You know that. And I happen to think Nancy's cool.''

''You know she was pregnant?''

''I overheard, yeah. So what?''

Hannah's mouth sagged open. ''So *what?* You don't have a problem with this?''

''What? That Dad and Nancy decided to get married? That

they're having a baby?'' Hands up, Schuyler shook his head. ''And how is this our business?''

Nancy felt strangely detached, as if watching a play. While Hannah's pain was obvious, she surmised that Schuyler's supposed indifference only served to mask his true feelings. A clue would be nice, right about now, some inkling of what to do or say to get them through the next ten minutes, at least.

Suddenly, Hannah pointed at Nancy. ''It's our business because she doesn't love him. Just like Mom, just like Myrna. So, once this kid is born, she's probably gonna walk out, too, and then what?''

''Hannah—'' Nancy pushed herself off the sofa and started toward her, hoping the right words—any words—would be there. Except suddenly, the screen went blank.

Rod had assured Belle she didn't have to come along, that Nancy was fine, that Hannah had called because they just needed help getting the cats over here, that's all. Frankly, he wasn't sure he could have survived the ten-minute trip with Belle in the same car with him and not strangled her. Ever since Nancy and the kids had left, the woman had followed him around like an itch you can't get rid of, questioning, nagging, nit-picking—she had that one down to a science. That Nancy hadn't ended up completely neurotic was a miracle in itself. And if he got through the next day and a half without exploding, it would be even more amazing.

But, for his as well as Nancy's sake, he had no intention of letting Belle get to him.

Stretched out on the sofa, Nancy had just about come to by the time Rod arrived, although the kids were still green around the edges. He didn't have the heart to point out that their stories—told simultaneously and with red faces—didn't exactly dovetail, although who was covering whose rear, he didn't know. Or care to know, at the moment.

His stomach twisted as he sat by her knees, gently stroking her hand. It hadn't once occurred to him she wouldn't sail through the pregnancy, as energetic as she was. Now, however, she looked more fragile and vulnerable than ever, a state she wouldn't be in if he'd listened to his head instead of other parts of his anatomy several weeks ago.

"Oh, hell," she said after a minute, licking her lips. "I fainted?"

He'd meant to let go of her hand, but her soft, warm fingers closed around his, and he found himself returning the favor. "Or pulled off a damn good imitation thereof. When did you last eat?"

"Please do *not* mention food. Ever." She covered her eyes with her hand. She tried to sit up, groaned, lay back down. Looked up at the kids. "Oy. You two look worse than I feel."

He twisted around to find both of his children staring at them, Schuy in this macho hands-on-hips pose, Hannah hugging her middle with one arm, gnawing on a hangnail. He turned back. "My guess is you scared the bejeebers out of them."

A faint smile flickered across Nancy's lips, then died out. "Didn't do myself any favors, either." Then he caught the apology, the helplessness, in her eyes, and realized immediately it wasn't due to her fainting.

"Guys," he said to the kids, "Why don't you load up the beasts in the Rover while I get Wan Wanda back on her feet, okay?"

Didn't have to ask them twice. Once the room was devoid both of cats and kids, Rod asked for her version of the story.

She picked at his coat sleeve, a small, inconsequential gesture that tugged things he didn't want tugged. "I feel a bit like I just got off a roller coaster," she admitted. "First they were leery, then they warmed up and we were getting along fine, and then Hannah guessed I was pregnant and everything fell apart."

"She'll get over it—"

"No, Rod, it's more than that." She folded her hands together over her middle, not looking at him. "She…knows this isn't a love match. I mean, she came right out and asked me.

I couldn't lie to her, and now she thinks I'm refrigerator sludge.''

Rod rubbed the back of his neck, but it would take dynamite at this point to break the knot of tension lodged between his shoulders. Not to mention the wall of it between the two of them.

Nancy broke the silence first, carefully sitting up, then swinging her legs past his hip to set her feet on the floor. "Come on…let's get out of here." The weariness, and sadness, in her voice nearly did him in. Impulsively, he brushed her cheek with his knuckles.

"This isn't a mistake, Nance."

She met his eyes. But said nothing.

Not surprisingly, she threw off his attempts to help her to her feet. She gathered her coat and purse, told him he'd better get the bags of litter and food from the garage, then glanced over at what he realized must be the portrait. "That goes into storage," she said simply, then made her way to the front door. When they got outside, he loaded the supplies into her car, then tossed Hannah the keys to the Rover.

"Think you can manage?"

His daughter's face split into a huge grin as she raised the keys in a triumphant gesture, then scrambled into the car before he could change his mind. He turned to meet a pair of questioning brown eyes. "She just got her license a couple months ago," he said, steering Nancy toward the sedan, then put out his hand for the keys. Clearly in no mood to argue, she dug in her purse for a moment, then handed them over without a word. "And you need a break from each other for a bit."

Once settled into their seats, he said, "I think you tried to accomplish too much in one afternoon. And Hannah's brain exploded. But she'll get over it." He reached over, patted her knee. "You'll see. We all just need some time to sort things out."

He decided to attribute her lack of response, not to mention her grimace, to her physical condition.

* * *

"Oh, Schuy—for crying out loud. You know as well as I do why this is, like, a total disaster." Hannah crept along the wet road, secretly grateful there was virtually no traffic and that the Rover was built like a tank. Dad must've wanted them out of there *real* bad to have trusted her to drive. Of course, she'd had driver's ed, and had even driven with him in the snow several times, so it wasn't as if he didn't know she could handle it. Still, she wasn't about to do anything crazy.

Meows—and occasional thumping as somebody tried to claw his or her way out of the carrier—winnowed through the sounds of Metallica on the car stereo. Schuy frowned, his arms crossed. "You really think she doesn't love him?"

"I don't know. I mean, that's what she said, but she looked so sad…" She could feel her brother's accusing gaze, hot on her face. "Well, how was I supposed to know she was going to faint?"

"You knew how she was feeling, Han. Maybe you could've been like more diplomatic or something?"

Her lungs stung when she sucked in a breath of icy air to keep her composure, since now would not be a good time to let her vision blur. She tightened her grip on the wheel as she carefully turned onto the road leading to the mansion, wishing she could maneuver her thoughts as easily. "You really like her, don't you?"

"She's crazy, but she's not weird, you know? So, yeah…I like her. And I bet you do, too, if you'd get over yourself long enough to admit it."

"Shut up, Schuy," she said, but without much enthusiasm.

Chapter 8

Most of the first six weeks of her marriage could be summed up in one word: *blech*. She'd had no idea a person could feel like something that had been regurgitated and still be considered healthy. But Ruth, the businesslike English midwife Rod's doctor had recommended, had assured her that the nausea simply indicated a good high hormone level, which meant the pregnancy had taken quite nicely. She'd also reassured Nancy that, long about week twelve, both her appetite and sex drive would return. In spades.

In the meantime, Rod treated her like a guest who'd become indisposed and couldn't get home again, Elizabeth tut-tutted and brought her soothing teas and things but was kind enough to not mention that *she* hadn't as much as burped during *her* first trimester, and Cora and Maureen kept sending her home every time she dragged herself into work. The days had bled together in a blur of nausea and dizziness and misery, punctuated by brief bouts of fake cheer when she had to talk to her mother. Otherwise, Belle was sure to blame her, somehow, for feeling so lousy.

Not to mention for getting herself into this predicament to begin with.

Then, one Friday morning in April, she woke up to discover she actually felt human again. Fighting her way from underneath the cats, she sat up. Granted, she recoiled from her own reflection when she caught a glimpse of herself in the guest room—yes, that's where she'd ended up—mirror, but her stomach stayed calm. She stood. Walked across the room. Twirled.

Nancy laughed out loud, so thrilled to feel normal again that nothing and no one was going to get her down. Then she smiled, her hands cradling the beginnings of a rounded tummy.

She was going to have a baby.

As in, she was going to be someone's mommy. Not an aunt, honorary or otherwise, but an honest-to-God mother with leaky breasts and stretch marks and a labor story and everything. And okay, so maybe she and Rod didn't exactly have what you'd call a real marriage—shoot, they didn't even have a real relationship—but he was good and kind and considerate and didn't have an extra head or anything, so things could be worse.

New life surged inside her, through her, making her feel capable of anything. Whatever the circumstances that had brought Rod and her together, she was determined to squeeze every drop of good out of it she could. Rod was *not* going to regret marrying her, she decided, pulling on a pair of jeans— which she could no longer button—and if it took everything she had, she was going to wipe the worry and fear and regret right out of those honeyed eyes. They'd be friends. Good friends. And good parents to this baby.

She looked around the guest room, still papered in faded ballerinas, and instantly chose it for the nursery. The way the light streaked in from the pair of windows would make it a great room for a child to play in, grow up in....

A daughter. She'd like a little girl, please. *And, God? Do the kid a favor—give her Rod's hair, not mine.*

Or…maybe a little boy. Rambunctious and energetic, like Guy's two. Yeah, boys were loud, but she could handle loud.

At the moment, she could handle anything.

Humming to herself—which merited a pained look from two of the cats—she slipped a bright red sweatshirt on over the jeans, yanked her hair back into a banana clip, then skipped down the front stairs through a feline waterfall.

She found Rod in the kitchen, seated at the kitchen table, communing with the morning paper. Sunlight glanced off the silver strands threaded through his golden-brown hair, highlighted all that fabulous bone structure, toyed with some interesting rippling going on underneath that mustard-colored chamois shirt. Just like that—bam!—desire streaked through her. Heart-racing, core-tingling, nipple-tightening, your-bed-or-mine lust.

Ruth knew whence she spake.

Odd to think they hadn't had sex since That Night. Odder still that she didn't quite know what to do about, or even *think* about, this conjugal-relations business. The past several weeks, sex had been a moot point. But now…

Now she had to think about it, because her hormones were, as Hannah would say, like majorly in her face. Hyper-hormones notwithstanding, however, she couldn't just hop into bed with Rod without thinking this through.

Crazy, huh? Why had it seemed more acceptable to make love with him when she *knew* it was a one-shot deal than it did now that they were married, but only for the baby's sake? Maybe because, in a weird sort of way, that first time had at least been honest. Then, neither was looking or hoping for anything more than a few hours of companionship and sexual release. Or so the story went. But now…now that they'd committed to providing a home for the ''more'' those few hours had produced, when they had a license to share a marriage bed, the idea somehow caught in her throat, like a bite of spoiled food you didn't quite know how to get rid of. Having sex just *because* you were married…well, it just didn't seem kosher.

Somehow.

Her stomach growled, as if to say, "Yo—you don't want to take care of other parts of your anatomy, fine. What's that gotta do with me?"

"Hey!" She waltzed into the kitchen with a huge grin plastered to her face. "What's a girl gotta do to get breakfast in this joint?"

His coffee mug landed with a muffled thud on the table as his eyebrows shot up, though whether at her demand or her sudden joie de vivre, she couldn't have said. "You're *hungry?*"

"Starved. As in feeling like I haven't eaten in weeks."

Relief—and something else—glinted in those golden eyes. "There's a reason for that. Ruth told me at least twenty times what you'd gone through wasn't unusual, but lady, I have to say—you really had me going there."

When was the last time someone—as in a *male* someone—cared enough about her to be worried about her?

Pushing down feelings best ignored, she sashayed over to the refrigerator and yanked open the door, thrilled to discover she could look at food and not puke. Oh, yeah...the sun was shining, the birds were a-twittering, she was hungry...life was *good*. Or could be, if she chose that option. "Yeah, well, I wasn't exactly having a blast, either," she said, pouring herself a glass of orange juice. She surveyed her choices, frowning. "I don't suppose there are any frozen waffles hiding in here, huh?"

Rod had come up behind her, which led her to the immediate and profound realization that her husband smelled better than anything she'd ever smelled in her entire life. Every single nerve cell in her body jerked awake like a kid hearing the dismissal bell at school. So when he gently shoved her aside and pointed to the bar stool, part of her breathed a great sigh of relief, while lots of other parts of her, well, didn't. Whatever it was she needed to figure out, she realized, she'd better figure it out like *yesterday*.

"Frozen waffles," Rod muttered into the refrigerator, pulling out the eggs. "You want waffles, I'll show you *waffles*."

"Oh, Rod, no—I can get breakfast myself! You've done nothing but wait on me for the last six weeks."

He actually glowered at her. "You're carrying my child. The least I can do is feed the two of you. So sit, dammit, and let me do my thing, okay?"

So she sat, dammit, and watched, her chin propped nonchalantly in her hand, as he did all sorts of tantalizing things with eggs and milk and whisks and copper bowls, afraid if she spoke, she'd break the spell. Or blurt out, "Oh, by the way, after breakfast? How's about having your wicked way with me?"

"By the way…" Rod started, and her heart stopped. "Your mother, Maureen and Elizabeth all called this morning." He poured batter into the waffle iron, lowered the top.

"Mmm," she said around a mouthful of juice, dreamily contemplating the chino-clad tush in front of her, then swallowed. Twice. Any moment now, she was going to wake up and realize…what? That she was hankering after her own husband? Or that she was setting herself up for a fall? If she made a pass, what if he rejected her? What if he didn't reject her, and they fooled around, and she discovered it wasn't enough? What if this was more than lust? What then? And what was this, Twenty Questions? Nancy had long since learned trying to change a man's mind was a waste of time and energy. Whatever Rod's reasons for remaining emotionally detached, t'weren't nuthin' *she* could do about it. *Find something else to think about,* she scolded herself, watching his hands. Oh, did she remember those hands. A shiver scampered right up her spine, popping up her nipples, which remembered those hands very well, too.

"Cora's throwing Elizabeth a baby shower," she said distractedly. "Next weekend, I think." One hand found its way to a coil of hair that had wriggled free of the comb, which she now twisted around and around her finger. "I can't believe she's due in a month. Probably why Maureen's calling, too—

we're supposed to go to the mall tomorrow to shop for baby stuff.'' An auxiliary little thrill ran through her at the prospect of, for the first time in her life, being able to look at things for her *own* baby. ''I'm going to try to set an appointment up with the Randalls in the morning, though, to look at some houses. I've neglected them long enough. Oooh, is that ready?''

''Uh, yeah…'' A brief frown flicked across Rod's face as he set her breakfast down in front of her, along with apricot syrup and a small dish of powdered sugar. ''Nance…you don't have to work, you know.''

Well, that sure whapped the old libido all to hell. She cut into the waffles, eyeing him warily. ''Please don't tell me you're one of those throwbacks who doesn't think his wife *should* work.''

He glowered again, then took her empty glass, poured more juice into it. ''Just an option. Thought you might want to take it easy. That's all.''

''Thanks, but I've had all the easy-taking I can stomach for one lifetime. You're busy most of the day, and the cats aren't exactly up on current events. I'd be bored stiff if I stayed home and watched my belly grow. Besides, my job's the only thing I'm good at—why on earth would I give that up? Oh, Rod…these are wonderful! Mmm—'' she waved her fork at him ''—these are no ordinary waffles. You know what people would pay for a breakfast like this?''

''What on earth are you talking about?''

''These are terrif—''

''Not the waffles.'' He leaned close enough for her to see a vein pulsing at his temple. To smell freshly showered man, tinged with the fragrance of browned butter and vanilla and a spicy aftershave that seemed to zing straight to her…

Oh, hell.

''Your work,'' he continued, his voice edged with irritation, she thought. ''About its being the only thing you're good at.''

''Well, it's true. Everything else in my life, I've bombed out on, one way or another. Just ask my mother.''

She jumped when he reached out, grabbed her free hand, his thumb flicking over her knuckles. Cold fury simmered in his eyes, although his voice stayed low, controlled. "Honey, please don't take this the wrong way, but your mother's full of it." Then he dropped her hand as if he'd been stung, walked back to the stove. "Want more?" he asked, spatula poised, voice strained, eyes averted.

Oh, *hell.*

Oh, yeah, she wanted more, all right. Not that seduction was her strong suit—their one tumble in the sack notwith-standing—but somehow, she had the feeling if she were to stand up right now and take Rod by the hand and lead him to his bed, he wouldn't put up much of a fuss. But there was *more* as in more than she had now, which was nothing. And there was *more,* as in more than she'd probably ever get.

And then there was *more* as in, here they were, married for the love of Mike, and they didn't know each other worth squat.

"So tell me about *your* parents," she said, surprising her-self.

"They're both dead," he said after a good two or three beats, lifting out his own breakfast from the waffle iron. "There's nothing to say."

But right as she was about to remark that he'd just said a lot, the phone rang. She only half listened to the conversation as she finished off the waffles, seriously considering licking her plate when she was done. While she was wondering how soon she could reasonably have lunch, she noticed Rod had hung up, and he was doing that scowling thing again. Not at her, though.

"What's up?"

He sighed. "That was a client in New York. A software manufacturer. He's been nagging me to come out for several weeks. I've been putting him off, but now I guess, since you're better…"

Hmm. Great timing, huh? "Oh, for heaven's sake, go," she said, smiling like the first runner-up in a beauty contest. "The cats and I'll be fine."

''He wants me to come out tonight, spend the weekend with him and his wife out on the island. But it's my weekend with the kids. Claire'll have a cow if I try to change plans now—''

Her smile froze in place. She'd said maybe two dozen words to his kids since the wedding, and none of them had been particularly parental, as she recalled. This making-the-best-of-things business could be a real pain. ''No problem. We'll manage.''

''You're...sure?''

''Sure I'm sure.'' She slid off the stool, carrying her dish over to the sink, her giddiness of a half hour before rapidly disintegrating as she rinsed off the dish and set it in the drainer. But not the determination to see this through. Once again, his hands came to rest on her shoulders. This time, she shut her eyes as need arced through her bloodstream, sharp and bittersweet, her body keening for what her soul could never have.

''You're petrified and you know it,'' he said, into her hair, his breath warm, delicious against her temple.

Truer words were never spoken. Not that any of this was going to undermine her resolve, you understand. But she *was* petrified. What if she'd bitten off far more than she could chew with this marriage, this convenient arrangement? How far was she willing to go to ensure the best for her child? How much of herself could she reasonably sacrifice and not end up eaten alive with what-might-have-beens? Her mother still ragged her about her decision, Elizabeth and Maureen did a lousy job of concealing the concern in their eyes, and Rod's daughter still clearly thought of Nancy as an interloper, extraneous, something to be put up with but never accepted as part of a whole.

And who could blame her? There was no *whole* to this family, and never would be. Just a bunch of parts and pieces that didn't fit together, no matter which way you arranged them.

No.

For thirty-four years she'd managed to hold on—sometimes by nothing more than her fingernails—to her dream of a real family, one whose members actually gave a damn about each other. A weaker woman might be tempted to believe that dream had been shattered. A weaker woman might believe the most she could hope for was to avoid getting cut by the broken pieces.

She hadn't survived this long by being weak.

"I'll be fine," she announced, drying her hands, an action that released her from Rod's touch. Then she turned to him, inwardly cringing at the look in his eyes. "Hey—I'm one tough little broad, and don't you forget it."

He bent over, kissed her, then left the room before she even had a chance to catch her breath.

Rod threw his suitcase on his bed—the bed he'd been sleeping in by himself for far too long—and cursed. Why on earth had he kissed her?

Well, hey—think it might have had something to do with the fact that she was totally irresistible when she was standing there, all perky and sweet-smelling and vivacious like that?

And needy. Lord—yearning fairly blazed in her eyes. It hadn't been difficult to ignore his own ache when she'd been feeling so awful, but now that she was better...

And clearly interested... He hauled a half-dozen folded dress shirts from his drawer, rammed them into the case. Who knew she'd go from *green* to *glowing* overnight? He'd caught those little shivers whenever he came close, the little catch-breaths of arousal. He remembered how Claire had been, especially around the middle of the pregnancies. A dream come true, for many men. Most men. And Rod hadn't exactly suffered in the obliging, as he recalled. But this was different. Dangerous. Whatever this attraction was he felt for Nancy, it was more than sex. Had been, even that first time. Her smile, her touch, the intent way she had of listening to him, that little line settling between her brows—

Come to Mama. Let me take you—

He sank onto the edge of his bed, his head cradled in his hands. He wanted to make her happy, to not regret this marriage. He wanted her, period, as much as he had the night they conceived their child, as he had from the minute he laid eyes on her. But to truly *have* her, he'd have to let go.

And that simply wasn't an option.

"Hey, this is cute." Nancy held up a sleeveless black jersey maternity dress splashed with huge red poppies. "But it doesn't really look like you."

Rod hadn't been gone two hours, and Nancy already missed him. Except that missing someone who wasn't likely to miss you back was not good. Not to mention she'd never felt that kind of attachment to anyone. So Elizabeth's unexpected visit, her arms laden with maternity clothes, came as a welcome distraction. Now, doing a splendid imitation of a ready-to-harvest pumpkin in a huge orange cotton sweater, Elizabeth shifted in her corner of the purple sofa—which had finally found its way here, into the den—and shook her head.

"A lot of this stuff comes by way of one of Guy's sisters-in-law, who's about our size. After four kids, Cindy practically threw the clothes at me, as if getting rid of them would destroy the curse—Jake!" she shouted as the jeans-and-sweatered six-year-old zoomed past in the hall, hot on the trail of one of the cats. "Calm down, honey! They've only got nine lives."

The dark-haired child muttered something resembling "Sorry, Mama," then took off down the uncarpeted hall, sneakers thumping.

"You really ready for this?" Elizabeth asked, one hand massaging the unborn hooligan jostling inside her.

Nancy grinned back. "Are you ready to add to the chaos?"

"Honey, at this point, I pray for labor. All I want is to be able to get up the stairs within less than five minutes. Not to mention get reasonably close to my husband again." Her hand made slow circles over her tummy. "And I can't wait to meet this little person."

Yeah, Nancy could relate. That part of her life, at any rate, was something to smile about. She pawed through the pile of clothes on her coffee table, feeling like a kid at Christmas.

Unlike Elizabeth, whose clothing preferences ranged from understated to conservative, this sister-in-law of Guy's had great taste. "How come you're giving me all this stuff now?" she asked, holding up a white T-shirt with a big Under Construction sign on the front.

"Between Cindy's contributions, what I bought, what my mother bought, and what Guy bought, I have far more clothes than I could ever wear. Besides, I'm down to about five outfits I can still fit in. No, four. That navy dress went by the side of the road last week."

"Aunt Nancy!" Breathless and flushed, Elizabeth's ten-year-old stepdaughter Ashli ran into the room, sweeping a hank of dark blond hair behind a tiny ear, showing off what Nancy knew was a brand-new gold stud in the lobe. "There's all sorts of flowers 'n' stuff coming up in your backyard, did you know?"

She smiled for the child, even as she realized she herself hadn't yet linked the possessive pronoun "her" to anything about this house, including the yard. Her clothes, her furniture, her cats were all in Rod's house, not hers. And certainly not *theirs*. "I haven't been out there in a while. We'll have to go look, later. Must be spring bulbs coming up."

"Daffodils and hyacinths," Ashli pronounced, grinning. "Like in our yard." Then she turned to Elizabeth, eyes shining. "Is the baby moving, Mama?"

"Actually, yeah. Come here."

Ashli scampered across the room, plopping herself beside her stepmother, who placed the small hand on her belly. After a second—even Nancy could see Ashli's hand jump—she giggled. "That is so cool," she said, as Micah came in, clutching the little calico by her armpits.

"She likes me," he announced as Elizabeth quickly reached to rearrange the poor beast in his arms before her eyeballs popped out.

"Well, she might like you a little more if she can breathe, okay?"

"C'n we get a cat?"

"Don't push it, big stuff," Elizabeth said with a mock frown, ruffling his blond curls. "Einstein's big enough to count for at least ten pets. Besides, you just got the hamster."

"But I want a kitty!"

"Yeah, me, too," echoed Ashli, who'd latched on to Pita.

"We can't always have what we want, guys. So deal with it." Elizabeth then kissed two pairs of pooched-out lips before sending both children back out of the room.

Nancy slowly folded the last of the garments, carefully laid it on top of the pile. With any luck, perhaps the child she carried would be as affectionate as Elizabeth's stepchildren were with her. But would she ever see anything other than wariness in *her* stepchildren's eyes?

In her husband's eyes, for that matter.

It was true. You can't always have what you want. What Nancy wanted to know was, though, why she *never* seemed to get what she wanted. Not what she most wanted, at any rate.

Elizabeth's warm touch on her wrist made her jump. "When you're this quiet, it's a dead giveaway something's wrong."

Dissemblance was wasted on Elizabeth. "What on earth have I gotten myself into?" she asked quietly.

Elizabeth let out a weighty sigh, crossing her arms over her protruding middle. "Give it time, honey. Give Rod time—"

"You think this was a bad idea, don't you? The truth."

Pursed lips preceded Elizabeth's reply. "It's not the idea itself I think is bad," she said carefully. "It was the motivation and timing that concerned me. Criminy, Nance—living with someone, dealing with his children, is hard enough when…"

"The parties involved actually love each other? Yeah, well, since when have you known me to do anything the easy way? Besides, it's not as if the pregnancy could be put on hold until…" Her eyes burned as she rose from the sofa. She walked over to the window, scanning the grounds that weren't hers, watching the children chase each other, their voices shrill and free and happy. "Rod only married me because he thought it was best for the baby."

Elizabeth had come up behind her, her hands braced on her lower back. "Yeah, I kind of figured that. So why'd *you* marry *him?*"

The question threw her. "Because…I decided he was right."

"Bullpucky. No one's ever been able to tell you what to do and you know it. So my guess is, you married him because you wanted to. Because maybe you see some potential in this relationship, even if he doesn't."

Nancy hugged herself, cold despite the unusually warm day. "Dammit, Liz," she said softly to the only person in the world she could confide in. "I'm so scared. Just because I want this to work, that doesn't mean it will."

"So. You're in love with him?"

"No." At Elizabeth's startled expression, she said, "I can't fall in love with a man I don't know." She let out a harsh laugh. "At least, not any more. Did that once. Have noooo desire to do it again. But I do care for Rod. A lot. Probably a lot more than I should. And I'm—" She blushed.

"Hot for him?"

"You could say that."

Elizabeth shrugged. "So work with what you've got."

That merited an incredulous look. "This from the woman who was a virgin, like, forever?"

Another shrug. "Different situation, different people…different modus operandi." Elizabeth twisted around to perch on the window sill, her hands braced on either side of her hips. "Okay, hear me out. It took a while, but I finally figured out why Rod and I didn't click. I mean, besides the obvious karmic thing that he wasn't the One," she added with a smile. "Rod didn't *want* anything to click. Not really. I mean, he really did want us to get together, to get married, but passion was never part of his game plan. Of course, at the time, I didn't think it was mine, either—" another smile "—but still, I think he thought I was safe. That he could have this nice little conservative wife to keep him company—because he does need company, Nance. In fact, I think he's one of the loneliest people I've ever known—but without the messiness of being really involved. The reason his plan didn't work was because I wanted more than I thought I wanted. More than he was willing to give. Or pry out of me.''

She watched her tummy undulate for a second. "Guy's made me, I don't know…more than I was before, I guess. More willing to take chances, to be myself, to be crazy. I guess what I'm trying to say is, Rod needs someone to do for him what Guy did for me. And as far as I can tell, you're the perfect choice.''

"Oh, right. I've been looking for love my entire life, and he's been fighting it. *And* we're polar opposites. Uh-huh, a perfect match—''

"Hey! Hey! Let's remember who you're talking to!" Elizabeth interjected, laughing, and Nancy huffed out a sigh. True, at first glance, who would have thought the ultraprim, ultraconservative woman in front of her would have hooked up with a long-haired, pierced-eared man whose favorite color was *loud*. But Elizabeth and Guy were right for each other. Anyone could see that. Nancy and Rod, on the other hand…

"It's not the same thing," she said simply.

"Actually, you're probably more alike than you know," Elizabeth said, a hairline crease marring her smooth brow. "I mean, if my hunch is correct." She paused, as if carefully choosing her words. "In all the times we went out, Rod never once talked about his childhood. But sometimes, when he didn't know I was watching him? I felt as if I was looking at a sad, lonely little boy."

So. Nancy wasn't the only one who saw it. Still… "Sorry. I'm not getting the connection here."

"That's because you're too close to the situation," Elizabeth said, as if anyone could figure *that* much out. Really. "Your childhood was sucky, too, don't you see?"

"Too?"

"Well, isn't it obvious? I mean, if he won't talk about it?"

Nancy had to laugh. "I think you're reaching, *bubeleh*."

"I think I'm *right*."

Actually, so did Nancy. She sat on the sill next to Elizabeth, picking at the hem of her sweater. "It's just so weird, you know? In the past few weeks, Rod's been kinder to me than any man I've ever known, certainly nicer than any man who *said* he loved me, when he had—has—every right to be angry. Or at least annoyed. He's even cleaning the litter pans since I can't while I'm pregnant! I've never known a man who seems so determined to do what's best for everybody, but at what price?"

Fear gnawed at her heart. "It's not natural, the way he keeps putting himself second. Or third or fourth. And if what you say is true, what's gonna happen when he suddenly realizes he's made one sacrifice too many? When he realizes he's got a wife and kid underfoot he never wanted to begin with?" She shook her head. "I know, in here—" she pushed one fist into her chest "—this is a disaster waiting to happen. And if I had any sense, I'd walk out now, before things got more complicated than they already are. But I can't."

Tears pricking her eyes again, she faced her friend, who gently pushed back a strand of hair from Nancy's face. "Even knowing this is doomed to failure, I can't leave. And I can't let Rod see I'm afraid, either. Isn't that nuts?"

"Your wanting to stay?" Elizabeth shook her head. "No. I think you know you're needed, whether Rod sees that yet or not. But the not letting him see you're afraid part, *that's* where you keep getting balled up. You wanna talk self-sacrifice? Shoot, lady, you've got a corner on the market. This may come as a shock, but you don't have to subjugate your feelings to make a man happy. Or—*or*—to keep him from dumping you. You're worth more than that. So you've got to be honest with him. You want this to work, you can't pretend everything's peachy keen when it's not."

"If I want this to work, I can't ever let him think he made a mistake!"

"Oh, you are so full of it, you know that?" Elizabeth's

eyes sparked with enough indignation for the entire female sex. "Being dishonest is the mistake, birdbrain! Not telling the guy what you're really feeling!"

"I can't do that, Liz. Not now. Not ever. How can I burden him any more than I already have?"

The kids' rushing into the room at that moment was probably the only thing that saved her from being throttled, such was the fury blazing from Elizabeth's green eyes. But Nancy was determined—if this marriage was to work, on any level at all, she'd have to keep her fears to herself. She'd do anything for this marriage, except put her heart on the line.

"Aunt Nancy!" Jake yelled. "I think Hannah and Schuyler are here!"

"Damn," Nancy muttered. "They're early." She headed toward the front door, Elizabeth lumbering behind her, her ducklings darting in and around her and bugging her about getting pizza.

"You ever met Rod's ex?" Elizabeth asked, after giving the kids a weary "We'll see" about the pizza.

"No." Nancy opened the front door; Elizabeth's brood all tumbled out and onto the steps, Micah bursting into pity-me tears when Jake knocked him into the stone planter off to one side. With a grunt, Elizabeth hauled the wailing child up into her arms.

"I have. And I'm gonna split before I get a chance to get reacquainted." With that, Elizabeth and her little entourage vanished down the stairs into the Volvo, and were gone.

Nancy watched them leave, choking down the feeling of dread lapping to and fro in her gut. This was not sounding good. Especially as, since the tall woman unfolding herself from the mauve Caddy had to be Rod's ex, it appeared Nancy's luck wasn't going to hold.

"Get your stuff out of the trunk while I talk to your father," Nancy heard her say to them in a nicotine-roughened voice. The tightly pulled-together blonde, whose hair was several shades lighter than her leathery skin, stopped short when she saw Nancy staring down at her. "Oh. You must be Nancy. Where's Rod?"

Nancy ordered her mouth to smile. "He was suddenly called out of town on business. His plane left too soon to catch you and tell you his change of plans. But we figured this would give Hannah and Schuy and me a chance to get to know…each other…" Her gaze drifted to the car, and the kids, and the rapidly growing mountain of luggage on the driveway.

What the hell—?

Nancy's eyes shot up to Claire's, the Gong of Doom sounding in her brain. "What's going on? Why did they bring so much stuff?"

She saw something like delight sparkle in Claire's washed-out blue eyes. "Rod didn't tell you?" she said, too slowly, as an overly glossed mouth slowly spread into a smile across her weathered face.

"Tell me…what?"

"Honestly, this is so like Rod, not bothering to tell anyone what's going on." Claire shrugged underneath her silk blazer. "Men, huh? Whatcha gonna do with 'em, right?"

"What's going on?"

"I'm getting married. On Sunday. In Mexico. I can't believe he's making me tell you this," she added more or less to herself, then looked back at Nancy. "Then we're spending three months at Rafe's villa in Cancun. When I asked Rod, he said, sure, no problem, the kids can stay here until we get back. I mean, I wasn't sure, what with having to take them out of school and everything, but kids are so adaptable, don't you think? Well, I'd love to stay and shoot the breeze, but I've gotta get back. Hannah's got a number where I can be reached after Sunday. "Nice to meet you, by the way." She waved a hand tipped in five perfectly squared-off red nails. "Ciao!"

Feeling as if a hole had just opened up underneath her feet, Nancy watched, open-mouthed, as Claire spun around in her classic Dior sling backs to say goodbye to her children, then left.

The kids hauled their bags to the steps. ''Here—let me help you,'' Nancy said to Hannah, reaching out. But the girl only shot her a nasty look, then trooped past in total silence.

Chapter 9

Nancy didn't know what was going on, or who was telling the truth, but since none of this was her fault, she refused to bear the brunt of Hannah's anger. At least Schuy, who was clearly every bit as ticked off as his sister, had deigned to acknowledge her presence. Once he'd drifted off toward the kitchen, however, Nancy headed straight to Hannah's room, banging open her door. The girl whirled around, eyes sparking.

"Hey! Whatever happened to privacy?"

"Whatever happened to *manners,* is what I'd like to know. You got a problem with your mother, that's one thing. That doesn't give you the right to waltz in here and snub me like I'm the hired help."

Hannah yanked open the top drawer to her bureau, sweeping her hair over her shoulder. It slipped right back. "Oh, right...like you want me here?"

"How do you know what I do and don't want?" That got a wide-eyed look, for a second, until the teenager turned her back, obviously uninterested in pursuing the conversation further. Nancy, however, was hardly going to back down before some pissed-off adolescent.

"Okay, let's get something straight, right now. You will not storm in here and pretend I don't exist. Since it looks like I'm the closest thing you're going to have to a mother for the next three months, I suggest we not start our life together this way, got it?"

The teenager ripped open the zipper to her large, soft-sided bag, yanked out a pile of shirts, crammed them into the bureau drawer. Nancy recognized, all too well, the anger imprisoning tears the girl was determined not to let loose.

"Hannah, look at me," she said gently, then waited as pride and obvious need warred it out underneath all that shimmering blond hair. Finally, need won out; the teenager turned around, defiance hardening her mouth. Nancy crossed her arms and drew in a deep breath. "Okay, I'm gonna put my tush on the line here, since you might worship the ground your mother walks on, for all I know, but far as I'm concerned, what she just did to you was pretty crappy."

Shock popped those eyes wide open.

"Yeah, yeah, like you've never heard the word before. Since I know how I feel right now, I can imagine how you feel."

Now bitterness burned off the shock. "So. I was right. You're not exactly thrilled about having us, are you?"

"What I'm not thrilled about is not being told. What I'm not thrilled about is being manipulated. And of being lied to. And what I'm most not thrilled about is that someone who's supposed to have her children's best interests at heart could do something like this to you guys."

The sound of shuffling behind her caught her attention; she pivoted to find Schuyler standing in the doorway, his expression blank. "Lied to?" Hannah asked, recapturing Nancy's focus. "By whom?"

"You really think your father wouldn't've told me, if he'd known?"

"See?" Schuyler interjected. "What did I tell you?" He

turned to Nancy, his braces gleaming in the weak light. "I told Hannah Dad would've been really hot if he'd known Mom was planning on doing this. Especially since it meant taking us out of school."

"Oh, cripes!" Nancy blew a stream of air through her lips. "I hadn't even thought about that! How much is left of the school year?"

"Two months," Hannah spat out, then threw herself into the stuffed armchair in one corner, her hands forking through her hair. "I had straight A's this year, too. Now what? Everybody knows no two schools teach a subject exactly the same way! And—" She stopped, a blush pinking her cheeks.

Ah. Someone had set her sights on a boy, was Nancy's guess, and now her darling mother had ruined her life. From somewhere deep and naughty came the sudden realization that Rod's ex had done her a supreme favor: there was little Nancy could do, inadvertently or otherwise, that would hold a candle to what their own mother had just done to them. In this case, t'weren't the *stepmother* who was the wicked one. So, if she could just keep from beating them and sending them to bed with nothing more than a crust of moldy bread for dinner, she might actually have a shot at coming out on top.

"Look, guys…we've got all weekend to sort this out. Let's just deal with dinner for the moment. Maybe go see a movie afterward. And, yeah, I'm going to spoil you rotten for the next two days. Just don't get used to it. But I promise, somehow, it's gonna be okay. The local schools are actually quite good out here."

"Local schools?" Hannah looked ready to throw up. "As in public schools?"

"Yeah. You know…where the common people send their kids?" Another blush washed up the girl's neck, but she didn't apologize. If Hannah intended on playing Spoiled Rich Kid while she was here, she was in for a rude awakening. "This may come as a shock," Nancy said, "but kids who go to public school can actually get into top colleges and everything."

Hannah squinted at her. "You're being, like, sarcastic, right?"

"Actually, I'm starving and pregnant, which means I'm closer to bitchy than sarcastic, but I'll work with that if you will."

Behind her, Schuyler chuckled, and Nancy realized she'd just made a huge blunder by making her comments in Schuy's presence. How many times had her mother torn her down in front of Mark? The anger and humiliation of those encounters—and there had been far too many of them to be called "isolated"—still stung, after all this time. Nancy turned to the boy, told him the number to the pizza place was pinned to the kitchen bulletin board, that he could order whatever they usually liked, then apologized to Hannah as soon as she was sure Schuyler was out of earshot.

For a second, it appeared the girl might drop her defenses at least long enough to accept the apology. But only for a second. Hurt had burrowed too deeply into her soul for a single apology—or the promise of pizza and a movie—to ferret it out, let alone heal it. She popped open her suitcase on the bed, began whipping garments out of it, still on their hangers.

"Tell you what," she said, smacking a half-dozen dresses up onto the closet rack. "Whenever everybody decides what to do with Schuy and me? You get back to me, let me know, okay? But right now—" she scooped up another armful of clothes, oblivious when a slippery white blouse escaped the bundle and slithered to the floor "—how about everyone just leave me alone? The last thing I'm in the mood for tonight is some dorky flick."

Nancy bent down and picked up the blouse, actually a silk tunic with exquisite mother-of-pearl buttons. She shook it out, then laid it carefully on the bed, all the while acutely aware of Hannah's gaze boring a hole through her. Then she looked at the girl, wondering why—how—she felt as calm as she did, decided it must have something to do with the pregnancy. "And when *you* decide I'm not the enemy, you know where to find me."

Then she walked out, leaving Hannah to her misery.

* * *

Hours later, the clatter of chocolate chips tumbling into a glass bowl prevented Nancy's hearing Hannah come into the kitchen.

"Whatcha doin'?" the teenager asked, and Nancy yelped, jerking up the bag so chips went flying, pattering like hail on the counter and floor. She cursed, then laughed, squatting to gather them off the floor before the cats got them.

"Sorry," Hannah said behind her.

Something told Nancy the child was apologizing for more than startling her. She pushed herself to her feet with a grunt. "S'okay," she said, shoving her hair off her face, then held up the bowl. "And I'm making microwave fudge, to answer your question."

"Now?"

It was past midnight. In fact, they were both in their pj's, Hannah in a red flannel nightgown and fuzzy slippers, Nancy in a pair of man-tailored pajamas underneath a white terry-cloth robe. "The pregnant stomach knows no timetables," she said, punching two holes in the top of a can of condensed milk. "Where's Schuy?"

"Asleep, probably. He's usually out by eleven." Hannah came closer, her arms crossed. "You sure you're supposed to be eating stuff like that?"

"As long as I don't eat the whole batch in one sitting, it's okay. Besides, I figured you and Schuy might help me—oh, right," she said when she saw the corners of the girl's mouth turn down. "You don't do junk food."

Hannah shook her head, now sliding up onto a bar stool, watching with more or less interest as Nancy poured out the can of milk over the chips, then stuck the bowl into the microwave. "I'm a lousy cook," Nancy said, wondering if she'd missed when the truce was called, "but I do a mean microwave fudge."

That got a bit of a smile, which quickly turned into a frown.

"I'm sorry," Hannah said again. "Not about the fudge. About the way I acted earlier."

Nancy thought for a moment before opening her mouth—a first—then said, "Yeah, well, I seem to remember a few times after my mother pulled one of her numbers on me, I wasn't exactly the epitome of graciousness, either. Forget about it." The microwave dinged; Nancy pulled out the concoction, decided it wasn't melted enough, shoved it back in.

"You had trouble with your mother?"

"What *had?* There've been times I've seriously considered getting an unlisted number."

"Why? What does she do?"

Maybe this wasn't the window of opportunity Nancy'd expected, but what the hell, right? "How long you gonna be around?"

"That bad?"

"Worse. I mean, I love the woman, don't get me wrong, but somehow, no matter how hard I try, I never seem to do whatever it was she thought I should be doing. Not to mention a short, skinny, Brillo-headed daughter wasn't exactly what she ordered." The microwave dinged again, but she ignored it, having far too much fun watching the you-mean-I'm-not-the-only-one? expression on Hannah's face. "*And,* to make matters worse, my brother is, like, God's gift, can do no wrong, married the right girl, got the right job, knows the right people...you get my drift." Hannah nodded. "So, no matter how we start out, the conversation always ends in this Mark-doesn't-do-these-kinds-of-things diatribe."

"Man. At least Mom doesn't do *that.* Compare Schuy and me, I mean."

"Well, then—" Nancy lugged the bowl out of the oven "—I win."

"No way," Hannah said with a half smile, sinking her chin in her palm as she watched Nancy stir the melted glop, then add chopped pecans and a teaspoon of vanilla. "She thinks we're *both* losers. Wow. That's it?"

"What? Oh, the fudge. Yeah, isn't it great? Turn it out into a buttered pan, stick it in the fridge, two hours later you got heaven.''

''That's really amazing.'' She gave a little laugh. ''You should see the production Dad goes through to make fudge.''

The pan filled and slipped into the refrigerator, Nancy heaved herself onto the bar stool next to Hannah, grabbed the bowl, then blithely started chipping away at the already-set streaks of chocolate with a spoon. She was beginning to get the picture. For better or worse, Hannah needed a friend. Better yet, an ally. And it appeared Nancy had been so appointed. Part of her was tickled to death—teenagers were harder to reel in than cats—but part of her was terrified. At least she knew what to do with cats. Some dry food, change the litter as needed, a quick scratch behind the ears or on the tummy— *bim-bam-boom,* bonded for life. Somehow, she didn't think Hannah wanted her ears scratched.

''Your father making fudge...let me guess,'' Nancy said, sucking on the spoon, then waving it. ''He probably grinds up fresh cocoa beans, blending them with refined sugar, grates the vanilla, churns the butter, then shells each nut by hand. And then he cooks it all in some fancy pot that costs more than my first car.'' She hacked off another piece of chocolate. ''Am I close?''

Hannah actually grinned. And reached over to pick off a dollop of soft fudge from the edge of the bowl. ''Pretty much. Mmm...this isn't half bad.''

''Enjoy it, honey. This is about as domestic as I get.''

The Persian mewed at Hannah's feet, asking to be picked up. Hannah obliged. ''What's this one's name again?''

''Schmutz, since she looks like a giant dustball.'' The cat turned its owl-like head to Nancy, gave her an offended expression. ''Yes, you do,'' she said to the cat, who just blinked at her, then curled up on Hannah's lap. ''I think she's made you hers.''

''Wow.'' Hannah tucked a hank of hair behind her ear. ''Should I be all honored and stuff?''

''*She* certainly thinks so.''

After a moment, Hannah said, more to the top of the cat's head than to Nancy, "I'm glad you're feeling better."

"*You're* glad? Honey, I wouldn't wish another six weeks like that on my worst enemy."

Concern swam in the blue eyes. "It's not always like that, is it?"

"Nah. My mother swears she breezed through carrying my brother, although of course she said she nearly died with me. But my friend Elizabeth didn't have a bit of sickness, morning or otherwise."

"I remember her," Hannah said. "She used to date my father, a few years ago. Frankly, she's the last person I'd expect to have a batch of kids."

"That's what she thought, too. Until she met her husband."

That got another grin. "Oh, right—the cute guy with the earring and those killer eyes." She let out a wistful sigh. "He was so sweet, at your wedding, the way he'd hover over Elizabeth, always touching her and stuff."

Nancy had returned her focus to the few flecks of fudge left in the bowl, trying to ignore the ache in her chest. "Nice to see it really can happen, huh?"

"So...what about you and Dad?"

Nancy slipped off the stool, carrying the bowl over to the sink. "Haven't we had this conversation before?"

"That was six weeks ago."

For a few seconds, the running water put off having to answer. "Nothing's changed," she said at last, then turned fully expecting another outburst. Instead, Hannah simply said, "Then I guess I just have to keep asking until I get the answer I want."

Drying her hands on a dish towel, Nancy walked back over to the island. "I know this is hard for someone your age to believe—God knows, I sure didn't at sixteen—but love isn't the only reason people get married."

"You were attracted enough to Dad to get pregnant."

"Attraction isn't the same as being in love, honey."

"Then why'd you bother getting married?" Genuine puzzlement, more than anger, fueled the words.

"Because we both feel that's what's best for the baby."

The girl sank her face into the cat's fur. "Pretty lame reason, if you ask me. I mean, it's not like parents *stay* together just because they have kids. So why should they get married to begin with, just because there's a baby coming? Especially if they don't love each other?"

Nancy bit back a wry smile. Here Rod had been so adamant about setting an example, and Hannah seemed to think the whole thing was stupid. She sat back on the stool, her head cocked. "This really matters to you, doesn't it?" Hannah nodded. "Why?"

"Because…" Nancy saw the tears well up in the girl's eyes, had to fight to keep her own at bay. "Because for once I'd like to be part of a family that teases and laughs and hugs, like Elizabeth and Guy's family, like some of my friends' families do. I mean, it's not like I think life's a sitcom, every crisis solved by the end of the half hour. But I know happy families exist. I've seen them. It'd just be nice to be part of one, for once, you know?"

Anguish twisted Nancy's heart as she reached out to her new stepdaughter, but Hannah shrugged off her touch. She let the cat drop to the floor, then, hunched over her folded arms, shuffled out of the kitchen.

Her thoughts bumping into each other like drunken moths, Nancy wandered out of the kitchen and upstairs, frowning hard enough to give herself a headache if she wasn't careful. She started to pass Rod's bedroom on the way to hers at the end of the hall, but it was as if a force of some kind actually grabbed her, making her look inside, flip the switch that lit one of the bedside lamps.

Wasn't as if she hadn't seen the room before, one of the few areas in the house Rod had already redone. With its rich taupe walls and carpeting, it was understated and elegant— like its occupant. A mixture of antique and contemporary, warm and cool, light and dark, gleaming wood and nubby silk.

Nancy walked in, turning on more lights as she breathed in Rod's scent—refined, reserved and instantaneously arousing. A shudder zipped through her as she settled into one of a pair of persimmon velvet armchairs flanking the dark marble fireplace. She tucked her feet up under her as she surveyed the room, thinking that, beautifully appointed as it was, it was missing something.

Her eyes lit on the bed, a lacquered pine four-poster smothered in a lusciously thick ivory down comforter, and she smiled.

Her.

Chilled from the cold spring rain, Rod shivered as he made his way to the Range Rover, safely tucked away in a long-term parking garage a few minutes from Metro airport. Seconds later, fee paid, he pulled out into the slashing rain, heading home…to a woman he wanted so badly his teeth hurt.

Oh, man, was he in trouble. Big-time. Despite five days crammed with software demos and meetings and conference calls and more meetings, remarkably absent was the rush of accomplishment that usually came from pulling together all the elements that would, inevitably and successfully, put a client's product into the hands of millions of unwitting consumers. Instead, there was nothing but this aching void, a void only one person could fill: Nancy.

Nancy. That bundle of irrepressible energy and sass with the cutest little fanny in the lower forty-eight, with those soft, sweet breasts that would be swollen and tender and even more sensitive with the pregnancy…

He almost laughed. Horniness, that's all this was.

Yeah, right. While the thought of hearing those delicious little moans in response to his touch certainly had something to do with his haste to return home, he'd missed her smile, and her laugh, and the way she tilted her head, concentrating, when he talked to her. Like she was actually listening.

Like she gave a damn.

Okay, so, yeah, he wanted her body. But he'd missed her friendship.

He'd missed *her*.

By the time he pulled up in front of the house, he could barely breathe. Or walk, for that matter. Behind that door was a woman who did things to his head, among other parts of his body, he didn't think a woman could do. He'd never let a woman get close enough *to* do. Just as he'd feared, she awakened feelings in him that far outdistanced physical need, feelings that kept him off balance, a state at once exhilarating and terrifying.

He could have her in his arms in a matter of seconds, in his bed, maybe, soon after—that is, if he could get out of the damn car—but was that fair to her?

He let out a long, heartfelt sigh. Marrying her had been a mistake.

The thought of not being married to her made him ill.

Why was it the more he tried to straighten things out, the more tangled they got? The more he tried to do what was right, the more wrong everything felt. The harder he tried to keep his emotions safely tucked away, the more this woman's vulnerability and honesty chipped away at his resolve, like a child picking at a scab.

With a sigh, he finally pushed himself out of the car, dashing through the deluge toward the house—yes, it would be nice when the garage enlargement was complete—up the stairs and inside. Bruiser trotted over to him, rubbing his ankles for a second until he realized Rod was wet. The cat darted away, clearly disgusted. Rod could relate. He slipped off his wet coat, hanging it on a coat tree by the front door. "Nance?"

From the back of the house, he heard laughter, his brows knotting when he recognized Schuyler's unmistakable croak, Hannah's shriek of mock outrage.

So much for sweeping his wife off to bed. And what in heaven's name were the kids doing here on a Tuesday, anyway?

He walked quickly down the hall to the kitchen. No one

noticed him at first, all three thoroughly engrossed with something involving graham crackers, chocolate bars and roasting marshmallows on stretched-out wire hangers over his restaurant-quality gas range. Nancy, in a coffee-brown tunic and leggings, a narrow tortoiseshell headband making a valiant—and unsuccessful—attempt to hold back her humidity-frizzed hair, looked like a sparrow hopping about between a pair of baggy, saggy storks.

And they were all, clearly, having a good time.

"Honestly, Schuy," Nancy said, laughing when the marshmallow on the end of his wire burst into flames. "It's supposed to be toasted, honey. Not cremated." She grabbed the hanger, blew out the inferno, then brandished another impaled marshmallow in the kid's face. "Observe, please."

With a flourish, she held the marshmallow over the flame, turning it this way and that until it turned a perfect golden brown. "See?" Her smile was as boundless as the sky. "Am I good or what? Okay, okay—Cora told me this joke at work today. This old man, like ninety-six or something, is dying. Lying in bed, so weak he can barely breathe, he smells something absolutely fabulous drifting upstairs from the kitchen."

She paused to smush the marshmallow between two graham crackers, waving it as she continued. "After a couple seconds, he realizes—" her splayed hand slammed to her chest "—Ohmigod! It's chocolate chip cookies, which was like his favorite thing in the whole world. Well, almost," she said with a grin, eliciting giggles from both kids. "So, anyway, he decides, before he pops off, he's gotta have one last chocolate chip cookie, right? So he hauls himself out of bed, crawling on his hands and knees to the stairs, then somehow drags himself downstairs and to the kitchen."

She shimmied up onto the counter and took a bite of her s'more, chewing for a second before continuing. "Crawls over to the kitchen table, where his wife's just laid out two sheets of warm, moist cookies, right from the oven. With his last ounce of strength, he reaches up to pluck one off the sheet,

when his wife smacks his hand with the spatula. 'Hands off!'
she says. 'They're for the funeral!'"

As the kids groaned, Rod let out a laugh, which brought all
three sets of eyes zinging in his direction. Immediately, Nancy
slid down from the counter, dusting off her hands as she approached him. Hannah and Schuy hung back, though, as
though not sure how he was going to react.

Without thinking, he gently flicked a graham-cracker crumb
from her chin. "You supposed to be eating stuff like that?"

"Hey, I've shoved so much milk and fruit and veggies into
my system today, the sugar in that one s'more couldn't find
its way to this kid if it tried." She cleared her throat. "I suppose you're wondering why the kids are still here."

He glanced at his children, returned his gaze to hers. "The
question had crossed my mind."

"Maybe you should sit down," she said.

In Rod's place, Nancy supposed she would have exploded.
Yet only the iron set to Rod's jaw, the look of stunned dis-
belief in his eyes, gave a clue as to how ticked off he was.
Although, at the moment, Nancy wasn't sure whether his ire
was directed more at Claire for her little stunt, or Nancy for
not having told him before this.

He'd muttered a few words to the kids before leading Nancy
out into the hallway, where they wouldn't be overheard.
"You're telling me she just dumped them on you?"

"On *us,* not *me.* Although I don't know that *dumped* is the
best word here."

Long fingers forked through his damp hair. "From her
standpoint, believe me, she dumped them." Now, in his shoes,
Nancy would have had some pretty choice things to say about
Claire, who had figured in some pleasant fantasies involving
Montezuma's revenge and/or large, nasty insects. But Rod
only asked, "How are they taking it?"

"It's been touch-and-go," she admitted. "They've alter-
nated between being pissed and philosophical—"

"You had no right to keep this from me, Nancy," he said,

cutting her off. "You could have called me, e-mailed me, *something*."

"Well, shoot the messenger, why doncha? You were busy, we were coping, and there wasn't a damn thing you could do, now was there?"

He clamped his mouth shut, pushed one hand across his jaw. "We'll discuss this later," he ground out, then returned to the kitchen as if she'd been dismissed.

The kids had migrated to the family room to watch TV. Nancy stayed in the kitchen, arms tucked against her ribs, telling herself she was more sensitive these days because of the pregnancy, that he didn't really mean to snap at her. Yeah, well, tears were tears, and these were burning the hell out of her eyelids. She watched as Rod approached Schuy and Hannah, now slouched into opposite corners of the sofa. Hannah looked up, a whole mess of emotions tumbling from those bright blue eyes. Fifteen minutes before, they'd both been yukking it up and having a blast, but the minute Daddy reentered the picture, everything Nancy'd worked so hard to establish over the weekend went *poof*.

Or was she just being paranoid?

They were both in his arms before he was even fully seated between them. Children still, even in those supersized bodies, Schuyler with the brain of a forty-five-year-old physicist, Hannah a combination of beauty, intelligence, and athleticism that would knock the world on its ear someday. Maybe Nancy sensed an awkwardness to the embrace, from both sides, as if no one was quite sure now what to do, but there was no doubting the connection.

So where was her place in this family tableau? Maybe she'd filled in while Rod was gone, but he was back now, and she simply wasn't needed. Or so he clearly thought. And she thought of the clothes she'd moved into his closet, her makeup neatly arranged on the right side of the master bath's double sink, the fantasies she'd entertained during the past few nights she'd spent in his bed, and she felt like a foolish little girl whose dreams had been, once again, shot to hell and back. He hadn't even kissed her when he'd come in. Shoot, they'd at least been up to that when he left—had five days away blown what little progress they'd made?

Or had she simply wanted so hard to believe in happily-ever-after endings, she'd deluded herself once again?

Damn him! No, it wasn't his fault he wasn't here when Claire pulled her number, but the least he could do was acknowledge that Nancy had survived the weekend intact. She'd pulled more tricks out of what she'd thought was an empty bag than she'd ever dreamed possible—getting them enrolled in their new schools, cajoling them into working on the garden, taking them shopping, *feeding* them, even. Feeding them food their father might actually approve of. Well, besides the s'mores. And he just…just brushes her off with a "Why didn't you call me?"

Well, forget this. There was a perfectly good mystery calling to her, lying where she'd left it in the den. She'd just go read, was what she'd do, give Rod and the kids a chance to hash things out and over and whatever. But they'd be in bed by ten, ten-thirty at the latest, and then, just as Rod had said, they had some serious discussing to do. Time to pin the man down and find out exactly what he thought her place was in this house, in the lives of the people she now lived with.

Then she was going to just have to change his mind.

Chapter 10

Nancy gave the kids an extra half hour—they'd both come in to say good-night—before hauling her little bod upstairs and into the master bedroom. Rod's suitcase was open on the bed, his tie loosened. Something Baroque and soothing hummed softly in the background. She could smell her own perfume hanging in the air, saw Oprah's latest pick lying open on the nightstand by "her" side of the bed. How could he not have noticed?

Or had he?

She saw the weariness in his eyes when he looked up, the slump to his shoulders, and her anger vanished. For the moment, at least. Right now, she just wanted to take him in her arms, give him a back rub. Do things to him, for him, with him—things her mother had probably never even *heard* of.

"You should have contacted me," he repeated.

She let out a harsh sigh. "I made a judgment call, okay? We had things under control, there was nothing you could do—"

"They're my kids, Nancy!" She watched as he choked back

the anger. "I want to know everything that concerns them, no matter how trivial it might seem."

"Who said anything about trivial, for the love of Mike? I just thought, being a grown-up and all, I could handle it without bothering you!"

He stared at her, hard, for a moment, then looked away. "Claire blew it, far as I'm concerned. I'm filing for full custody in the morning."

Nancy stood at the foot of the bed with her hands on her hips, unable to decide whether to be ticked off or not. *Not* was not winning. "Yes, I agree, that's an excellent idea, thanks for asking."

She must be losing her touch, since her sarcasm—if not the whole blamed comment—was apparently lost on him. However, she caught the extra snap to his movements as he grabbed several shirts, went into the dressing room next to the walk-in closet, tossed them into the wicker hamper, then came out again without commenting on the fact that two-thirds of his closet now held girl stuff.

The guy was either blind or seriously preoccupied.

"She had no right, none, to do that to them," he said through a tight jaw, not even seeing *her,* let alone her clothes or a book. Ah. Preoccupied. Did he know he'd wadded up a shirt in his hands? His eyes found hers. "Or to you." Then again, maybe not *that* preoccupied.

"I realize I'm sticking my nose in where it doesn't belong," she said, "not that that has ever stopped me before…but why did Claire ever get full custody to begin with?"

A hint of a smile, as if he'd expected the question, played around his mouth. "Because, simply, I gave it to her. At the time, it seemed the easier way to go for everyone, especially the children. She'd've made things ugly otherwise, and I couldn't see putting the kids through that. Not on top of the divorce."

"But—pardon me—she's a lousy mother."

"She wasn't always," he said softly, then lifted his eyes to hers. "And if I'd had any idea then the only reason she wanted custody was because of some personal one-upmanship thing, I would have fought harder to keep them.'' There went the hand, up to the back of his neck. ''At least, I think I would have. Hindsight is a bitch, you know?''

What was a bitch, Nancy thought, was discovering that what you thought was the best thing for your children hadn't been, at all. That you'd made a mistake, possibly one with far-reaching consequences. For a man of Rod's integrity and deep-seated desire to avoid causing the people in his circle of responsibility any pain, such revelations were the stuff of nightmares.

Hanging on to his gaze like a toddler with a bright penny, Nancy walked around the bed, pried the shirt from his hands, then threaded their fingers together. Took a *reeeeal* deep breath as heat from the simple touch seared through her, the subtle widening of his pupils setting those five gazillion hormones to break dancing. Man, anger and lust were a deadly combination. ''Let it out, Rod.''

''Let what out?''

''What you're feeling. Yell. Throw something. *Swear,* even. But do something, for heaven's sake.''

He disengaged his fingers from her grasp, returning to his task. ''I'm fine.''

''Like hell,'' Nancy shot back, not giving herself even a second to react to the obvious rejection. ''Tell me you wouldn't like to rip Claire's guts out right now.''

''Then,'' he said in that irritatingly patient way he had, ''I'd only be admitting she could still push my buttons. What on earth would getting angry accomplish, except to raise my blood pressure?''

''Well, keeping it all bottled up sure isn't going to do you a whole lot of good, either!''

''I'm touched by your concern, Nancy, but I'll deal with Claire and the kids in my own way, okay? There's no reason for you to get so involved—''

''You're *touched by my concern?* You think you're talking to one of your clients, what? And what is this *you-don't-want-*

me-getting-involved garbage? I'm your *wife,* Rod, for whatever that's worth! Hannah and Schuy are my stepchildren—''

"In name only," he said, and her blood ran cold.

"What did you say?"

After a moment, he let his gaze touch hers, just barely, as if afraid to let her see what was in his eyes. "This marriage is for *this* baby," he said at last. "I never expected you to have full-time stepmothering responsibility, to get that involved with Hannah and Schuy—''

"I'm already involved, you twit!" she exploded, her hands flying into the air. "Okay, so maybe things haven't gone the way we'd planned, but so what? We're all in this together, and I, for one, would like to make this work. So trust me, *bubeleh*—I'm involved.''

"And what if this *doesn't* work out?"

Fear stuttered in the air between them, though whether his or hers, she couldn't have said. Still, it took a moment to untwist her heart and get it beating again. And when it did, she saw Rod through a furious haze. "Whatever happened to *I don't make conditional commitments?* I made a promise to you, to our child, to raise him or her with you. As you did to me. I'm hardly going to back out simply because someone upped the stakes.''

"Nance—calm down. This isn't good for the baby.''

"Oh, please, Rod—that went out with confinement and keeping a mother flat on her back during labor. Besides, I'm not gonna change who I am just because I'm pregnant. Or because it makes you uncomfortable.''

Then she stood there, waiting for the next volley. When none came, frustration roared through her. "Fight *back,* dammit!''

"I don't fight." The words came out stiffly, overenunciated. Yet even as they further infuriated her, she sensed they arose, not from weakness, but from a strength born of events she didn't know or understand. "Fighting only gets people hurt.''

"Well, I got news for you, buddy—so does acting as if what the other person says isn't important enough to merit a reaction! Why do you pull the plug on arguments before they're over, start things you can't finish?''

Something almost like horror flashed in his eyes, as she apparently hit a bull's-eye she didn't know she'd been aiming for.

She sank onto the padded bench at the foot of his bed, momentarily deflated. ''What do you expect from this marriage, Rod?'' she asked quietly, then twisted around to capture his eyes. ''From me?''

Sharing breathing space with this woman was like being caught in a revolving door. She made his head spin, his heart pound, and God knew she probably was the worst thing possible for his blood pressure.

And now she'd gone and wormed her way into his children's hearts. Oh, he had no doubt there were problems to be worked out, but even he could see how much more relaxed Schuyler was, could hear how the defensive tone in his daughter's voice had faded almost to nothing. In five days, he had to admit, Nancy had paid more attention to his children, had made them feel as if they mattered, more than he or Claire had done since the divorce. And that had singed a nerve he hadn't even known was exposed. Not to this extent, anyway.

If he wasn't real careful, she was going to make him need her.

''Well. Guess that answers that question,'' Nancy said as she rose, and he realized she'd misinterpreted his silence.

Just as he realized he was one screwed-up dude, as Schuyler would say.

He grabbed her hand, twisted her back around to face him, and suddenly she was more than just in front of him, in the same room with him. Her scent, her being, flowed through him and into him, as a pair of huge, dark eyes, tinged with longing and sadness, searched his. Of its own accord, his hand sought her face, his thumb that luscious lower lip.

''I honestly don't know what I want,'' he whispered, his voice ragged even to his own ears. When her hand rose, her fingers scraping along his evening-roughened jaw, he swallowed. "So I'll turn the tables—what do *you* want?"

He watched as she struggled with her answer, although it surprised him that she'd have to think about the question at all.

"Go back into the closet," she said at last, a smile playing on her lips, "then come tell me what you see. Go on," she encouraged when he didn't move.

So he did, only to wonder a second later how on earth he'd missed five thousand female garments when he'd come in before.

She'd moved in. Lock, stock and L'Oréal.

He walked out. Stared at her. Sure enough, she was twisting her hair around that finger hard enough to cut off the circulation.

"I want to feel like your wife," she said. "At least, in some ways. I want to feel I belong here, not like a guest, or the poor cousin no one really knows what to do with. I want to feel…as if I matter, that I'm appreciated, that I at least have some say in what happens around here. And most of all, I want you to make love to me, right here, right now, because I'm sick and tired of feeling as if I've been sent to the Ferndale Home for Unwed Mothers to wait out this pregnancy."

"Except you're not unwed."

"Then how's about we stop acting like I am, okay?"

He hadn't even realized he'd closed the distance between them, but he must have, because her face was less than six inches from his, a study in strength and resilience and absolute determination, with just a touch of please-don't-reject-me to take the edge off.

"And what if I say," he began, running his hand up and down her arm, scooting the loose tunic sleeve out of the way so he could feel her smooth skin, "that as much as I want you, our going to bed wouldn't change anything?"

He saw a thousand thoughts flicker through her eyes. "I'm not asking you to fall in love with me," she whispered. "Just make me your wife."

''And will that be enough for you?''

She broke away, walked over to his door and shut it, pushing in the knob to lock. She turned around, one hand still on the knob. ''I come from a long line of women who know how to make do.''

He'd made a vow to keep her happy, he remembered as he approached her, unbuttoning his shirt, slipping it off, flinging it to God knew where. To put her first. They both understood the ground rules, after all, he reminded himself as he drew her into his arms, covered her mouth—warm and giving—with his. And he remembered, as he had every night since the night this baby had been conceived, every curve of her slender body, her responsiveness, her eagerness to please as well as be pleased. And he wanted her—Oh, man, how he wanted her!—more than he probably should, more than he thought he could ever want a woman.

More than he'd ever dare let on.

If all she really needed was sex and respect, to feel appreciated and wanted—hell, he could do that, no problem.

He slid one hand underneath the plush tunic, unhooking the front clasp of her bra to cup a breast so soft he could barely feel it, the nipple already alert against his tingling palm. He knew she was still tender, took care to be gentle as he caught the nipple between his thumb and forefinger, barely squeezing it; she stiffened as if shocked, sucked in a quiet, eager breath. Shuddered.

She'd given him a sort of power over her he didn't want, couldn't ignore. Didn't want to ignore. No woman had ever responded to him the way Nancy did—with everything she had. As much as that scared the hell out of him, it also thrilled him. And, hey—as long as she wasn't asking for his heart, it wasn't as if his body had anything better to do, right?

His hands ventured down, breached the elastic waistband of her leggings, stroked the sensitive area at the base of her spine before slowly peeling away the stretchy fabric. He brushed kisses across her sweetly rounded tummy, down her thighs. Sandalwood and roses and woman-scent filled his nostrils, made him crazy. She stepped out of the leggings, a soft sigh floating from her lips when he cupped her bottom, teasing her with his mouth through gossamer silk and lace. Purple, he briefly noticed. And barely there.

He slipped them down, too.

"Rod...please..."

"Stop?"

Her fingers dug into his shoulders. "Not hardly."

So he kept going. Probably not the way she'd intended, but he doubted she'd argue. A nuzzle, a nip, a little trick of the tongue he'd almost forgotten about, and...oh, *yeah.* She cried out, startled, then laughed.

He sat back on his heels, stroking her thighs. "How's that?"

Breathing erratically, she held up one finger, her other hand still gripping his shoulder. "Let's put it this way." She swiped back her hair. "I haven't decided whether to kill you or have you declared a national treasure. But, um, I'd kind of been thinking more along the lines of, you know, making love in a *bed?*"

"Oh, trust me, honey—" He stood, bracing his hands against the wall on either side of her shoulders. "We'll get there. Eventually—hey!"

For such small hands, they were remarkably adroit. And fast. He hadn't even heard the zipper being undone, yet there were his trousers, puddled around his ankles. She tilted her head, contemplating the arousal straining against his briefs. "Hmm. That looks promising—"

Her last word ended on a cross between a laugh and a yelp as, not even bothering to extricate himself from his pants, he tugged her down onto the plush carpet at the foot of the bed. The rest of their clothes soon dispensed with, he hefted himself above her, his gaze raking over her fuller breasts, the nipples and areolae dusky, enlarged with the pregnancy; the taut roundness of her belly, arousing in its implications; her smile.

"Make me your wife," she whispered, her fingers tracing his cheekbones, then his jaw as she opened to him.

"It's the least I can do," he whispered back, easing himself inside her, giving over to that sweet, tight heat, feeling even then like a paratrooper about to leave the plane, torn between thrill and terror. It's just sex, he told himself, beginning to move inside her, slowly, exquisitely, the thick carpeting abrading his knees, his heart stuttering when her legs wrapped around his back, enclosing him. Just sex, he told himself, less emphatically, when her eyes closed in concentration at the sensation beginning to build inside her, around him. Just…sex, he managed to repeat, barely, watching her face contort as she caught the wave of her own climax, riding higher… higher…higher, her cries of release detonating his own as she yanked him over the edge with her.

Just sex? he wondered, when, seconds later, he lay with her tucked against his chest, his chin resting in that riot of curls so she couldn't see his frown. If this was just sex, then why did he feel as if someone had ripped a hole the size of a football field in the center of his chest?

A sudden craving for fudge had driven Hannah out of bed and down to the kitchen. On the return trip, she noticed the handle of the master bedroom door was turned to the locked position. Not to mention a muffled sound or two which didn't take a rocket scientist to identify.

Cheeks blazing, she hurried down the hall, barged through her brother's unlocked door, clicked on his light and plunked herself down on the edge of his bed.

Schuyler lurched up in bed, shielding his eyes. "What the hell—?"

"I think Dad and Nancy are *doing it*," she whispered.

"Oh, *gross*—"

"It is not! It's great! And keep your voice down, dweeb!"

He looked at her as if she'd truly lost it this time, then sank back into his pillows with a groan, shutting his eyes. "You mean you woke me up to tell me that?" He shuddered, tugged the covers higher over his T-shirted shoulder. "Trust me on

this, Hannah—" he opened one glaring eye "—I don't want
or need to know about my father's sex life, okay?"

"Oh, don't be such a prude, Schuy. Don't you see what
this means?"

He glared at her again.

"I don't mean *that*. I mean, what it could mean to us. As
a family."

With a sigh, Schuyler once more hauled himself up to a
sitting position, his hair fanning out around his head like a
cheap wig. For the first time, Hannah noticed a little peach
fuzz on his upper lip. "Hannah," he said, doing his far-too-
smart-for-his-age number, "you're doing it again. Getting
your hopes up."

Yes, she was. And damned if she was gonna let her brother
dash them. "This time is way different, Schuy, and you know
it. I know Nancy's in love with Dad. I just know it, even
though she keeps denying it and stuff—"

"Han," he said on a yawn. "Stop." He hunched his legs
up under his chin, clasping his arms around his knees. Rubbed
his eyes. "Nancy's cool, and I think she does really care about
Dad. But it's Dad we have to worry about, you know? So
they're getting it on?" His shoulders hitched. "So what? I
mean, so did Dad and Mom, obviously, or we wouldn't be
here. People, like, have sex and stuff and still get divorced."

Shaking his head, he skootched back down underneath the
covers, nearly knocking Hannah off the bed when he jabbed
his feet into her rump. "Now, I don't know about you, but
I'd like to be able to stay awake in class tomorrow, so I'm
going back to sleep." With that, he clicked off the light,
plunging the room in thick darkness. "Good *night,* Hannah."

Well, what did he know, anyway? Rubbing her hip as she
carefully picked her way over assorted piles of stuff to get to
the door, she muttered, "You're just an old pook, you know
that?"

"I prefer to think of it as being pragmatic," came the sleepy
reply from a few feet away, and Hannah humphed. What sort

of thirteen-year-old uses words like *pragmatic,* for crying out loud?

Smart ones, she thought with a pang, then headed back to her own room.

Eventually, they did make it to the bed. Nancy supposed that eventually, as well, they'd be able to keep their hands off each other.

But not yet.

They could afford to go slow now. And Rod, it seemed was an expert at *slow.* Okay, so he was no slouch at fast, either, but slow was…

Well, Nancy was sure there was a word for it, but God knew if she could think of it at the moment. Not while his hands were stroking like this, and his lips were suckling like that, and his tongue… Somebody should patent that tongue.

Never had a lover been so careful, considerate, concerned.

Or more detached. Ironic, wasn't it? Rod was, indisputably, the best lover she'd ever had, would ever *have,* yet even as he coaxed and teased and aroused her to trembling before guiding her onto him, luring her into yet another brain-melting climax, she knew only part of him was in this bed. Physically, he held nothing back, as finely attuned to her needs as someone who might have shared her bed and body for years. But still he kept his soul to himself, like a child willing enough to share the whipped cream on his sundae, but not the ice cream underneath.

Afterward, they lay together, a sheen of perspiration all that separated their bodies, but Nancy knew they were as far apart as they'd always been. Just as he'd said, this had changed nothing. And now she knew, unequivocally, that it would take powers far beyond her ken to crack open the unassailable vault in which Rod kept his heart locked away. He'd even said, at one point, how much this was for *her.* So was that the comment of a generous lover…or a man simply doing his frustrated wife a favor?

The slow, even breathing under her ear alerted her that Rod

had at last succumbed to not being seventeen anymore. She jacked herself up onto one elbow, smoothed a hunk of hair off his forehead, then got up and slipped on the most boring nightgown ever made. Instead of crawling back into bed, though, she opened the door to let in Ditzy, then settled in one of the chairs in front of the fireplace with the calico in her lap.

Her eyes swam as she thought of Elizabeth and Guy, the joy and love they shared, and envy clawed at her determination to be grateful for what she had, which she reminded herself yet again was so much more than most women had. But still, why was it she could never seem to find someone who really needed her, someone willing to bare his soul to her?

Why was it that no matter how hard she tried, she was never good enough?

And why had she married Rod, knowing upfront what the limitations would be, what he could and could not—would not?—give?

She had no idea when the answer came to her, sitting there in the dark, stroking a purring cat while her husband slept on the other side of the room. Certainly, she didn't need Rod's protection, or his money, or even his assistance in taking care of their baby, when it came right down to it. Or even her mother's blessing. No, Elizabeth was right: the real reason she'd agreed to marry Rod was because, no matter how often her heart had been trampled, she still held out hope that somehow, some day, she'd find that man who'd need her the way Guy and Elizabeth needed each other.

Now all she had to do was figure out why on earth she'd pegged Rod Braden as that man.

He'd heard her get up, the floor creaking even underneath the thick carpeting as she went into the dressing room, padded back out, let in one of the cats. Was very aware, as well, that she hadn't come back to bed.

It would be easy enough to take the coward's way out and pretend to still be asleep. As he supposed they would both pretend, for his children's sake if nothing else, that a marriage based on respect, friendship and physical attraction could work just as well as one based on something as unpredictable, ephemeral, and potentially volatile as love.

Nancy was like an experimental medicine, he decided, that, while it might prove to be the miracle cure for some long-standing disease, could very well make things worse, as well. In some ways, he ached to let her inside, give her a shot at healing his tattered soul as he'd never let another woman before her. But he was afraid. Afraid to be vulnerable again, afraid to trust, afraid to untie the bands that had constricted and restricted his emotions for all these years. Afraid to find out just how much of his mother's child he was.

Or his father's.

He rolled over, tried to focus on her in the charcoal light, thought maybe she was sitting curled up on the chair, like a hurting child. "Nance?" Her head turned, although he couldn't see her face. "Come back to bed, honey."

She didn't move right away, as if considering her options. After a minute, though, he heard the soft thud of a cat being deposited on the floor, then saw her rise, move toward the bed, her nightgown ghost-white in the darkness.

Wordlessly, she lay down, settling on her right side, facing away from him. Rod spooned himself around her, his arm tucked over hers, his hand cradling their growing child. Comforting. Protecting.

Pretending.

Nancy burst into the sunlight-flooded kitchen at nine the next morning, eyes wide, hair wild. On her, frazzled looked good. "Why didn't you wake me up?"

"Because you needed the sleep," Rod said. "So I got the kids off to school, then called Cora, told her you wouldn't be in today."

Rod caught her flummoxed expression as he crossed to the refrigerator and withdrew a pitcher of freshly squeezed orange juice.

"You did what?"

He handed her a glass of juice, then leaned back against the counter, arms crossed over his favorite knit shirt. "Sprung you."

Her gaze riveted to his, she gulped down her juice before responding. "And...does this sudden spurt of machismo have anything to do with last night?"

It was hell being married to a perceptive woman. He'd lain awake half the night, trying to figure out ways to make her feel more like she belonged. Like she mattered. Because she *did* matter, a great deal. "In a way. I thought maybe you and I should spend some time together. Out of bed, that is."

She stared at him, stone-faced, for a long moment, then set her glass on the counter, assuming a mirror pose to his. "You don't have to work?"

"The world had me all weekend." He picked up his half-finished cup of coffee, took a long swallow. "Today is for us. You. What would you like to do?"

Something very much like suspicion flashed in her eyes, just for a second, before a smile finally softened her features. "Okay. You're on. I'd like to go out to that nursery off Highway 60, maybe get some bedding plants for the front yard, now that it's warm enough. I mean, if that's okay."

He frowned. "If what's okay?"

"Doing something with the garden. It's your house, after all."

"*My*—" Annoyance heated his neck. "Why on earth would you think that?"

He noticed her worrying her wedding ring with the fingers of her right hand. "I guess...I'm just not used to the idea, is all," she said softly. "Of this being, um, mine."

"Well, *get* used to it," he said with a huff of annoyance, placing his coffee cup inside the dishwasher. "You can do anything you want with the garden. With the inside, too, for that matter...Nancy?"

He turned to see she'd slipped outside, onto the deck off the kitchen, her hand shielding her eyes from the sharp morning sun as she surveyed the long-neglected gardens. A few bedding plants for the front, she said. Uh-huh.

They'd take the Rover.

Forty-five minutes later they were off, Nancy in a butter-yellow jumper in some soft, clingy fabric with a row of white buttons down the front, worn over a white T-shirt, white rope-soled shoes on her feet. And scrunched over her curls, a wide-brimmed straw hat, the front pinned to the crown by an enormous, constantly trembling, white fabric rose. She sat beside Rod in the Rover, her hands laced in her lap, the soft fabric tenderly cupping her tummy as the wind from the open window teased her hair. It was one of those perfect spring days that doesn't feel quite real, the temperature flirting with seventy, the sky postcard-blue, the air scented with damp, freshly turned earth. A day, Rod mused, designed to delude one into thinking no problem was too big or scary to resolve.

"I've dreamed of a garden of my own since I was a little girl," Nancy confessed a few minutes into the half-hour drive. Rod was glad to see her relaxed, even if only for this little while. Even if it didn't last.

"I thought you said you lived in suburbia, growing up?"

"Oh, my mother wouldn't let me near her garden. Not after I sprayed the wrong stuff on her petunias and nearly killed the lot."

His brows dipped. "And how old were you when that happened?"

Her mouth twisted into a wry smile. "Ten. But they were very rare petunias. Or so she said." A breeze caught one of her curls, slapping it over her mouth. She snagged it in the crook of her index finger, pulled it free. "To give credit where it's due, my father went to bat for me, won me a square-yard plot in the back corner of my very own. But everything I planted there looked so puny and scraggly next to the 'real' garden, and I got so tired of hearing my mother's criticisms of everything I did, I eventually gave up, moved on to other interests."

Rod swallowed down a wave of empathy. "Such as?"

She let out a short laugh. "Boys, mainly. Turns out, though, I should've stuck with my scrawny tomato plants. Oh, look— a dairy farm!" She twisted slightly in her seat to get a better look as they zipped past it, then back around. "That might be a fun place to take the baby, when he or she gets bigger."

Gets bigger. Every once in a while, it hit him this arrangement wasn't just for a few months, until the baby came. Even he and Claire would have to deal with each other for the rest of their lives, because of the children they'd made. He glanced over at Nancy, who'd lapsed into what he took to be contemplative silence, and found himself unwilling to accept his and Nancy's relationship would end up like that. He nearly lost his breath for a moment when he realized just how much the responsibility lay in his camp for what did, or didn't, happen this time.

"How'd the kids seem this morning?" she suddenly asked.

He thought of the furtive glances darting between his offspring, the leading questions lobbed his way, and chuckled. "Basically okay. But I'm pretty sure they know about last night."

Nancy looked at him, frowning for a second. Then a flush swept up her neck until her cheeks were red as cherries. "Oh. I thought they were asleep."

"Well, you thought wrong," he said, unable to resist the grin.

After a moment, she shrugged. "Well, I guess it's no big deal, really. I remember being able to hear my parents going at it." She laughed. "Of course, it took me a while to figure out what was going on, and then I was embarrassed to death for about a year or so. But I got over it." She turned to Rod, rubbing one hand over her middle. "So. You ever hear your parents having sex?"

Every muscle in his back tightened. "No," he answered tightly, hoping she'd take the hint.

She didn't. "You know, I don't even know their names."

His hand tightened on the steering wheel. "Lawrence and Susan."

He could feel, more than see, her frown. "That was supposed to have been an opening, Rod," she said gently. "I tell you about my dysfunctional childhood, you tell me about your perfect one. You know—getting to know each other?"

"What makes you think my childhood was perfect?" he barked out, immediately realizing he'd played right into her hand. Damn.

"Call it a fantasy of mine," she said mildly, smoothing out her dress. "Since mine was so rotten, I figure most people's had to be better."

Neither Claire nor Myrna had ever seemed to care about his past. Which was what came from marrying shallow women, he supposed. Which Nancy was definitely not. Now she'd put him in the position of either lying, telling the truth, or backing away from the conversation entirely. Great choice, huh?

"There's the nursery," he said, veering off the highway and onto a gravel parking lot in front of a green-painted building nested in a million pansies, while rows and rows of baby trees stretched out forever off to one side. He cut the engine, realized he wasn't breathing properly. He started when Nancy laid her hand on his wrist.

"You might find this hard to believe," she said with a shaky smile, "but occasionally I do stop yammering long enough to listen. Talk to me, buddy."

After a moment, he turned to her, lifting one hand to touch her hair. "Remember when you told me to let you know if certain topics were off-limits?"

The smile faded. She turned around, arms linked over her middle. "Oh." He could hear the hurt in that single word, the incomprehension. "Why? Because you don't trust me?"

"Nancy...no. *No.* Like I've said all along, this has nothing to do with you."

Her hands shot up. "You can feed me and sleep with me, but you can't talk to me. For God's sake, Rod, even *friends* talk to each other!"

She swung open the car door, got out. Rod scrambled from his side, reaching her before she could get far. "Nancy—" He grabbed her hand, so tiny and fragile in his, and was nearly overwhelmed with the memory of his response to those tiny, fragile hands the night before. But when she lifted her dark, expressive eyes to his, the eyes of a little girl whose mother had never once praised her scrawny tomatoes, his heart nearly cracked.

There were no words.

Several seconds passed before she let out a soft sigh, then squeezed his hand. "I'm sorry," she whispered, shaking her head. "What kind of a friend am *I,* getting mad at you for sticking to the rules I set, huh?"

No. The question was, what kind of husband was he, demanding his wife abide by those conditions to begin with?

He leaned over, brushing his lips against her forehead. "You may find this hard to believe," he said softly, "but I am trying."

That got a bit of a smile. "I know, Rod. I really do. And like I said, I know how to make do."

Guilt constricting his breathing, he draped one arm around her shoulders. "Come on, honey. Let's go buy some flowers."

Like Hannah and Schuy the first time they saw Disneyworld, Nancy let out a gasp of anticipation and wonder at the vast field of color twinkling like a mass of gemstones in the splotches of sunlight leaking through the building's slatted roof.

"Oy," she breathed. "I don't know where to start." With that, she drifted out into the field of bedding plants, the breeze catching the soft fabric of her jumper, whipping it out behind her legs.

"May I help you, sir?"

Rod turned to the smiling young man at his elbow, then nodded toward Nancy, whose hands were already full. "My wife wants to get a few things for our garden. But she's kind of new at this. If you could sort of follow her around, answer questions for her, make sure she gets the right plants, that would be a big help.''

''No problem.'' The young man loped over to the cashier, grabbed a red wagon, presumably for Nancy to stash her haul until they were ready to pay. But Rod shook his head, pointing to a six-foot-long flatbed a few feet away.

''Think maybe that's more the size you're going to need.''

The kid grinned back. ''Yes, *sir,*'' he said, dropping the red wagon handle with a clatter, then grabbing the flatbed, expertly pivoting it through the tables of plants to Nancy. When she saw the kid with his truck, she looked over to Rod, her eyebrows raised in question.

''Just be sure to leave a few things for the other customers,'' he called, his heart catching in his throat at her enormous grin in reply.

Chapter 11

Keeping busy, Nancy decided as she sat staring out her now miniblinded office window instead of doing whatever it was she was supposed to be doing, was the remedy for most ills, even those that were self-inflicted. And heaven knows there'd been plenty to keep her busy since the kids' coming to live with them three months ago.

Elizabeth had given birth with a minimum of fuss, if nearly two weeks late, to an eight-pound baby girl at the beginning of May. Chloe Elizabeth. Daddy's blue eyes, chick-fuzz blond hair. Maureen and Hugh did get married, secretly, but Cora and Nancy threw the couple an after-the-fact wedding reception. Nancy and Hannah had overseen the renovating and re-decorating of the rest of the house. The exterior had been sandblasted to reveal a warm, silvery-gray stone, and the garage could now comfortably hold four cars and was connected at long last to the kitchen by means of a glassed-in breezeway. Claire had returned from her honeymoon, sputtered and groused about Rod's bid for custody for a week or so until her new husband apparently convinced her to back off. And, despite the expected occasional skirmishes occasioned by a pair of teenagers suddenly living in a household with—gasp!—limits, both Hannah and Schuyler seemed to be adapting well to small-town life. Both finished the school year with honor-roll grades and new friends, and the high-school girls' basketball coach had practically promised her firstborn to Hannah if she'd join the team.

So, if it hadn't been for this little chink in the works called her *marriage,* Nancy's life would have been just about perfect. Oh, on the surface, things were harmonious enough. Rod continued to be kind and considerate and careful not to reveal one iota more than he wanted her to know, while she continued to pretend to be so busy it didn't matter. Her husband was also spending more and more time away on business, something else he rarely talked about. In fact, instinct told her his heart didn't seem to be in that, any more than it was in their marriage.

And damned if he wasn't taking out his silent frustration on their sex life. Like late Friday night, when he'd come home after a week away. She'd heard the garage door close, gone downstairs to meet him in her nightgown and robe. As always, apprehension hummed in her veins as she wondered what he expected of her.

He'd already reached the entryway, tugging at the knot in his tie. Even in the dim light in the stairwell, she could see the emptiness in his eyes. And the desperate, overwhelming need. He didn't smile, but hunger flared between them, provoking an instant and reciprocal response in her woman's soul.

She continued down to the bottom step, her hand at her throat, watching as he approached her. A breeze from somewhere stirred the heavy scent of roses she'd arranged in a crystal vase nearby; his hand lifted to finger her hair, her heart keening at the sadness etched in his handsome features, the loneliness he wouldn't let her ease.

He kissed her, testing. She put a hand to his cheek. Waited.

''Where're the kids?'' he asked.

''Out. Spending the night at friends' houses.''

"Good."

He lowered his hand, eased aside her robe, the gesture no surprise. She knew what he wanted, what she'd give, had known since that first glimpse of him, seconds ago. The gown was white voile, nearly transparent, her nipples erect and aching in the chill of that elusive breeze. She closed her eyes, sucking in a sharp breath at the lightning his touch ignited, even though the knuckle grazing her nipple through the sheer cotton was more promise than caress. "I missed you," he whispered.

"So I gathered," she said with a smile.

There were no more words, gentle or seductive or otherwise, only the rustle of hastily rearranged clothing, the scrape of a cast-iron table leg against marble, her gasp when Rod lifted her, enabling her to wrap her legs around him as he filled her, fiercely, sweetly, right there by the front door, the cats mewing, perplexed, at their feet.

Take me, was her wordless plea as he sank himself into her, as if to bury whatever fears he wouldn't share, bury them deep inside her where they might be incinerated in the raging heat of her own need. *Take what I have to give* was the message she willed him to hear through her kisses, her caresses. Her tears.

Let me love you.

Wrapped safely in those strong arms, in the arms of a man who would deny her nothing except *himself,* she cried out, not from fulfillment, but from the hollowness of a loveless mating.

His kisses afterward were gentle. Apologetic. Tears swimming in her eyes, she'd clasped his face in her hands, searching. Pleading. She'd give him everything she had to heal his soul, but he couldn't—wouldn't?—take it.

Even her *everything* wasn't good enough.

He'd sent her back to bed, claiming to be too wound up to sleep.

And his eyes had screamed *forgive me...*

A flurry of commotion outside Nancy's office snapped her out of her brooding. Knuckling tears from the corners of her eyes, she pushed herself out of her chair, an activity that had become increasingly difficult as the weeks passed, peered out the door. Beaming for all she was worth, Elizabeth stood by the reception desk as her mother, Cora, and every other female in the office cooed and clucked over the snoozing infant nestled against Guy's shoulder. Nancy's hand went to her tummy; the baby, as if sensing Mama needed reassurance, squirmed inside her. But it wasn't enough to stop her heart's slow, painful turn in her chest. Especially when she saw the glance that passed between Elizabeth and Guy when Elizabeth patted the baby on her back, then said something to her husband. He nodded, after which Elizabeth, her petite figure fully restored and shown off to perfection in a rose-colored jersey tank dress, made her way back to Nancy. She grinned, nodding at her outfit. "That looks familiar. And are you ever filling it out!"

Nancy glanced down at the navy-blue maternity coatdress, complete with gold-colored nautical buttons. The color was death with her olive complexion, but she was rapidly reaching the point where she didn't care.

"I feel like I'm going to a costume party, dressed as you," she said, which got a short laugh, followed by an invitation to lunch. Nancy glanced back at Guy, cradling his daughter's wobbly head as she surveyed the horde of clucking women staring at her. Chloe sneezed, which immediately brought up no less than a half-dozen hands to tuck her little blanket more securely around her tiny shoulders.

"What about Snookums?"

"Snookums doesn't need me for another three hours. Come on." Elizabeth linked her arm around Nancy's, tugged her out of the office. "You need to get out of here. Let's take both cars, though, since I've got errands to run afterward."

Ten minutes later, they were seated in a booth at the Lakeside Diner, a once charming eatery—or so Nancy had convinced herself—that could benefit from being completely regutted. Still, at noon, the place was jammed, the ambiance a jumble of conversations and clanking crockery, occasionally punctuated by a waitress's raucous laugh, an order screamed out to the short order cook behind the counter.

"What nobody tells you," Elizabeth said between delicate sips of homemade vegetable soup, "is that your brain melts when you give birth." She sighed. "For the first three days, I just kept staring at Chloe, as if I couldn't believe she was mine. That Guy and I had made her. And I cannot tell you how glad I am you're pregnant so I can say all this stuff and know you're not going to feel left out."

The spoonful of chicken-noodle soup on the way to Nancy's mouth stopped in midair, like a halted ski lift. "Why would I have felt—"

"Oh, come on, honey. I may be blond, but I'm not *that* dumb." Affection, and compassion, danced in her friend's eyes, even as a smile lifted the corners of her mouth. "Ever since you moved here, I know you've been uncomfortable around Guy and me."

Nancy felt her face flame. "That's ridiculous—"

"No, it's not ridiculous," Elizabeth continued. "And I felt terrible about it. I've been so involved with Chloe, I've sort of neglected you these past few weeks. But you've been on my mind. A lot. Especially in the middle of the night, since thinking's about all you *can* do with a baby attached to your breast. Anyway, I keep getting these little updates from Mother and Cora and Guy, and the consensus is you're not doing s'hot s'good for someone who should be wallowing in prenatal bliss right about now."

Nancy wasn't sure she could swallow her last bite of soup. Eyes stinging, she focused her attention on the terra-cotta tub of white petunias outside, knowing that looking at her friend would be disastrous. Images of Rod and her, that last time, darted through her thought, slicing through her heart. Why, how, could he come so close, only to edge away, over and over and over?

"Honey..." Elizabeth touched her wrist. "Talk."

She was torn, not wanting to admit she'd screwed up—again—yet so desperately needing someone to dump on. Her liverwurst on rye blurred in front of her as she realized she could no longer deny the one thing she'd promised herself wouldn't happen: that she'd fallen in love with her husband. And some time ago, too, although she couldn't exactly peg when it had happened. But it had. And there wasn't a damn thing she could do about it.

"It's as if there are pieces missing," she said in a rush, poking at the sandwich with one finger. "Like adding two plus two and only coming up with three. We get along fine, don't get me wrong. In fact, I think it's safe to say we actually enjoy each other's company, laugh at each other's jokes…" She swallowed back the tears, unwilling to make a fool of herself in public, at least. Not that anyone would notice in this place.

"And you're in love with him."

Eyes burning, she nodded. "He's a good man, Liz. A kind man, which you know." She stopped, pressing one shaking hand to her mouth.

"But…there are three little words conspicuously absent from his vocabulary?"

Nancy fought for control, then said, "I understood that wasn't part of the bargain going in. So what's wrong with me that I'm not content with everything that *is* right with this marriage?"

"Not a damn thing," Elizabeth said, leaning forward. "And don't ever let me hear you say that again. You think you don't deserve to be loved, is that it?"

"Considering my track record, I'm beginning to wonder."

"Oh, please." Elizabeth blew out a sigh. "You have to *make* the man fall in love with you," she continued in that authoritative way of hers that made even those who loved her seriously consider gagging her from time to time. She glanced around the restaurant, signaled to the waitress for the check.

"Oh, right. And how do you propose I do that?"

Elizabeth scanned the check, then clicked open her purse, fished out her wallet. "Wear him down," she said at last, sliding out of the booth, the check clutched in her hand. "You're a salesperson—don't let him go until you've closed the deal. Oh, shoot," she said, glancing at the clock over the front door as they made their way to the cashier. "Look at the time! I've got to get a move on before the next feeding!" Elizabeth paid the check, kissed Nancy on the cheek, and was gone.

Nancy took in a shaky breath, then wandered outside, her tender eyes stinging in the sudden glare of sunshine, where she literally ran into Sybil Bennett, Spruce Lake's other real-estate agent and the thorn in Millennium Realty's side.

"Nancy! My, my," the frizzy redhead crooned, dull blue eyes slithering over Nancy's swollen form, "aren't you looking positively *ripe* these days? You short women really do stick straight out in front, don't you?"

God. Nancy's mother could take lessons from this woman.

"How's business?" Sybil wheezed, one chunky hand pressed to her rayon-shrouded bosom.

A trickle of sweat meandered into Nancy's bra. She'd rather lick the sidewalk than discuss business with the Realtor, whose pointy little nose had been out-of-joint ever since Millennium's expansion. "Fine. Look, I'd love to chat, but—"

"You wouldn't happen to know of anyone looking to buy a restaurant, would you?"

Only years of training enabled Nancy to pick up on the subtle desperation behind Sybil's words. "Not offhand, no," she started to say, shielding her eyes from the blistering summer sun, but from somewhere in the morass of confusion and self-pity, a tiny light bulb flickered to life. "But I'll certainly…keep an ear out. Where is it?"

Sybil jerked her head to the right. Twice.

Nancy's eyebrows shot up. "The *diner?*"

"Owners want to retire. Immediately. We're talking *extremely* motivated."

"How motivated?"

Sybil mouthed the asking price. "That includes the equipment, everything. Of course, it would take a bit to redo, the condition it's in. But still quite a bargain. And with the increase in our population since Shadywoods…"

Well, Nancy couldn't blame the woman entirely for getting in a dig about the development that had taken Millennium Realty out of Sybil's league. But Sybil had a point. Not the one she thought she was making, granted, but that was neither here nor there. That increased population—young, upwardly mobile, perpetually busy and with plenty of disposable income to spend on dining out, would be the perfect clientele for a trendy, but not overly so, little restaurant right in the middle of town.

"Well, I'll keep an ear out," Nancy said. "You never know."

She shook Sybil off, then walked back to the sedan—she couldn't get in or out of the MG anymore—her heart thumping inside her chest like a dreaming dog's tail. This was too good a deal to pass up, that was for sure. Now all she had to do was make sure Rod thought so, too.

Right now.

Rod was tempted at first to ignore the doorbell, but Bruiser had other ideas. Every time the bell rang, the cat would dash up onto his desk, scattering papers to kingdom come, plant his huge face in Rod's and issue a strange, guttural hey!-you-deaf-or-what? meow. So he gave up trying to come up with searingly brilliant marketing ideas for some celebrity Mexican-food line and trooped to the door, brushing cat hairs off his chinos as he went.

"Elizabeth!"

"Okay, I've got no more than twenty minutes before Chloe freaks out, so I talk, you listen, and if you have any comments, you make 'em to your wife, okay?" With that, she slipped inside, heading for the den.

Rod followed, wondering what had happened to the quiet, demure woman he'd dated for two years. Thought of Guy and answered his own question.

Once inside, the former Miss Quiet and Demure turned on him, eyes blazing. "Now, if you weren't married to my best friend, I wouldn't be here, putting my fanny on the line. But since you are, the least I can do is fill you in on a few things you probably don't know about your wife, because she's too bullheaded to be honest with you.''

Rod heard a nervous laugh, realized it was his. ''What on earth are you talking about? Nancy's the most honest person I know.''

''About other people, sure. And she's a pushy little twerp, too. But her bravado covers up a boatload of insecurities.''

He leaned against the arm of the purple sofa. ''I know that.''

''Yeah, but what you may not know is how often Nancy's bounced back in her life. You've met Belle—imagine growing up with that? Imagine never having your own mother tell you she was proud of you, that you were worthwhile or special. Imagine being made to feel you had to compete against your own brother for your mother's approval, and never, not once, getting it.''

He crossed his arms in a vain attempt to quell the nausea beginning to roil in his gut. ''I don't have to,'' he said quietly, but she didn't give him a chance to explain.

''Then imagine a series of disastrous relationships,'' Elizabeth went on, ''every single one of which ended with the discovery that your boyfriend or lover or husband couldn't be trusted. But if you're Nancy, you keep believing that, maybe tomorrow, maybe just around the corner, you'll find that person you can finally trust, who'll see all your good qualities, not just your flaws. And because you keep believing in *some-day,* because you don't want anyone to feel sorry for you, you keep picking yourself up every time someone knocks you down, plaster a smile on your face and keep going. Then one day, you meet someone who, by rights, should be everything you'd ever dreamed of, and you take one last chance.'' She paused, caught her breath. ''Do you have even a *clue* how unhappy your wife is, Rod?''

''Elizabeth!''

They both turned at the sound of Nancy's voice. Her face reddened, she stood in the doorway to the den, her fists balled at her sides. "Where the hell do you get off coming here, interfering in my life?"

Through the agony crushing his chest, Rod had to hand it to Elizabeth. Even caught in the act, she didn't flinch.

"Well, sweetie," she said gently, hiking her purse over her shoulder, "somebody had to." She made her way to the door, her features crumpling when Nancy, brows knotted, stepped out of her path, not looking at her. Elizabeth opened her mouth as if to say something else, then apparently thought better of it and simply left.

Even as the brutal truth of Elizabeth's words rang in his ears, Rod vented his frustration on his wife. "And where," he said coolly, "do *you* get off telling tales out of school, Nancy? Whatever is going on between us is between *us*. It's no one else's business."

Anger flared in Nancy's eyes as she lowered herself into a wing chair. "Don't let anyone suspect that life isn't all sugar and spice, you mean?"

"Our problems are not for the world to see—"

"Elizabeth is hardly *the world*."

"Oh, right. Like she won't say anything to Guy, or her mother?"

"She doesn't *have* to say anything! Oh, for God's sake, Rod! Wake *up!* Anyone who cares about us can see something's wrong! And if you think otherwise, you're in serious denial, buddy."

Bands of fear constricted his chest; he took a deep breath, letting it out slowly as he walked over to the window. "Is it true, that you're unhappy?"

Several beats passed before she replied. "And if you have to ask, doesn't that indicate exactly how bad things are?"

He squeezed his eyes shut against the stab of pain, the acrid taste of failure in his mouth. "I knew we still had some things to work out—"

She sighed. "It's more serious than that, Rod. And not being the stoic you seem to be, I confided in one of the few people I can trust. Not that I had any idea she'd come blabbing to you about it, but I have no one else to talk to.''

He turned to her, suddenly desperate to be someone else, to be that man Elizabeth had talked about, the one who'd be what Nancy needed. ''How about your husband?'' he asked, even as he realized how empty the words were.

''Oh, and like that would do any good?'' He saw the tears now, glistening in her eyes, despised himself for being the one who'd put them there. ''We don't even do that anymore. All we do now is occasionally get it on, whenever the mood strikes you, spending most of our time keeping up appearances, trying not to step on each other's toes. Three months ago, I thought maybe we could make this harebrained arrangement work. Now I'm not so sure.'' She sighed, smoothing a hand over her belly. ''I'm not sure of much anymore, to be honest.''

They heard the front door slam shut; seconds later, Hannah swept into the room, her hair damp from summer basketball practice. ''Hey, Nance, what're you doing...home?'' Blue eyes, far too wise and understanding, darted from one to the other, before, with a loud, extremely unladylike curse, she stormed from the room.

''I'll go to her,'' he said.

''You do that,'' Nancy quietly replied, not looking at him.

Chapter 12

A little later, Rod found Nancy out back, kneeling underneath a willow, putting in a bed of impatiens from a flat she'd bought over the weekend. She'd changed out of her work clothes into a flowered one-piece romper and sandals, her hair scrunched up on top of her head in a leather gizmo that looked like something Wilma Flintstone might have worn. Judging from the way she was jabbing the trowel into the earth, he figured maybe he shouldn't get too close.

He approached slowly, not sure what to say. He couldn't change who he was—what circumstances had made of him, he amended—but neither could he bear to see her so miserable. Elizabeth was right: she did deserve better than that. And he had been...aloof these past few weeks.

Okay, terrified.

She was getting to him. A little more each day. Like termite damage, he thought with a rueful smile. She was chipping away at his reserve, at the protective barrier he'd maintained so diligently for so long.

She was making him care. And he didn't know what to do about that.

His shadow fell across her work area, making her look up, but only for a moment. "Hannah okay?" she asked, setting in another bedding plant.

"Are teenagers ever okay?" he parried, squatting beside her.

"Probably about as okay as pregnant women."

"Nance—" He reached out, stroked one knuckle along her cheek.

"Rod...don't." Her mouth thinned. "I'm still ticked, and very confused, and your touching me only makes things worse."

He laced his fingers between his knees. "I can't change who I am, Nancy."

"Neither can I, Rod." She sat back on her heels, a crease marring her brow. "Besides, I'm not asking you to change. All I'm asking is to be let in, and you won't do even that much." Worry flickered in her eyes. "If you can't love me, I suppose I can deal with that. Even though—brace yourself— I've fallen in love with you. But I can't deal with the way you shut me out."

He wasn't sure how he was breathing. "Oh, Nancy, honey...don't love me. Please."

She pinned him with a gaze at once steady and incredulous. "You say that as if I had a choice in the matter. We don't choose who we love, although God knows, I tried. Not to love you, that is. I have no shame, Rod, in case you haven't noticed. My heart is yours. Do with it what you will. Or don't. Whatever. But I guess, when it comes right down to it, I was at least a little bit in love with you when we made this baby."

"That's illogical, Nance."

"So's aerodynamics, but damned if people can't haul those huge metal things up into the air." With a shrug, she picked up the next container and tapped out a baby plant with hot-pink petals. "I know it doesn't make sense, maybe, especially since I really don't know what's going on in your head. But what can I say? I fell in love with what you *did* let me see.''

"You're wasting your time, then.'' He saw the hesitation in her movements, her breath catch in her throat. "I told you from the beginning what I could give. My heart isn't part of the package.'' He snagged her chin in his hand, his gut wrenching at the disappointment in those enormous eyes. "Just being honest.''

"Why are you so afraid to feel, Rod?'' she asked, her eyes hooked to his. "To let go and trust? Even if…even if I'm not the one you eventually love—''

"Sweetheart, don't do this to yourself. You're not a way station, if that's what you think.''

She pulled away, stuffed another plant in the ground. "Well. At least we've identified the problem, huh? I can't help being in love with you, you can't help not being in love with me. So where do we go from here?''

Rod leaned over and kissed his wife gently on the temple, then stood, his knees popping. "We take it day by day, honey. Figure it out as we go along.'' After a moment, when he realized there was nothing left to be said, he started back to the house.

"Rod?''

He looked back, saw her kneeling, her middle cantilevered over her knees, her chin raised. "For the record, I don't consider loving someone a waste of time.''

He had absolutely nothing to say to that.

Nancy didn't let the tears come until she was sure he was back inside. She sank back to sit cross-legged on the grass, her arms wrapped around the unborn child she already loved with all her heart as she rocked and sobbed, feeling as alone as she'd ever been in her entire life.

Why wasn't she good enough for someone to love? Really, truly love?

Oh, God—if it was the only thing she ever accomplished on this earth, this child would know how much he or she was loved and cherished and appreciated for who he or she was, every minute of every day.

"Nancy?"

She hurriedly swiped at her tears with the heel of her hand, then rummaged in her pocket for a tissue. Hannah knelt beside her, as Rod had done earlier, concern puckering her mouth. "Nance, hey—you okay?"

Nodding, Nancy blew her nose. "Hormones."

Hannah snorted. "I'm not totally stupid, you know."

Nancy collected the empty six-pack containers, then hauled herself to her feet, dusting dirt off her bottom. "That makes one of us, then," she said, carrying the containers over to the shed in the back of the garden, dumping them in the recycle bin. She sucked in the sweet summer air, then pointed to the row of black-potted plants along the side of the shed. Gardening had been her salvation these past few months. "Help me decide where these rosebushes go."

Hannah came up beside her, her arms crossed. "Dad said you weren't fighting, when I came in a little while ago."

Nancy glanced at her, then picked up one of the pots, carrying it over to a spot on the other side of the garden. "Depends on your viewpoint. I was trying to, but he wouldn't meet me halfway." At Hannah's horrified expression, she managed a short laugh. "Fighting's not necessarily bad, you know." She plunked down the rose, in a spot just outside Rod's office window. "That's a Peace. Yellow with pink edges. Think it'll look good there?"

"Uh, yeah, I guess—Nancy?" Hannah wrinkled her nose, squinting in the slanting sun. "Please don't take this the wrong way, but are you nuts?"

"You mean there's some doubt?" She winced, pushing down a foot or something. Was it her imagination, or was this baby unusually large for six months? "Hand me that shovel, would you? Over by the shed?"

Hannah looked around for a minute, then fetched the shovel. She nodded toward Nancy's middle. "You sure you should be doing this?"

"Watch me." As she suspected, the soil was loose and rich over here, and the shovel slid in with no resistance. "For your information, fighting's only bad when someone gets hurt. The kind of fighting that gets problems out in the open, where everyone can deal with them, is a good thing." She swiped her forehead with the back of her hand, looking up at her stepdaughter. "You have to care about someone to get angry with them, you know."

Hannah seemed to consider this for a moment. "So…did you and Dad get things out in the open?"

The hole dug, Nancy sprinkled in some fertilizer, then loosened the rose from its pot, lowering it into the soil. "Here— you shovel while I hold it."

Hannah did as she was told, her eyes more on Nancy than her task.

"Yes, Hannah. I think we got some things out in the open."

The shoveling stopped. "And?"

Nancy spread the soil around the root ball, building up a short wall of dirt with her hands to make a well to hold the water. "I don't know."

Hannah squatted beside her, fingering the rose's baby leaves. "You love Dad now, don't you?"

Nancy looked up, smiling at Rod's beautiful, wise daughter through a scrim of tears, and nodded. "Got a soft spot in my heart for his kids, too."

Hannah rolled her eyes, but Nancy could tell she was pleased. "Okay—me, I can see. But Schuy's such a geek."

"The world needs geeks, too."

Hannah plopped in the grass. "I suppose."

Nancy regarded the girl thoughtfully for a moment, then awkwardly lowered her rump into the grass beside her. "Answer me something."

A shrug. "Sure."

"You know how your dad loves to cook?"

Brows dipped, puzzled. "Yeah…"

"He told me once he'd wanted to have his own restaurant, at one time."

"Really? Cool. So why didn't he?"

"I'm not sure. He was kind of vague about it. But something tells me, deep down inside, he'd still like to."

Hannah lay down on her side, chewing on a piece of grass. "Huh." She sucked in a deep breath. "He sure doesn't seem all that happy with what he's doing now."

"I don't think so, either. Well, as it happens, I heard today that the Lakeside Diner's up for sale."

It took the girl a moment, then she made a face. *"Ewww…"*

"Well, of course, *ewww,* the way it is now. But think about it. It's a great location, there's lots of people who'd love to have someplace right in town where they could get a really fancy meal, and imagine the decorating possibilities. I was going to mention it to your dad when I got home, but then things got a little crazy…." She stopped, reined it in. "Anyway, whaddya think?"

She shrugged, a teenager's seal of approval. "Sure, I guess. I mean, he might go for it, you never know. Then again…"

"What?"

Hannah turned worried blue eyes to Nancy. "Have you ever noticed the way Dad never seems to care enough about *anything* to fight for it? Not even Schuy and me, you know?"

"Hannah—he just requested full custody for you two, remember?"

"Yeah, *now.*" She fell silent, then said, irritation edging her words, "I know all about why Dad didn't contest Mom's original custody claim, all that crap about trying to protect us because Mom would have made such a stink. I mean, that's *so* Dad, you know? Trying so hard be some sort of hero, keeping the peace, even though everyone ends up hurt, anyway."

Nancy had nothing to say to that. And Hannah's next words didn't make her feel any better.

"Like what he did when he married you. Right? I mean, he thought he was doing this big atonement number or something for his screwup, but he doesn't love you. Not the way you obviously love him. So how is that *right?*" Brow knotted, she shook her head, then sighed. "I just don't get it. I just don't get *him*. I mean, he obviously cares about us, I know that, but he's never once said, *I love you guys*. Why does the idea of loving somebody freak him out so much?"

"Oh, Hannah. I wish I knew, honey." She leaned back on her hands, rubbing her belly. "But people like that need our love the most, don't you think?"

"Even if they don't love us back?"

Over a tight throat, Nancy managed, "*Especially* if they don't love us back. But I have no doubt your father loves you both, very much. He just doesn't know how to say it, maybe, but that has nothing to do with how he feels. Besides—and this may sound like something out of some self-help book— we don't love someone because of what we expect to get back."

"That doesn't sound like much fun."

Nancy gave a short laugh. "Depends on your definition of fun, I suppose. Come on—help me put in the other two bushes."

For the next half hour, as if by mutual consent, the conversation bounced safely from school to boys to the baby to basketball to movies and back to boys.

"By the way," Hannah said as they tamped down the soil around the last bush, "Heather and I were supposed to go to a movie tonight, but she can't get the car. You think I could borrow one of yours?"

Stretching out her aching back, Nancy thought a moment, then nodded. "I don't see why not. As long as you're back by midnight."

"One?"

"Midnight."

"Twelve-thirty?"

Nancy tried to maintain a stern expression, but considering the "child" was nearly a foot taller than she, it wasn't easy. "Twelve-thirty," she allowed, which earned her a squeal and a peck on the cheek. "Tell your Dad I said it was okay. The car is his decision. And no, the MG isn't on the short list."

As Nancy watched the girl lope off across the yard, a thin thread of worry winnowed through her brain. So far, it seemed she was doing a lot better at stepmothering than wifing. Okay, so she'd done the honesty bit and told Rod how she felt, and she really meant what she said, both to him and his daughter, about not expecting love to be returned. But, well, that didn't mean she didn't *want* it to be returned, did it? And now that Rod knew, hadn't she only widened the emotional chasm between them? She'd put him on notice, she realized. Maybe that wasn't what she'd intended, but the result was the same.

And in doing so, she'd just made things ten times worse.

Not even at the beginning had Rod gone into marketing for the money. His mother's fortune was safely and well invested, allowing him the option of retiring at any time with no appreciable decline in his standard of living. But for years, his career had often been the only aspect of his muddled existence he knew he could count on to give him some sense of satisfaction.

Perhaps he didn't have a clue how to relate to humankind up close and personal, but lumped together in nice, neat demographic niches, he knew people inside out. Knew what pushed their buttons, what caught their attention, what sorts of products they craved to make their lives easier. It was a gift, he supposed. And he'd lapped up that first praise from Star's head of marketing when he'd started there, the ink not yet dry on his MBA. There at last he found recognition for his talents, a venue in which he actually received kudos for his efforts. He was good at what he did, and his superiors rewarded him accordingly. After a childhood of constant criticism, this was nirvana. And, as time passed, as his expertise became more and more valued, his dependency on the praise grew. When a merger stripped Star Motors of its autonomy and the new parent company decided to dispense with the in-house marketing team, opening his own consultancy was a piece of cake. Within a month, he had more clients than he could handle. He could pick and choose those projects that interested him, could continue reaping the praise, the approval, that had become his life's blood.

Now, however, the praise he'd once craved no longer seemed as important as it once had. Maybe he was growing up at last, he thought as he rubbed his eyes, the demographic spreadsheet in front of him blurring more and more as the night wore on. Whatever the cause, not even he was so blind as to ignore the warning signs of burnout. He still made his clients happy, still reaped their accolades, but found himself deriving less and less pleasure from his work. He was bored, frankly, his ennui verging on irritation each time he had to kiss up to some executive, spend a week living out of his suitcase, devise a fool-proof campaign to sell a zillion units of some product he wouldn't use himself if someone threatened to break his kneecaps.

Yet, the idea of letting it all go terrified him.

The quarter-hour chime from the small brass clock on the mantel—one of the few things Rod had of his grandmother's—snagged his attention. It was a quarter past one, rather than midnight, he realized with a start, which meant Hannah was now forty-five minutes late. Apprehension trickled through his bloodstream, making him shudder slightly underneath the cotton sweater he'd pulled on to ward off the slight evening chill. He snatched off his reading glasses and rose from his desk without a conscious thought, going upstairs to find Nancy sitting up in bed, reading. She hadn't heard him, he assumed, since she didn't look up. Instead, concentration puckered her brow as she read, worrying one knuckle between her teeth.

She loved him. The words slammed into him from out of nowhere, immediately followed by a sense of regret so heavy it hurt to breathe.

She would listen. She would listen to his worries, his confusion. Help him sort it all out. Offer advice, if he asked. Which he'd never done before.

Or maybe she'd be appalled at the idea of his wanting to chuck it all.

The thought caught him up short, that he actually did want to chuck it all. That he wanted something...else.

But what?

He knocked lightly on the door frame, as if this wasn't his room. As if she wasn't his wife, soon to be the mother of his third child. She lifted her gaze to his, brow still furrowed. Annoyed he'd interrupted her? "It's after one," he said. "Did you know?"

"I've read the same paragraph a dozen times." She sliced the pages with a bookmark, laid the novel on her nightstand.

"Do you know where they went?"

"The movies, she said." Nancy combed her fingers through the hair lying heavily against her neck. "Which should have been over long ago."

She flipped back the covers, awkwardly pulled herself out of bed. The bedside lamp illuminated the thin fabric of her cotton nightgown, silhouetting her nakedness underneath. He found the combination of ripeness and delicacy unbelievably erotic, though this was probably not the time to mention it to her. Or show her. Even if Hannah's missing her curfew hadn't been their primary concern at the moment, Nancy's comment about their sex lives this afternoon had smacked him between the eyes with how she read his need. Since he couldn't begin to explain it himself, neither had he defended it. He did know that her terse assessment of their relationship had never once entered his mind. He just didn't know what to call it. Unfortunately, it still wasn't enough. Not for her.

And strangely enough, not for him, either, although he'd yet to allow himself permission to follow that train of thought, see where it led.

A faint shudder passed through the house as the door from the garage breezeway opened, then shut again.

"Finally," Nancy muttered. She slipped on her cotton robe, her slender, clever fingers jerkily managing the row of pearl buttons down the front. "She better have a damn good reason for this, is all I have to say."

"Let me handle this, Nance," Rod said quietly. "She's my daughter—"

"Forget it," she huffed as she lumbered past him on her way out the bedroom door. "Hannah broke a promise to *me*."

Her eyes widened when Rod caught her hand, stopped her short. "And I'll take care of it. My way. You look ready to chew her up into little pieces."

"Yeah, well, somebody shaves a year off my life, that's what they get!"

"I'm not letting you fly off the handle, Nancy. Not in your condition. And not in my house."

Pita mewed at Nancy's feet; after a moment, she bent down as far as she could to pick him up. "Fine," she said. "Your daughter. Your house. What does any of this have to do with me, right? In that case—" she walked back to the bed, began unbuttoning the robe "—since I'm not needed, I'll just go back to my gestating, if that's okay with you."

Irritation jolted through him. "That's not what I mean, Nancy, and you know it!"

She hauled her book back into what was left of her lap, leveled a deceptively cool gaze in his direction. "Do I?" she said, then calmly returned to her reading.

Rod didn't return to their bedroom that night, opting to sleep—if you could call it that—in the guest room. The next morning found him groggy, cranky and determined to straighten out at least some of this.

Nancy was already in the kitchen, feeding cats. She looked about sixteen in that puffy-sleeved lavender maternity dress and her white espadrilles, her hair caught up into something like a ponytail with one of those scrunchie things. It struck him how big she already was for only being this far along, how uncomfortable she must already be. He supposed it was because she was so tiny to begin with. Her eyes darted to his, then away, when he came in. She slowly straightened up, using the counter edge to brace herself as she stood.

"Kids still asleep?" he asked.

"Far as I know. Hannah's got practice later."

Silence.

His hand found its way, yet again, to the back of his neck. "Aren't you going to ask me what happened?"

"Why should I?" she asked, closing the cat-food bag, shoving it with more force than necessary back into the cupboard.

"Nancy. Look at me."

After a moment, she did, her face expressionless.

"I screwed up. Okay? It was late, I was exhausted and upset with Hannah, and I wasn't thinking clearly or I would have never said what I said. But it irks me that, after all these months, after everything I've said to you to completely refute this insane notion you have that you don't matter, that you're not a real part of this family, you still twist everything I say. I wasn't trying to keep you from saying whatever you needed to to Hannah, only trying to keep you from flying off the handle. For everybody's sake, don't you see? That didn't mean we weren't equally as ticked off with her, or that I was somehow blowing off your opinion. We are in this together, honey. And frankly," he added with a hopeful smile, "it would have been nice to have you there with me to absorb some of her indignation when I grounded her for two weeks."

Her arms folded across her tummy, Nancy looked down, but he could see the smile teasing her lips. "I would've made it a month," she said at last, then met his gaze again. "Except then I probably would've wussed out after a week, anyway, and backed down."

He chuckled, then held out his arms. She drifted into them without a word, filling his very being with her scent and softness and fire. Fear and contentment shot through him simultaneously; he decided to ignore them both.

"So," she said after a moment. "What did Hannah say? About being late?"

He sighed. "They decided to drive around, though where they'd go in Spruce Lake is beyond me. In any case, they lost track of the time, she said."

Nancy leaned back, frowning. "There's a clock in the car."

"Exactly. Which is why she's grounded." That got a sigh,

which prompted him to ask, "You have breakfast yet? I could fix you an omelette."

"No," she said quietly, pulling away. "I've eaten. And, no, not a Pop-Tart."

Rod took hope he knew he didn't deserve from her small joke. He went about putting on coffee she couldn't have, grateful to be past the stage where the smell made her sick. "That would be tricky, since we don't have any."

"Says who?"

He clicked on the coffeemaker, shot her a look. She just smiled. But it still wasn't her normal smile. Just a small one. A Band-Aid on the wound, was all his little speech amounted to. The wound itself was still there. He wondered if he'd ever see her smile for real again. What it would take to make that happen.

The rich aroma of fresh coffee mingled with her perfume and the honeysuckled air drifting in the open window, the combination nearly making him dizzy with longing. And nostalgia. His grandparents' house had smelled much like this on those summer mornings he'd spent there as a small boy.

"Evelyn coming today?" he asked, referring to the cleaning lady they'd finally hired last month, who they knew was angling for a full-time position.

"At nine. I gave her a key the other day. So neither of us had to be here."

"Good idea." He hesitated. "Sit with me while I have my coffee?"

Confusion stirred in her eyes—they'd spent few mornings together these past weeks—but she nodded. She poured herself a glass of grapefruit juice, then sat across from him, her slender fingers worrying the straw place mat as they talked about this and that for several minutes. Then, casually, Rod suggested driving her to her prenatal appointment that afternoon.

Brows lifted. "You're keeping track of my appointments?"

"Ruth's assistant called yesterday to remind you. While you were in the garden. I guess I forgot to mention it."

Her mouth pulled at the sides. "Now I know where Schuyler gets it. Not that I needed reminding." She took a small sip of juice, both hands clamped around the glass. "But you don't have to take me. I've got a spare inch or two to go yet before I get stuck behind the wheel."

"I want to go, Nance. I said I wanted to be in on this, and I meant it."

"You mean, pretend we're the happy couple awaiting the birth of our child?"

He looked down into his coffee. "Guess I had that coming."

She massaged a spot in the center of her forehead. In the stark morning sunlight flooding this part of the kitchen, he could see spiderweb creases at the corners of her eyes, tiny crescents bracketing her mouth.

"I'm sorry," she said, then looked up at him. His heart lurched at the pain in her eyes as he wondered if they'd ever be able to have a conversation not punctuated with apologies. "I'm not having a good morning. I should be thrilled you want to come along, that you want to be involved." She drew in a slow, quiet breath, let it out. "But I'd gotten into such a habit of keeping at least some of this to myself, thinking that was the only way I could hang on to at least a shred of my sanity—" She paused. "Until I realized it wasn't doing any good, anyway."

He looked up, questioning.

"It finally hit that what went in is inevitably going to come out. I don't want to be drugged, because I don't want to do a single thing that might even be remotely dangerous for this baby, but I'm also a huge weenie when it comes to pain. Especially my own. And now Ruth's telling me this baby might be too big for me to deliver naturally, which means a C-section..." Her eyes filled with tears. "Oh, Rod...I'm so damn scared."

"For God's sake, Nancy—" he reached across the table and tucked her hand inside his "—why didn't you say something?"

"Because I'm the dumbest person on the planet?"

''I'm beginning to wonder,'' he said, which actually got a little laugh. She grabbed a napkin off the table and blew her nose, then said, ''The appointment isn't in Ruth's office. She wants me to go to the medical center for an ultrasound.''

''An ultrasound?'' He knew Nancy'd been resisting any technical interference, even though Ruth had assured her of the ultrasound's safety. ''And you thought you'd actually get away with seeing our baby for the first time by yourself?''

''Yeah, well, this is just kind of a preview. And you know the way you always fast-forward through video previews until you get to the movie itself? I figured this was kind of the same thing.''

He was living with the world's craziest woman.

''No, Nancy. Not even remotely.''

She nodded, finished off her juice, then stood up, gathering her purse and keys from the counter.

''Honey?''

She turned, her face a mask.

''For better or worse,'' he said, ''we are in this together. Please don't shut me out.''

She looked at him for a long time, then opened the door leading to the breezeway. ''Right back atcha, *bubeleh*. Right back atcha.''

Chapter 13

Honestly. No matter how hard she tried, Nancy couldn't distinguish anything on the ultrasound monitor. All she could make out was a bunch of wiggly, squirmy blobs. A bunch of wiggly, squirmy blobs that seemed to be causing her midwife a great deal of amusement. Ruth stood grinning at the monitor, her salami-esque forearms crossed underneath breasts that made Nancy's puny little things whimper in shame.

"Is it safe to assume nothing's wrong," Nancy said, "or do you just have a sick sense of humor?"

The midwife glanced at Nancy, then at Rod. "I take it you can't tell what you're looking at?"

"Not a clue," they both said at once.

"Okay, folks, pay attention. See this?" She pointed to one of the wiggly blobs. "That's a heart."

"That much I figured out—"

"And that, my dear, is another one."

"Ohmigod! The baby has two hearts—?"

Ruth roared with laughter. "No, no, no—not one baby with

two hearts, love. Two babies. One heart each. Two beautiful, healthy babies, with two beautiful, healthy hearts.''

Nancy found her voice first.

''Are…you…sure?''

''Yep. That's why you're so big.''

''But I'm in my seventh month! You mean, you couldn't tell before this?''

Ruth patted her shoulder. ''Most of the time, yes. But you didn't want an ultrasound, and they've been lying in such a way I couldn't tell. Since Rod is tall, I thought maybe it was just a big baby.'' She shrugged, then grinned. ''Surprise!''

Nancy could barely think over the shrill buzzing in her brain. ''You mean to tell me,'' she said at last, ''I'm lugging *two* kids around in here?''

''Aren't you glad you only have two and a half months left?''

''Yeah. Thrilled. Don't they gain the most weight these last months?''

''That's what we're hoping. But if it's any consolation, twins often come a little early. Gets too crowded for them.''

For…*them.*

Rod had yet to say anything, although she did have to pry her hand out of his before he crushed her fingers. He was in shock, would be her guess. Nor did he say anything until she'd gotten dressed again, received a whole new set of instructions for taking care of herself now that she was carrying twins, and they'd wandered off in a daze down the hall toward the exit.

''I feel like a Volkswagen stuffed with a pair of elephants,'' she said as Rod cupped her elbow and guided her outside. When they reached the car, however, he started to laugh. She eyed him warily for a minute until she was sure she didn't need to go back inside and fetch someone. After a minute or two, his laughter subsided enough for him to gather her in his arms, give her a hug. The second hug of the day. Wow. Her eyes burned with the unexpected affection, with the sharp realization of how much she just wanted to feel this man's arms around her from time to time.

And to hear his laughter. He had a wonderful laugh, one that hugged a person's soul the way his arms did her body. She could get used to hearing it a little more often.

"There's an up side to this, you know," he whispered into her hair.

"Oh, yeah? And what's that?"

He chuckled. "Just think how many kids might be in there if you *hadn't* been using a diaphragm!"

"*Twins?*"

Hannah and Schuyler looked from one to the other, their mouths gaping. Since they were having dinner outside, this increased the likelihood of fly consumption. "You're gonna have twins?" Hannah repeated.

Nancy handed her the ultrasound photo, which she'd looked at no less than a hundred times in the past couple of hours, as if trying to convince herself as well. "See for yourself. No—" she turned it around "—this way."

"At least," Rod said as he dished out the salad, "now you won't have to fight over who gets to hold the baby." He handed Nancy a wooden bowl filled with things she'd never even seen before, let alone could identify. "One for each of you."

Hannah tossed him a *yeah, right* look, then returned to scrutinizing the picture, her brow scrunched. "Uh, Nancy...I don't know how to break this to you, but all I see here is a bunch of wiggly blobs."

"Here, let me see that—" Schuyler snatched the photo from his sister, wiping his hand on his jeans. "Kinda weird lookin' little dudes, huh?"

Nancy snatched the photo back as Rod said, "So were you at this stage."

"What *were?*" Hannah interjected, then wet her index finger, marking an imaginary point for her in the air.

This is as good as it's going to get, Nancy thought as she listened to the gentle, relaxed banter over the early-evening birdsong, the breeze soughing through the nearby maples and pines. An oasis of normalcy in the emotional minefield of this so-called marriage. Rod got up to turn the steaks and skewered vegetables on the grill, the sweet, pungent smoke billowing into the air. Like some lovestruck adolescent, she followed his every move, admiring the way he performed the most mundane task with almost a dancer's grace. The kids had finally talked him into wearing a T-shirt and jeans, rather than his usual "casual" uniform of polo shirt and chinos, and the result was nothing less than startling. Of course, they gave him grief because he insisted on the garments' actually *fitting.* And fit they did, hugging various muscle groups in ways that made Nancy's mouth water for far more than steak.

The babies jockeyed for the best position inside her, already vying for attention. Reminding her that they were the reason she was here to begin with.

The only reason.

"So," Hannah said, "do we know what they are? Besides babies, I mean?"

"No," Nancy said, smiling over the tightness in her throat as Rod plopped plates of food in front of them. "Well, they said they could guess at one, but the other one wasn't giving anything away. Besides, I don't want to know. Not yet."

The phone rang. Schuyler grabbed the mobile from the center of the table, only to turn it over to his father. Rod took the call, then excused himself, his expression immediately souring. When he was out of earshot, Schuyler said, "Would someone please tell me why Dad keeps doing this if he hates it so much?"

"I know," Hannah said before Nancy could react. "And it's getting worse. Watch—when he comes back, he's going to be all grumpy and stuff. Hey, Nancy—" she turned, her face alight "—tell Schuy your idea!"

"Oh, no…I don't think—"

"What idea?" Schuyler said. "About Dad?"

After a moment, Nancy glanced over her shoulder to be sure Rod wasn't standing right there, only to have Hannah reassure her she could see him in his office from where she was and would keep an eye out. So she told Schuyler about the restaurant, adding she wasn't at all sure Rod would go for it.

But Schuy only shrugged. "What could it hurt to mention it to him, right?"

Nancy poked at something orange and mysterious in her salad, then sighed. "I don't know. Part of me thinks he'd still like to give this a shot, but another part thinks he'd have done it by now, if he'd really wanted to."

Hannah took a swig of her tea, her face crumpled in concentration. "Not necessarily. I mean, what if he'd just gotten into the habit of doing this marketing thing, you know? Don't people like just sort of give up on ideas sometimes? You know, they don't do it when they were younger, so they go on to something else and sort of forget about it."

Nancy leaned as far back in her chair as she could, marveling at the young woman in front of her. "How'd you get to be so smart?"

She grinned shyly at the compliment. "I watch a *lot* of movies."

"Hey—why don't you and Dad go into town for sundaes or something after dinner?" Schuyler suggested. "Then you could like slip into the conversation how the diner's available, sound him out."

"Dad's made something fancy for dessert, Schuy."

The waning sunlight glinted off the boy's braces as he grinned. "But Nancy could say she's got a craving for something we don't have in the house. Then Dad would have to take her."

"Guys, guys..." She tried to shush them, since Schuy's voice especially had risen as his enthusiasm grew. "It doesn't have to be tonight—"

"You said yourself the property wasn't likely to last very long, since it was so cheap," Hannah pointed out. "So I think you should do it."

"Do what?" Rod said as he walked back out onto the deck, making all three of them jump. Nancy glared at Hannah. Some lookout.

"Oh, Nancy's got this craving for one of the Lakeside Diner's banana splits," Hannah said mildly. Nancy turned up the wattage on the glare. "But she didn't want to ask you to take her into town, since you'd already made dessert."

Rod expertly removed the skewer from his vegetables, shrugged. "I could probably make one here, if you'd like."

"We're…all out of bananas," Hannah said, sending a visual message to her brother that was so blatant, Nancy nearly cracked up.

Rod frowned. "Didn't we just buy some the other day?"

"We ate them all. Didn't we, Schuy?"

"Yep, sure did. May I be excused?"

Rod frowned at the kid's nearly full plate. "You didn't eat very much, Schuy."

"Uh, yeah, I know. But…I promised Jay I'd call him back by seven…."

With that, the kid disappeared inside the house, undoubtedly to dispense with the dozen bananas Nancy herself had seen an hour before. What he would do with them, she didn't want to know.

And what she didn't dare say was how much she hated banana splits.

"Well," Rod said, "Sure. I suppose we could go into town, if that's what you really want."

"Yeah, you two go on," Hannah said, munching on a piece of grilled pepper. "Schuy and I'll even clean up, how's that?"

An hour later, Rod sat across from her, his spoon hovering over a dish of strawberry ice cream.

"I can't just open a restaurant, for the love of Mike."

And if she'd been smart, she would have let it die, right then. But his dismissal was so immediate, her sales training clicked into place before she even thought about it. "Why not?"

"Because that was a dream of my youth. Not something I'd do now. I'm not the same kid with silly, impractical goals as I was then."

"No, you're a great cook with a marketing degree and plenty of capital who could make this work." She took a bite of low-fat vanilla yogurt, the only way Rod would let her have the banana split to begin with. "If you're willing to take the risk."

"Risk has nothing to do with it."

Yeah, right. And he didn't have the spoon in a death grip.

"Doesn't it?" She took a deep breath, hardly daring to look at him, and said what she'd been thinking for months. "Isn't that the name of the game with you? Minimize the risk, stick to what's safe, what you know, what you can control?"

He said nothing. She kept going.

"What you're doing now is a no-brainer, isn't it? Results guaranteed. You know you're good at it, that you can usually manipulate things to come out the way you want them to. But you hate it, Rod. Or at least, you've grown bored. Isn't it time to do something for yourself for a change?"

He actually paused before responding. "A restaurant's hardly the answer, Nancy. You have any idea the kind of hours that takes?"

"Yes, I do, actually. My Uncle Morty in Queens has a deli restaurant, open six days a week from ten to midnight. And he's there most of the time."

"I rest my case."

"Yeah, well, Morty has this problem with letting go, for one thing. And he's *meshugge,* for another." She leaned forward. "Oh, come on…haven't you always secretly wished to be an eccentric millionaire?" The shock in his eyes alone was worth the comment. "So don't think of this as a career move. Think of it as a hobby. Maybe just ten tables or so. Something tiny and very exclusive, maybe open just a couple nights a week…what are you doing?"

He flagged the waitress and asked for the check. "Leaving." His jaw set, he glanced at the check, pulled out a twenty from his wallet and left it with the check on the table, then helped pry Nancy from the booth. Hanging on to her elbow, he propelled her into the dusky evening and down the block toward the car, obviously forgetting not only that she was enormous with child, but that his legs were three times longer than hers.

"Hey! *Hey!*" She dug her flats into the sidewalk and jerked her arm back. "If you're gonna be like this, I'll walk home, thank you."

Rod sighed, planted his hands on his hips. "Leave it to me," he said, "to knock up the pushiest woman in the lower forty-eight."

She wasn't sure whether to laugh, cry, or slug him. "And don't you forget it, buddy. Now you listen to me—you love to cook, you said you wanted to have your own restaurant when you were younger, and now here's this place, just waiting for someone to adopt it. And the kids and I just thought—"

His eyes burned into hers. "The kids know about this?"

"There's a dozen bananas hidden somewhere in the house says they're a hundred percent behind the idea."

He didn't smile. Apprehension began to bubble in the pit of her stomach. "That was supposed to be a joke, Rod."

"I've had enough upheaval in my life this past year without throwing something like this into the mix," he said, and the apprehension turned immediately to ice. She stared at him for a moment, then turned and started back to the restaurant.

"Where are you going?"

"I don't know. Somewhere else. Away."

"Oh, hell, Nance…" He caught up to her, gently pulled her around to face him. "I didn't mean that the way it sounded—"

"Damn you, Rod! You tell me I'm overreacting, reading things into your words you don't mean, yet you keep making the same 'mistakes'! So how dense do you think I am? Never mind—don't answer that. But the fact is, suddenly you've got a wife you didn't want, not to mention two—count 'em, *two*—additional names to add to next year's tax return. Yes, you're being kind and gracious about it all, and I've been convenient to relieve the odd stress now and again. But otherwise we're like a couple of rubber balls in one of those Lotto bubbles. Sometimes we crash into each other, but most of the time we're zooming off in completely opposite directions, sharing the same space but not necessarily because we want to be there. And for someone who likes things as neat and tidy, life-wise, as you do, this has gotta be making you crazy.''

A car full of teenagers passed by, their laughter spilling out into the warm evening. For a moment, Nancy envied them.

''Yeah,'' Rod finally said on a stream of air. ''It is.''

The pain that sliced through her reminded her of the time she'd had to have an infected finger lanced when she was a kid. The cut hurt like hell, but she also knew it was the only way to get the bad stuff out.

''No one told you to marry me,'' she said over the lump in her throat.

He reached out, skimmed warm fingers down her arm, sending a shiver of need racing over her skin. ''No one told me how difficult this was going to be, either. I thought—'' He closed his eyes.

''You could control the situation?''

The hand dropped. ''Yeah.'' His eyes blazed with pain. And fear. ''You scare me, Nancy.''

''Why?''

At first, she took his silence as another rebuff, until a short, soft laugh arced between them. ''Because, if there ever was a woman I might fall in love with, it would be you. And that's something I don't dare let happen.''

His words spun out to her on a fragile thread of possibilities he'd so adamantly denied until this moment. ''Why?'' she repeated, the word barely audible.

Again, his hand lifted to her face, cupping her jaw. His expression was tender. Aching. Strong in its denial. In the glow of an old-fashioned streetlamp, just blinking to life, she saw a sadness so deep her heart twisted. ''It's a long story,'' he said.

''Then I need to sit,'' she said, marching herself to a bench in front of Hinkle's Hardware, lowering herself onto it. A breeze stirred the leaves of an overhead ash, releasing the scent from the petunias in the planter next to the bench. A tiny person shifted inside her; her hand went to the spot, massaged it. She looked over to where he still stood, hands in pockets, jaw set. "I'm having your babies, Rod. The least you can do is explain why you can't love me."

After a moment, he nodded, then lowered himself onto the bench beside her, his face creased with pain.

She wasn't surprised by the way his words rushed out at first, now that he'd finally decided to talk. She sat quietly, listening, as he skimmed through his early years as the only child of older parents—his father a high-profile defense attorney, his mother an automotive heiress—for whom his arrival was more of an interruption than a joy. How he'd spent a lot of time with his grandparents, until their deaths when he was still small. About his father's closet alcoholism, his parents' passionate attachment to each other, a relationship which began to show signs of stress when his mother, no longer able to shunt him off to her parents', finally began to take an interest in her son.

She heard the change in Rod's tone at this point, the near detachment giving way to a bitterness she understood all too well. "The more my mother 'babied' me," he said quietly, leaning forward, his hands clamped between his knees, "the more my father did everything in his power to put me down, to make me feel worthless, useless, stupid. So my mother would try to balance the scales by spoiling me. Unfortunately, this only compounded the problem, since it was crystal clear my father hated the idea of sharing my mother with anyone else. Even their own son. And I suppose belittling me gave him a warped sense of power. Control. Something."

Instinctively, she cradled her own babies. "He was a bully, in other words."

"You could say that."

He then told her of his years in boarding school, a haven of sorts, where he made friends and discovered he was anything but stupid. On weekends and holidays, however, he had to return home.

"I was about ten or eleven, I guess, when I began to notice changes in my mother's behavior. She always seemed about to apologize for something. Although she'd always been quiet and unassuming, now she acted like a frightened little bird. Especially around my father." He went quiet for a long moment. Then he reached over, slipped her hand into his. "It was the heavier makeup that gave it away," he said, and Nancy squeezed his hand, held on tight. "Except, what she didn't realize was that, sometimes, it didn't work."

"And no one else knew?" she asked quietly.

"At the time, *I* didn't even understand what was going on. Not completely. My father may have treated me like dirt, but he sure seemed like the perfect husband. Always bringing my mother gifts and flowers, tender and solicitous when she wasn't feeling well. How could I know—?"

He sprang up from the bench, as if the memories burned. However, now that the floodgates had opened, he apparently was in no rush to close them.

"Especially as he never touched me," he said, almost in wonder. "Not physically, anyway. Even though the barbs, the taunts, the put-downs grew more frequent, and more cruel, as I got older. Never mind that I was a straight-A student, that I lettered in several sports, that I kept my nose so clean the other kids thought there was something wrong with me. It was never enough.

"By the time I'd reached my mid-teens, I'd figured out what was going on. To a certain extent, at least. In any case, I finally understood Mother's entreaties to keep the peace, to not let my father see he was getting to me, were as much for her safety as mine. So, no matter what he said, how much it ripped me up inside, I didn't flinch, refused to give him that power over me. And you know what?" He let out a soft, sad laugh. "That was the only thing he ever complimented me on. Told me I was becoming a 'real man,' that those who succeeded in this world were the ones who never blinked, never let on when the enemy was wearing them down. *He* thought he was toughening me up, preparing me to face the world.'' He scraped one hand across his jaw. ''God knows what he thought he was doing for my mother.''

''And it became a habit,'' she said in a low voice. ''Not letting anything get to you, never letting yourself get angry. Keeping the peace.''

He sat beside her again, actually smiling. ''Figured it was better than smoking.''

She jumped when one of her passengers jabbed her. Rod laid a hand on her belly, stroking, soothing. She could feel the infant lean into his touch, just like the cats did when you reached down to pet them, and marveled at how much strength it took for a man to be this gentle.

''But things got worse, anyway,'' he said, removing his hand. He shifted to sit at an angle, facing her, one elbow propped on the back of the bench, his head in his hand. ''One Friday evening, shortly after my fifteenth birthday, I came home unexpectedly, since the kid I was supposed to spend the weekend with got sick. The housekeeper had already left for the day, so I let myself in.

''From upstairs, I heard my father yelling at my mother. Threatening her. For several seconds, I was paralyzed. Until I heard my mother cry. I remember running up the stairs, screaming my lungs out, reaching their bedroom door in time to see my father slap my mother hard enough to knock her down. She went sprawling, hitting her head on the radiator in their room.

''Then this powerful, respected man, the man people paid megabucks to defend a case, just stood and stared at my mother, as if confused about what he'd done. And this...*rage* exploded inside me, like something entirely separate from me, something with its own rules, its own volition, its own impetus. I went after my father like a rabid dog, and I know, to this day, if he hadn't been heavier and stronger than I was, I would have killed him with my bare hands. In the split second before he slapped me, I caught a glimpse of the cold-blooded fury in his eyes, and realized I'd discovered his little secret. His weakness. But what frightened me far more was seeing my reflection in his eyes, and understanding that I was *his son*.

"While I stood there, swallowing down the urge to puke all over the Chinese rug in their bedroom, my father burst into tears, falling on his knees by my mother and checking her to be sure nothing was broken, acting almost as if someone else had brutalized her. And my stomach turned as my bleeding, bruised mother actually *forgave* him, apologizing for God knows what."

Nancy realized she was barely breathing. "What happened?"

"My father called Arlen to come and 'take care of things.' And I could tell, from the expression on Arlen James's face, this wasn't the first time he'd been called."

"Oh, Rod...why on earth hadn't he reported your father before?"

Rod shrugged. "Because Mother begged him not to, was the only explanation I could come up with. I never asked at the time. And now they've been gone so long, it seems pointless to bring it up. I got the feeling, though, that Arlen's choice was either treat Mother and shut up, or refuse to treat her and not know if she was being cared for at all."

Nancy took in a breath, trying to keep from screaming. "Did you...did you try talking to your mother yourself?"

She could hear the acid frustration in his humorless laugh. "Only a thousand times. She swore she'd die if she left him, he needed her, she just had to be more careful not to rock the boat. That no matter how things looked, they truly loved each other. That she trusted him with her life. And, to be honest, things did seem to settle down after that. I thought, in my naiveté, maybe her near miss had put the fear of God into him, that the abuse had stopped.

"Then I came home for Thanksgiving, my junior year of college. Lulled into a false sense of peace, no doubt due in part to having one too many glasses of wine with dinner, I made the mistake of mentioning my idea of becoming a chef.

Up to that point, Father assumed I was going into law. I hadn't figured out how to break it to him that he could kiss that idea goodbye, but talking about opening a restaurant was downright stupid. As he let me know. But without blowing up, much to my surprise. It being a holiday and all, I backed down, we had dinner, I went back to school the following Monday.

"Two weeks later," he said quietly, "Arlen called me to come home. My parents had apparently been arguing when my father slapped my mother at the top of the stairs. She fell. Broke her neck. Shortly after Arlen got to the house, my father shot himself."

Nancy was trembling so badly her teeth were chattering when he turned to her, offering up the pain he'd held so long inside. "According to Arlen, at whose house the argument began, my parents died over a fight about my going into the restaurant business."

With a cry, Nancy hunched over as far as her protruding stomach would allow, her face buried in her hands. Rod stroked her spine, trying to comfort despite the numbness in his soul. He'd let the ghosts out, true. But he hadn't banished them.

She lifted her head after a moment, let out a ragged sigh. "Oh, Rod…I'm so, so sorry. What a horrible thing to live through."

"Not just for me. I know Arlen still blames himself for not intervening. In fact, he started up the Domestic Abuse Foundation soon after, volunteers his services at a woman's shelter in Detroit." He shifted on the bench, realizing he needed to tie up all the loose ends. "With my father's reputation, my mother's family name, the story made national news. I went into something like seclusion for nearly a year. Even changed my name."

"From…what?"

He looked at her. "Page. My father was Lawrence Page."

He watched as recognition reached her eyes. "Oh, my God," she said softly. "I remember now, hearing about that."

Then she frowned, a little. "And I think opening a restaurant would be the best thing you could do for yourself—"

"I can't do that, Nancy."

"Honey…it's been twenty years—"

"Takes more than time to heal some things."

"True." She got up, stretching out her back. "It takes courage. And resolve." She turned to him. "The kind of courage and resolve that kept a man from following in his father's footsteps, and I don't mean in his career choice."

"Then maybe, now, you'll understand why I told you all this to begin with." He remained on the bench, deliberately apart. "Why I am the way I am. I'm the offspring of two parents who were ruled by their passions, Nancy. My mother couldn't control her dependent, obsessive love for my father, which left her more vulnerable than any human being should ever be. And my father couldn't control his temper. In the weeks after their deaths, it hit me just how much I was their child. Even when I was little, I wasn't simply sad when something bad happened, I was morose. Things that would annoy other children would infuriate me. My feelings frightened me, overpowered me, left me feeling helpless. Emotionally, I was—I still am—a loose cannon. I'm like an alcoholic who doesn't dare take that first drink. And, I realized, the closer I get to someone, the more I run the risk of losing control completely."

He couldn't read her expression clearly, but he could guess. "So…you deliberately married women you didn't love?"

"Yes."

Nancy began to pace, slowly. "So why'd you marry at all?"

Leave it to Nancy to cut straight to the heart of the matter. "Because ironically, I hated being alone." He lowered his head into his hands, staring at the pavement beneath his feet. "Unfortunately, I discovered there wasn't a woman alive willing to play the game by my rules." He looked up, expecting…well, certainly not the compassion radiating from his wife's eyes.

"But you love your children." Statement, not question.

He smiled. "More than I dare let on. And the more I get to know them, the more I *like* them, too. But it's been hard, trying to figure out how to discipline them without ever letting them see me angry. I mean, *damn,* I was ticked with Hannah last night."

"Kids survive their parents getting mad at them, Rod, if it's the kind of anger that comes from truly caring about someone. You know, emotional investment?"

His eyebrows lifted. "You sound a little miffed yourself."

"Oh, I passed *miffed* a half hour ago. I'm up to royally pissed by now. At your parents for doing this to you, at you for armoring your heart rather than getting out there and really *feeling.* The good and the bad, Rod. Avoid one, you lose the other. Your parents were both *ill,* Rod. You're not. I mean, did it ever occur to you that your strong emotional reactions as a kid just might have had something to do with your home life? But instead of dealing with it, you simply shut down...Ooh!" She speared her fingers through her hair, shook her head. "I cannot *tell* you how frustrating it is to live with someone so afraid to rock the boat, he's forgotten how to live!"

"Spoken like the quintessential eternal optimist."

Her hands dropped. "Oh, please," she said with a smirk. "As many times as I've been dumped on, you have the nerve to say that to me? That doesn't mean I'm going to go curl up in a corner and suck my thumb, or give up on life."

He shot up from the bench, his heart racing as he planted himself smack in front of her. "If I'd wanted to give up, Nancy, I would have put a bullet through my brain, too! But I didn't. I kept going. I *survived.*"

"Barely!" she lobbed back. "If you call the inability to trust someone, to let yourself *be* loved, surviving!"

"This has nothing to do with trust."

"Oh, but I think it does." She placed a hand on his chest; he automatically covered it with his own. "I'm a survivor, too, Rod, in my own way. I've survived disapproval. Infidelity. Betrayal. With you, I don't have to worry about any of those.

I *trust* you, because you've proven yourself worthy of my trust. You're the first person who's ever totally given me permission to be *me*. But isn't that what falling in love *is*? Entrusting your heart, your soul, your being to someone else, and they to you? You can't, or won't, do that. And I certainly can't make you. But knowing you don't trust me the way I do you...frankly, that hurts."

He dropped her hand to fork his own through his hair, hating himself, hating that he had no solution to a problem that demanded one, and right now. "For the hundredth time, Nance, I'm sorry." He hooked his thumbs in his back pockets, staring across the street, wondering how they'd managed to be having the most serious discussion of their lives in the middle of Main Street. He turned to her. "I really do want these babies. And I want you in my life. Your trust...I don't deserve it, but it means more to me than you'll ever know. And the kids adore you. In so many ways, this feels like the family I'd always wanted, but never quite got. But—"

Nancy let out a soft laugh. "Oh, here it comes," she said, mostly to herself.

"But...I've already offered everything I can."

"As in, take it or leave it?"

"As in...I wish there *was* more."

She was silent for a minute, then said, "My back is killing me, and I've got to pee. Take me...home, Rod."

Once in the car, they drove in silence for several minutes before she said, "You know, all my life, I've had to settle for second-best. To make do. No matter how hard I worked, what I accomplished, what I was willing to do or give or be, it was never enough. So it occurs to me, at this point in my life, who am I to demand things maybe I'm not supposed to have, you know? Things like...a normal family life. A husband who *loves* me. And the ironic thing is, see, here we are, you and me and the kids, and the babies coming, and the dream seems *so* close, all except the husband-who-loves-me part. And you know what?"

She turned to him as they pulled into the garage. He refused to look at her, afraid to be ensnared by those eyes. "It makes me mad. It makes me feel selfish, and ungrateful, and let me tell you something, Rod—I really, really *hate* feeling this way."

She got out, slammed the car door shut. And Rod had to admit, punching the crap out of something would feel *real* good, right about now.

Chapter 14

The next morning, Guy stuck his head into Nancy's office and said on a single breath, "Elizabeth says she's sorry, she had no business poking her nose in like that, and she'll never, ever, ever do it again."

Nancy looked up, sighing at Guy's contrite expression. She sat back as far as she could, massaging a protruding foot. "Yeah. Me, too. I know she meant well. I've, um, been known to poke my nose in where it didn't belong a time or two myself," she added with a half smile. "So how come she sent you as emissary?"

"She said you wouldn't hit me."

"Shows how little she knows." Then, "She tell you what happened?"

Taking that as an invitation, Guy waltzed on into her office and sank down in the chair in front of her desk. A flock of winged pigs frolicked across his tie. "More or less." He frowned. "We're both worried about you, you know."

"Yeah, well, that makes three of us. And, to add an extra dimension to my own private soap opera—" she lifted her hands, a bright smile fixed to her face, "—ta-da! I'm having twins!"

Guy swore.

"Yeah, that was about my reaction, too." Then she slumped onto the desk, her head in her hands. "Elizabeth's right, you know."

"She usually is, but about what?"

Nancy straightened up, since she couldn't breathe in that position. "About how jealous I am when I see the two of you together." Guy's eyebrows shot up. "I know it's dumb, but there it is. I mean, I want this to work, with Rod and me, but it isn't, and I don't know how to make it, or even if I should be trying all that hard, considering…" She thought about telling Guy what she'd learned last night, thought better of it. That wasn't her confidence to reveal. "Anyway, there you two are, happy as those stupid pigs on your tie—"

"Hey!"

"—and I'm, well, *not*. And you know what? I don't *like* being depressed."

"Uh, Nance?"

"What?"

Guy leaned forward, his customary grin conspicuously absent. "Elizabeth and I have had our share of challenges. There's no such thing as perfect, no matter how cozy things might seem on the surface. You don't live with four kids in a house in a constant state of disrepair and not have some tense moments. Days." A wry smile tilted his mouth. "Weeks."

She knew where he was heading with this. "Guy, we're not playing on the same field. You and Elizabeth are nuts about each other. No matter what, you've got that to work with."

"And you're not nuts about Rod?"

Her face warmed. "I'm just nuts, period."

"*Ho*-kay," Guy said after a moment, linking his hands over his stomach. "Here's where I confess I know more about this than I probably should. If Rod's saying he doesn't love you, then all I have to say is, the man should be more careful how he looks at you when he doesn't know anyone's watching."

The thread of hope felt a little stronger, but not enough to carry any weight, she was sure. "Oh, right. My mother, when she was here, said he looked at me as if he was afraid of me."

"So? Elizabeth scares the hell out of *me,* after all."

"Doesn't count. Elizabeth scares the hell out of everyone."

Chuckling, Guy rose from the chair, tucking his hands in his pockets. "Believe it or not, women aren't the only ones with a sixth sense about these things. If my hunch is correct, the man needs you. Frankly, I think he *adores* you. But for some men, that's a very scary proposition. Just…hang in there." He glanced at his watch. "Listen, I've got a closing to get to," he said, heading out of the office, "but give Elizabeth a call. Make up. *Please.*"

After Guy left, Nancy sat motionless in her chair, fragmented thoughts playing bumper cars in her head, as they had since last night. For once, she really, truly had no idea what to do. She didn't want to leave Rod; she didn't know if she could bear living with him the way things were. But thinking she could care for *two* babies on her own wasn't exactly being realistic.

She looked down at the undulating mound responsible for all this. No, she corrected herself, *she* was responsible for her own mess. She'd asked Rod to make love to her, she was the one dumb enough to assume her diaphragm was still okay, she was the one, ultimately, who'd accepted his offer of marriage. If she was miserable, she had no one to blame but herself.

And what right did she have to make Rod even more miserable than he clearly already was? To demand, or even wish for, something he simply couldn't give her?

Talk about your rock-and-hard-place scenario. This one took the prize. What she needed, she decided, was some time to think, time away. Away from Rod, the kids, Elizabeth, the place she'd called home the last several months. The family she still wasn't quite sure was hers. But where could she go?

She sat, frowning at the floral watercolor on the opposite wall, thinking.

The answer that came to her was hardly the one she expected to hear. It was also the only one that made any sense. In a very warped sort of way, that is.

She hauled out the Yellow Pages, dumping it on top of her desk. Ten minutes later, she'd booked her flight. And since Rod had an early breakfast meeting in Detroit tomorrow morning, she could get away without his knowing.

This would be his last client. His final project. Not that Rod had known that when he went into the city this morning for his meeting, but he sure did by the end. Odd how this little voice—one with a decided New Jersey twang—just popped into his head, saying, "No more."

Definitely one of the more exhilarating moments of his life. If not one of the most frightening. Arlen would be pleased, Rod thought as he crossed Spruce Lake's city-limits sign, headed toward the center of town, rather than back out to the house. As would Nancy, he imagined, once she got over the shock. After all, she'd expended a great deal of energy hammering the idea into his hard head that he could do anything he wanted…as long as he wasn't afraid to take the risk. And there would be risk involved, no doubt about it. Some people would be surprised he hadn't done this years ago, when they found out. Others still wouldn't approve, he imagined. Old friends of his parents, most certainly. But dammit—he didn't need anyone's approval anymore, for or about anything. It had taken long enough, but he'd finally figured that out.

And it would be a fine tribute to his mother.

He'd decided this morning, actually, before he'd left for his meeting. He'd been standing in the garden in the filmy early-morning light, no one to keep him company save two of the cats and a host of birds, when it struck him how Nancy had brought life again to his hurting children, just as she had to this dead, tired garden.

To him.

Just as she said he'd done for her, Nancy Shapiro was the only woman he'd ever known who'd given him permission to be himself. Who, in fact, was forcing him to be more *himself* than he'd ever been in his life. To be *more,* period. All in all, he supposed, a good thing. If a bit nerve-racking at times.

She was wrong about one thing, though: trust and love weren't the same thing. In fact, in his experience, he'd pretty much discovered the two concepts to be mutually exclusive. After all, love led straight to jealousy, didn't it? Even Nancy had to admit that, considering her previous experiences.

She'd left out some tools, which he put away in the shed, since they called for rain later in the day, which is when he'd discovered her stash of Cheetos, Cracker-Jacks, and, yes, Pop-Tarts, tucked away between stacks of empty plastic pots. He could only hope all her prenatal vitamins counteracted the BHT running rampant through her system. At this rate, the babies would come out pickled—

Something nameless and breath-catching had knifed through him at that moment, as it had again, and again, all morning. An odd, not entirely pleasant sensation, a lumpy mixture of apprehension and anticipation, peace and terror. And here it was again, making his heart skip in his chest, his palms sweaty, as he parked in front of the diner and headed inside. He couldn't define it, he wasn't sure he liked it, but damned if it didn't happen every time he thought about his wife.

Cathy Jackson, the original owner's daughter, was happy to show him the kitchen after he'd introduced himself. Which, while a little long in the tooth, equipment-wise, was immaculate and airy. He had to check the place out, just to be sure, before he made his final decision.

"Stuff's kind of outdated, I suppose," she said, nodding toward the stove, "but it still works okay, so we never saw any reason to buy new." The woman forked one hand through cropped beige hair, her smile flickering on and off like a loosely seated lightbulb. "The agent told me I wasn't supposed to talk turkey with anyone without her say-so. But I can't see the harm in showing you around. I've seen you in here a couple times, haven't I? You married Nancy Shapiro, right?"

He nodded, opening the aluminum-faced refrigerator, pleased to find it science-experiment free.

"When's the baby due?" Cathy asked behind him.

"Babies," he corrected with a half smile. "We just found out we're having twins. In late September."

"Twins? Well, bless your hearts! And you with that pair of teenagers!"

While Cathy regaled him with tales of folks having late babies in her family, Rod inspected and considered and kept his expression neutral. Then he thanked her for her time, muttered a few noncommittal phrases, and left. And drove straight to the agency, hoping Nancy was there. Not that he knew what he was going to do or say once he got there, mind. He just wanted to see her. Touch her. Tell her what he'd decided, thanking her for giving him the kick in the butt to do something he should have done years ago.

There came that feeling again, stronger this time, constricting his breathing. He loosened his tie, slipped it out of his collar.

Maureen Louden—now Farentino, he reminded himself—greeted him with a bright, if puzzled, smile when he walked through the door. The petite, flawlessly put-together blonde held out her hand, her trim little brows dipped in confusion. "Rod! What can I do for you?"

"Just stopped by to surprise Nancy, that's all."

The brows dipped further as she lifted her left hand, weighted with an impressive pear-shaped diamond, to her throat. "Uh...she's not here..."

"Oh." Even he was surprised at the disappointment that slashed through him. "Do you know when she'll be back?"

"Rod." Maureen offered him worried amber eyes. "Nancy called in this morning, said she wouldn't be in for a few days. I assumed it was because of the babies...Rod? Rod—is everything all right?" he heard her call behind him as he dashed outside so quickly, he nearly knocked over the oversized Norfolk pine nestled in the sunshine to the right of the front door.

* * *

It was raining when the plane landed in Newark, the air so heavy with moisture, Nancy's hair frizzed before she even found the limo driver. Oh, yeah, she'd hired a limo, since no way was she schlepping out to Scarlet River on a bus in her condition. The flight had been bad enough. Nor had she thought it such a hot idea to call her mother, tell her she was coming. The longer she could put off the barrage of questions-recriminations-accusations, the better.

But she hadn't come home for peace. Obviously. She'd come home for answers, a chance to settle some things in her own head, lay others to rest, even if she had to pummel them into oblivion. Mental nesting, she supposed it was. Instead of readying a nursery for her babies, she was readying her head, cleaning out old thought-patterns and lopsided interdependencies before she became a mother herself. The belief that she needed a man to be complete was one of these; the belief she needed her mother's approval to be happy was another.

An hour later, she stood on her parents' front porch, telling herself she did *not* want to run after the driver, tell him to take her back to the airport. Believe it or not, she still had her key from her high school days, so barring her parents' having changed the lock—

They hadn't. In fact, they hadn't changed anything.

Same stark white walls, same olive shag carpeting, same gold-damask upholstered sofa and matching arm chair sheathed in vinyl slipcovers. Place even smelled the same, a mixture of mothballs and Pledge and chicken soup.

Nancy took a deep breath, then crossed the threshold into her past.

"How can you not know where she is? You're her best friend!"

Rod was aware he was on the edge of irrational, judging from Elizabeth's tight-lipped expression. They stood in her living room, her arms crossed over a baggy shirt that looked like it might be Guy's. Her hair was haphazardly pulled back into a ponytail, her contact lenses forsaken for the huge tortoiseshell glasses she used to wear. A spit up stain graced her left shoulder. "Her friend, Rod. Not the other half of her brain. I'm just as blown away by this as you are."

The oldest child—Ashli?—brought him a glass of tea, then ran off to play with her brothers, their shrill yells blending with birdsong, the sound of a lawn mower, a dog's frantic bark. The baby grunted in her swing; Elizabeth sprung her daughter, grabbing a receiving blanket from the arm of the sofa. She settled into a rocker in front of the fireplace, the baby now letting out a series of excited grunts, and Rod paled.

"Sorry," Elizabeth said, arranging the lightweight blanket to cover everything, including the baby, from her neck to her waist. "Feel free to talk, but if I don't feed her, we won't be able to hear a thing."

He decided now would be a good time to look out the window, catch a breath of summer air heavy with the scent of honeysuckle and new mown grass. Since Elizabeth didn't have any information, he could have left. So why hadn't he?

"She left a note, you said?" she asked.

He nodded. He'd called home from his mobile the minute he'd gotten back to the car. Hannah had read the note the housekeeper had found and was on the verge of losing it, he could tell, even more worried than he was. If that was possible. "Just that she'd be back in a few days. Not where she went." He sucked in a breath, keeping to himself the part about Nancy's needing to "think things through."

"Rod," Elizabeth said quietly, "she's not some fourteen-year-old who's run away from home—"

"She has no business gallivanting around as pregnant as she is!"

For several seconds, the baby's snuffling sounds filled the space between them. "Somebody sounds like he gives a damn," Elizabeth said mildly.

At that, he spun around. "Of course I give a damn! Oh…wait." He sucked in a breath, shook his head. "Let me guess. She told you everything."

"I don't know about everything, since we haven't talked to

each other since…the other day. In any case, you can't expect
the woman never to talk to *anyone* when something's bothering her. She'd explode. Or go mad.''

She had him there. Momentarily defeated, he sank into the
matching armchair across from the sofa. ''How much did she
tell you?''

''More than you ever saw fit to tell me,'' Elizabeth said
without rancor. ''And by the way—nothing she tells me goes
farther than this house, okay? I'm a confidante. Not a gossip.''

Yes, he knew that much was true. Then, for some reason,
he smiled. ''Makes me wonder, though, how much you said
to Nancy about me when we were dating.''

Elizabeth just smiled back for a moment, before fixing him
with an expression full of affection. And concern. ''Why are
you so afraid to admit how you feel about your wife, Rod?''

If he hadn't already been sitting, he would have fallen over.
''And what's that, exactly?''

''Exactly?'' she said with another smile. ''Now that, I can't
tell you. But picture this from my vantage point—Nancy tells
me you say you can't love her. But what I see in front of me
is a man totally freaked out because his pregnant wife's gone
off on her own for a few days. Hate to tell you this, Rod, but
the two don't jibe.''

He bolted from the chair again, began pacing the room, that
odd feeling once again slicing him into pieces. ''Please, Elizabeth—the last thing I need is a two-cent analysis from a
woman who's read every self-help book on the market.''

''Oh, get over yourself, Rod,'' she said with a laugh.
''You're forgetting who you're talking to. You think I can't
recognize the symptoms? If you recall, we were pretty much
birds of a feather, at least when we started dating. Neither of
us wanted our cages rattled, wanted something that would in-
volve more than the minimum emotional expenditure. And
why is that, do you suppose?''

''You already know the answer to that.''

''Damn straight. But so do you. The difference is, you're
not admitting it.''

"Stop talking in circles, for God's sake!"

"Fine. You, Rod Braden, are scared spitless of being hurt, of being abandoned. Just like I was. You're petrified of taking the risk of having your love thrown back in your face. In my case, I was scared of losing someone I loved, like my mother and I did when my dad died when I was twelve. I suspect in yours, your real fear is of being rejected, just like your parents rejected you."

"My mother didn't reject me," he said before he caught himself.

"Of course she did, in her own way. She could have accepted your suggestions to get out of that horrible situation, which would have shown you she loved you enough not to put you through that horror, as well as herself. Nobody's ever truly returned your love, have they?"

It took a second before her words sank in.

"You…knew?"

After a moment, she nodded.

"But if you haven't talked to Nancy for two days, how—?"

"You and I dated for nearly two years, Rod. At one point, I even entertained the idea of marrying you. Since you weren't exactly forthcoming about your background, I did a little digging around on my own. *I* knew who you were, even if you didn't."

His hands had turned to ice, even in the warm room. "Yet you never told Nancy."

"It wasn't my place to tell her. Like I said. I'm not a gossip."

"Even if it meant protecting her?"

"From what? From a man strong enough to put his past behind him, who never allowed anyone to consider him a *victim?*" She smiled, stroking her child underneath the blanket. "Seeing the two of you together was like finding the key to a room that had been locked for far too long. One with something priceless inside. You two need each other, just as the locked room needs that key. And Rod...believe me, Nancy would never, ever throw your love back in your face.''

''I know that.''

''Then you be damn sure to return the favor. She needs your whole heart, Rod. Not just the scraps you feel you can spare.''

Before he could respond, his mobile burred on his belt. Elizabeth's words reverberating in his ears, he answered it.

''We found her, Dad!'' Schuyler practically shouted. ''She went to her parents' house. I remembered she'd put it on speed dial, so I took a chance, called the number. Her father answered, said she got there a couple hours ago.''

The relief that flooded through him was so profound, he actually felt dizzy for a second or two. ''Good work, Schuy. I'll be right there.''

He disconnected the call, then told Elizabeth, who'd brought the baby to her shoulder to work out a burp. ''Sometimes I wonder about that woman,'' she said, cocking her head at him. ''And your next move is...?''

Rod grinned, already to the door. ''I'm way ahead of you on that one.''

''If you've screwed this up, Dad, I swear I'll never speak to you again.''

''Not now, Hannah.'' He stormed into his office, grabbed his Rolodex off the corner of his desk. She'd followed him, her arms knotted over her T-shirted ribs. Rod caught a slice of midriff between shirt and shorts, decided now was not the time to discuss it.

''Did you hear me?'' she said.

''Half of Michigan heard you, Hannah.'' Rod jabbed the travel agent's number into the phone. ''Now, if you don't mind, I'm in no mood to be dressed down by a sixteen-year-old....'' He cursed the damn tape recording, stabbed the appropriate number, then waited.

''What did you do this time to make her leave, Dad?''

''I didn't do anything...yes, this is Rod Braden—yes, Annie, good morning—what's the next available flight you have out of Metro into Newark?'' He checked his watch. "Anything after twelve, I guess. Yes, today..."

"Oh, and you think you're just going to play the White Knight and fetch her back, right?"

Rod cupped his hand over the phone. "You have a better idea, Miss Smarty Pants?... Yes?" he said into the phone. "Yes, that's fine. Credit card...just a minute..." He grabbed for his coat, which he'd laid over the back of his desk chair, wrestled his wallet from the inside pocket. A minute later, he was booked for a flight that left in less than two hours. With Hannah hot on his heels, he took off for the bedroom to throw some things into a carry-on.

"What if she doesn't *want* you to go after her? What if she just couldn't take it anymore, if she doesn't want to come back?"

He whipped around, feeling his face heat. "Dammit, Hannah—you think I haven't thought of that?" When her eyes went wide, he realized he was actually yelling at her. "But going after her is a damn sight better than sitting around and doing nothing, so you can jolly well get off your high horse right now. You're right—she might not want to see me. And maybe it is too late. And maybe I have screwed up. But I don't know any of that until I see her, do I?"

Tears quivered on her lower lids, making her blue eyes as bright as the cornflowers Nancy had planted outside, and he immediately regretted raising his voice. Ditzy and Schmutz meowed in concern at her feet; Hannah picked up the mangy Persian, then twisted away, swiping at her tears with the heel of one hand. "Oh, God, Hannah, baby...I'm so sorry—"

But, to his amazement, she dropped the cat and threw herself into his arms. "You're scared to death, aren't you?" she said into his chest. "You're absolutely terrified she won't come back."

The back of his throat burned. Unable to answer his daughter, he looked out the window, watching Pita chase a butterfly through the kaleidoscope of color and texture that was Nancy's garden. He remembered her grin underneath that ridiculous floppy hat after her initial plunder of the local nursery, how she'd bought some of everything that caught her fancy, planting things wherever the mood struck. Her amazement and delight that most of them thrived.

The result was pure joy. Crazy, yes, but you couldn't look at all these colors jumbled together and not smile. At least, he couldn't.

She was everywhere.

Including his heart.

Tears pushed over his eyelids, the first ones he'd let himself shed in more than two decades. So *that* was the terrible, wonderful feeling that had been stomping around inside him all day. Even before, he realized. When had it happened? When had this tiny, exuberant woman breached twenty years' worth of defenses to accomplish what he'd vowed no woman would ever do?

And why had he fought it so long?

He pried his daughter off his chest, planting a kiss atop her head. "I won't let her go," he said, pulling out a handkerchief to wipe away Hannah's tears. "I promise."

Hannah's smile was brilliant.

Chapter 15

Nancy had never realized before how adept her mother was at eating with pursed lips. Disapproval rolled off the woman in waves, chilling the little dining room far more efficiently than the ancient window unit wheezing in the living room window.

"You made your bed, little girl," Belle now said, spooning boiled potatoes onto her plate. "So you lie in it. You expect too much, is your problem, you know that?" she suddenly added, thunking the spoon back into the serving dish. "All your life, nothing was ever good enough for you."

Nancy stared at her dry, stringy pot roast for a beat or two as visions of Rod's veal marsala brought a lump to her throat. Not to mention the vision of the chef, the way his eyes always glittered expectantly when he presented a new dish for her to try. How he'd grin like a kid when she swooned in ecstasy at the first bite. Something else she'd never had to fake.

She lifted her eyes to her mother. "No, Ma, I think you got that backward." At Belle's raised, crookedly applied brows, she continued. "All my life, *I* was never good enough for *you.*

Well, guess what? I'm human. I make mistakes. Lots of 'em. I'm not Mark, I'll never be Mark, and the kicker is, I don't *want* to be Mark. And I'm sick and tired of trying to make you love me.''

"You're talking stupid. When have I ever said I wanted you to be Mark?''

Nancy just laughed.

"And what is this *mishegoss* about my not loving you?'' Belle said, bristling nicely now. "Of course I love you—''

"Then why do you *constantly* tear me down, Ma? Huh? Tell me, because I'd like to know. Because I need to know why it's taken me so long to figure out that I'm not worthless, that I have a right to make my own decisions. I get more respect and appreciation from a man who *doesn't* love me than I do from my own mother.''

Her mother didn't miss a beat. "Oh, you wait. You wait until you're a mother, how your heart breaks when you watch your children make fools of themselves. So you give them constructive criticism, make sure they don't screw up. Although, in your case, my words have obviously fallen on deaf ears—''

"Belle! Shut *up*.''

They both jumped at the sound of her father's voice. Belle flushed an odd shade of red. When she spoke, her voice quavered. "Since when do you tell me to shut up, David Shapiro?''

"Since now,'' he said quietly, spearing a potato.

"Nancy—you hear how your father talks to me these days?''

Nancy jumped again when her father's silverware clattered to his dish. "I hear how you talk to your daughter, Belle. Your own *daughter*. And it makes me sick. The girl is pregnant, for God's sake. And unhappy. So she comes clear from Detroit to maybe find some peace in her own home, from her own parents, and for this you kvetch at her like she's scum. You should be ashamed, Belle.''

Astonished into silence, Nancy could only watch her

mother's eyes fill with tears behind her glasses, which she removed. So everyone could get the full effect, Nancy presumed.

''Mark doesn't talk to me like this.''

Her father leaned forward, waving his fork, which he'd picked up again, in a more or less menacing manner. ''Of course not. Why should he? You treat him like a damn prince. Like he can do no wrong. When everyone knows he's no prince. So Nancy's made a few mistakes. Who hasn't? At least she admits them, tries to fix them, keeps trying to make her life better. Not like Mark.''

While her mother's color deepened to steamed lobster, Nancy brows shot up. ''What's this about Mark?''

''We agreed, we wouldn't talk about this while she was here,'' her mother said under her breath, glaring at Nancy's father.

''No, *you* said you wouldn't talk. I said no such thing.''

''What about Mark?''

With a weighty sigh, her father speared another glob of beef. ''Shelby left him—''

''Because she didn't know a good thing when she had it,'' Belle said.

''—because Mark was cheating on her,'' her father finished wearily. ''And I know it's true, because Mark admitted it. Says he wants to marry this girl. This Bambi.''

Nancy's hands flew into the air. ''I'm sorry I asked.''

''He said he wanted to *marry* her?'' her mother asked, her hand pressed to her breasts as if to keep them from flying up in her face. Then she turned to Nancy. ''And now you come home, seven months pregnant, because you need time to *think*. Like you couldn't have done that before you married the man? Or better yet, before…'' She dropped her face in her hands, muttering something Nancy figured she was better off not hearing.

Tears pricked behind Nancy's eyelids. ''Ma? Here's a flash for you.'' She tucked her teddy-bear studded paper napkin beside her barely eaten dinner, her throat tight with the effort not to cry. "This isn't about you, okay? Mark's cheating, my screwing up, none of it. We're not doing these things just to ruin your life, believe it or not. Now, I came home to think. Since that's not going to happen in this house, I'm going to go take a walk."

"In your condition?" her mother yelped.

"I'm pregnant, Ma. Not handicapped." She pushed herself up from the table, waddled out of the dining room toward the front door. Underneath her denim jumper, someone delivered a good, swift kick to her kidney.

"You didn't eat."

"I wasn't hungry." With one yank, she wrenched open the front door and escaped.

It was still light out, the air heavy and moist against her skin from the earlier rain, which had stopped an hour or so ago. A watery, pallid sun winked through the scrim of clouds still cloaking the town, an occasional ray setting a droplet-encrusted bush to sparkling. Kids raced and shouted and splatted in puddles underneath a canopy of wet maples that periodically shivered in the warm breeze, showering droplets on whatever hapless victims chanced to be strolling underneath. Tidy, neat little clapboard and brick houses seemed to nod at her from behind their tidy, neat little lawns as she slowly made her way to the corner store and a chocolate egg cream.

Frankly, she'd made her decision by the time the plane landed. Whether it was the right decision or not, time would only tell. And heaven knew how Rod was going to take it. But she'd weighed the pros and cons until her head hurt, and she always came back to the same answer—

"Yo! Lady! Heads up!"

Startled, she whipped around, ducking the stray softball that came within inches of glancing off her temple. The sudden move knocked her off balance, however, just as she was about to step off the curb. Her ankle wrenched underneath her; she grabbed at air, trying to right herself, but her extra load had severely repositioned her center of gravity. With a gasp that was more surprise than fear, she felt herself pitch forward into the street, wondering exactly how good the brakes were on the truck that had just turned the corner.

Shards of light flashed behind her eyes as she landed, her head hitting the curb. Pain stabbed from all directions at once—ankle, temple, belly. She heard brakes squeal, then a horrible crunching sound as the truck sideswiped another car; a woman's scream from across the street; a voice in her ear, soothing, reassuring.

And achingly familiar.

"Nance! Honey, it's okay, baby. I'm here. It's okay—"

She tried to focus through a blur of panic and pain and throat-closing fear as another spasm vised her abdomen. She cried out, clutched the arm that tightened around her and realized she wasn't hallucinating.

"Oh, Rod! The babies! I'm having contractions—"

Then, for the second time in her life, that damn screen went blank.

No one dared to mention visiting hours. As in, they weren't in effect at 5:00 a.m. In the past ten hours, Rod had perfected a glare that put Belle Shapiro to shame. Maybe bullying wasn't his thing, but this was his wife they were dealing with. His babies. His family. If they weren't worth putting the fear of God into a few medical personnel, nothing was.

The contractions had petered out on their own shortly after she was admitted, a godsend since, with her head injury, using drugs to stop them wasn't an option. Her ankle was badly sprained, but not broken, and while she'd have a nasty lump on her head for a couple days, she'd come to by the time the EMT team had arrived. A mild concussion, maybe, but nothing to worry about.

But talk about scaring the bejesus out of people. Man, she had that E.R. staff hopping, especially with the threat of premature twins. And she wasn't completely out of the woods, either. She'd have to stay another twenty-four hours, they'd said. Just to keep an eye on things.

Which is what Rod had been doing since they'd brought her in here, watching her as she lay in bed, head elevated, foot elevated, IV running, attached to blood-pressure monitors and fetal monitors and cardiac monitors, the damn things beeping and scritching and blipping like a nursery full of baby CP3-0s. How she could sleep was beyond him, but she was out like a light. Rod stood up to check on her, as he had a hundred times already, as if he didn't trust the monitors. Just a bunch of wires and doohickeys and thingamabobs, sophisticated, expensive, and—he hoped—reliable. But they weren't him.

They didn't love her.

Her expressive brows tucked into a small frown, she slept with her face slightly tilted, her left hand resting protectively over her middle. The plain gold wedding band gleamed like a smile in the dim light. Like a promise.

Carefully, not wishing to wake her, he fingered the end of one of those wayward curls, then bent over to feel its silkiness against his lips. Breathing in sandalwood and roses, he whispered words he would say aloud the minute she woke up, and a million times more during their lifetimes.

Hannah wasn't the only one who'd never forgive him if he messed this up. He'd blame himself for the rest of his life if he let Nancy go, if he let another day, another minute, pass with her believing he didn't, or couldn't, love her. For twenty years, he'd avoided, ignored, denied relationships and situations and feelings that had frightened him, that had even suggested a loss of control.

For twenty years, he'd existed. Not lived. Just as Nancy had said.

For twenty years, he'd come perilously close to letting his father win.

And Nancy had been the only woman strong enough and crazy enough and determined enough to love him in spite of all that.

God bless that defective diaphragm, Rod thought, tears welling in his eyes.

He let her hair slip out of his fingers, then silently pulled the chair up as close to the bed as it would go, never taking his eyes off her, even as he lowered himself into it. Then he waited for his wife—for the woman he loved with his whole heart, not just the scraps—to wake up.

Nancy came to with a start, panicked for a moment, fearing the contractions had resumed. Afraid to breathe, let alone move, she lay completely still, her eyes still shut, the pain of her bandaged ankle and head nothing compared with the terror of thinking something might happen to her babies.

She was just being kicked, was all, by one of those babies squirming into a more comfortable position. She could relate, aching to roll over.

As if she had anything to complain about. The truck had stopped. So had the contractions. The ankle would heal, as would her hard—

"Good morning, sweetheart."

—head.

Her eyes popped open. She *verrrry* carefully turned that hard head to see Rod sitting beside her. His eyes were puffy, his chin was stubbled and his hair looked as if it had sneezed, but the combination of the broad smile on his face and the fear in his eyes box-kicked her heart nearly out of her chest.

"You've been here all night?" she breathed.

He nodded, then took her right hand in both of his, brought it to his lips, kissed her palm. "I've got two things to say to you, Nancy Shapiro Braden, and I'm going to get them out before that mouth of yours is fully functioning, because maybe if I talk fast, I can change your mind. First off, don't you *ever* take off like that again and not tell me where you're going."

She shifted on her pillows to get a better look at his face, wondering if she dared believe what she thought she saw there. Deep inside her, hope stirred, like that mutt of Guy's and Elizabeth's when he thought maybe someone was going to feed him. "Wow. You sound really pissed."

"That's putting it mildly. You just shaved a good five years off my life, lady." He swallowed, and she saw tears glittering in his eyes. "Five years I'd really like to spend, along with the rest of them, with you."

Her breath caught in her throat. "And the second thing?" she whispered.

Rod stood then, but only to bend over, his hands clutching the bed rail. He lowered his mouth to hers as he tenderly cradled her jaw in his large, gentle hand. A kiss not meant to arouse, but to reassure, to cement something she wouldn't have thought possible twenty-four hours ago. A kiss to render earlier decisions moot.

He lifted his lips from hers, only to place another, gentle kiss on her forehead, near the bandage. "I want to thank you," he whispered, smiling, his thumb stroking her cheek, "for loving me even though *I'm* the dumbest person on the planet." He took her hand in his again, tucked it against his chest. "For making me fall in love with you."

She swallowed. "Please...don't say it unless you really, really mean it."

His smile was like a blessing. "I don't lie, remember?"

"Oh, hell." She blinked, his face becoming a blur. "Now I'm gonna cry."

Then she saw them. Tears. Not hers, but Rod's, tracking down those sculpted cheeks. He laughed, shook his head. Cleared his throat. "You have no idea how scared I was, Nance. First, when I read your note, realized you'd left...then, when I saw you fall, saw that truck. All I could think was...what if I lost you without ever telling you what an idiot I've been all these months?"

"Those are sweet words, buddy," she said, and he laughed. "But it takes a lot more than a knock on the head to do in this tough little broad." Tears welled again. "You came after me?"

"Damn straight."

With a watery smile, she laid a hand on his cheek. "Nobody's ever cared enough to try to win me back."

He pressed his hand over hers. "Well, now that I've let all

these feelings loose, I hope you realize you've created a monster. I even yelled at Hannah.''

"No! Why?''

"Because she was being a pain in the butt.''

"Ah.'' She tried to look serious. "And what was her reaction?''

One side of his mouth lifted. "She hugged me.''

Nancy chuckled. "She's gonna do all right, that one.''

He lay his hand, warm and strong, on her belly. "So are these guys.'' He kissed her again, and she thought how she'd never get enough of the taste of him. "I love you, Nance. Completely and forever and always.''

"Wow. I do like the way you do schmaltz, Mr. Braden.''

"So…does this mean I'm not…too late?''

"Late for what?''

"To change your mind. About…that decision you had to make.''

She let a couple seconds tick by, just for the hell of it, then said, "Well, I'm sorry, Rod, but I'm afraid it's way too late to change my mind.''

He went pale. Oh, it was tempting to let him suffer. But she figured worrying about her had been torment enough. For now. Besides, she was in her mid-thirties and carrying the man's babies. What was she, nuts?

"Okay,'' she said, "you can breathe now. See, I'd already decided to stay, to do whatever it took to keep this marriage going.''

"You…weren't going to leave?''

"Oh, that option made the short list, don't kid yourself. But it wasn't on there for long.'' She reached up, touched his face, loving the rasp of whiskers against her fingertips. Her husband's whiskers.

"I just couldn't give up on our marriage. On us. Even though I had no idea if I could ever convince you to let down those infernal barriers of yours, or even if you would ever love me. I finally realized it didn't matter, as long as there was even a shred of hope. It's like I told Hannah—we don't love someone because of what we expect to get in return. I figured maybe it was time I practiced what I preached.'' Then she grinned. ''Besides, what woman in her right mind would walk out on a man who can cook the way you do?''

Carefully, so as not to disconnect her from anything, he pulled her into his arms, his breath warm in her hair. ''I don't deserve you,'' he whispered.

She smiled through her own tears. ''Probably not. But you're stuck with me, anyway.''

His chuckle rumbled in her ear. ''Right back atcha, sweetheart—''

''Just you never mind,'' came the strident voice from the doorway. ''She's my daughter, I'll take her breakfast in to her. You just go do whatever it is you need to do, we'll be fine.''

In a flurry of polyester and costume jewelry, Belle clumped into the room, Nancy's breakfast tray suspended in her hands, which she clattered onto the bedtable. ''So,'' she said, squinting at Rod as she cranked up the table to accommodate Nancy's bulging middle. ''How is she?''

''Ma, hello?'' Nancy waved. ''I'm over here and not deaf. Ask me yourself. And how'd you manage to get in before visiting hours?''

Belle shooed her question away as something not worth thinking about as David shuffled into the room, his gray knit shirt already wilted in the summer heat. ''Thirty-four years you've known your mother,'' he said, pulling out a handkerchief to wipe his brow, ''and you have to ask?'' He walked over, kissed her on the forehead. ''How ya doing, sweetheart?''

She squeezed Rod's hand. ''Never better, Pop.''

''Well, you're just lucky, let me tell you,'' her mother started in, bustling around the room straightening up God knew what. ''Of all the idiotic things to do, going out by yourself for a walk in your condition. What were you thinking? Bad enough you got on a plane this far along in the pregnancy—''

''Ma—''

"Mrs. Shapiro," Rod said quietly, "that will do."

Nancy's gaze zipped to Rod, then to Belle, whose penciled brows had shot up, one of them a half inch higher than the other. "Excuse me?"

"I realize this might strain family relations for the next several years, but what the hell?" Hands in pockets, he moved closer to Nancy's mother, backing her into the bed table. "Maybe you've somehow missed it, but you have a terrific daughter. She's smart and kind and loving, and as far as I'm concerned, gorgeous, no matter what condition she's in—"

Nancy wasn't sure how complimentary that part was, but she let it go.

"—in spite of the fact that, from what I've gathered, you haven't exactly been the most supportive mother in the world. Did it ever once occur to you that belittling Nancy like that is a form of abuse?"

Three people gasped, including Belle, who'd turned crimson. "How dare you! I'd never abuse one of my own children! David!" She turned to her husband, her hand at her throat. "Are you just going to stand there and say nothing?"

"Sounds like he's doing just fine without my help," her father said, scratching his head as he settled into a chair with a little grunt.

"Thank you," Rod said to her father.

"Anytime," David returned with a little salute, then waved toward Rod. "Please. Continue."

So he did. "It's about time you appreciated your daughter for who she is, Mrs. Shapiro. Not for who you want her to be. And if you can't do that, I'm afraid you're not welcome in our home, because I'm not going to let you or anyone else ever make my wife feel she's unworthy of being loved, just as she is."

Wow. Talk about your pregnant pauses. Nancy glanced from her father, who was grinning, to her mother, who looked poleaxed, to Rod, who was standing there looking all heroic and stuff. And she knew what he'd done, in that quiet little speech of his: he'd stood up for her. *Even if it meant making someone else angry*. Even though he knew, and she knew, she didn't really need him to act as a buffer between her and her mother. Not that it didn't feel good, but that wasn't the point. The point was, he just proved to himself he could get angry—and act on it—without losing his cool.

Nancy leaned over, grabbed a bowl of something off the tray, decided she was too hungry to care what it was. She'd no sooner put spoon to mouth when her mother walked over to her, grabbed her face in her hands and planted a big kiss on her forehead.

"Congratulations, *bubeleh*," Belle said with a huge grin.

"Fo whad?" Nancy said around a mouthful of what turned out to be oatmeal. *Blech.*

"Took you long enough, but you finally got one with *co-jones!*"

They let her go home a few days later, although she practically had to sign in blood that she'd stay put once she got back to Detroit. The thought of being pampered for two months put her teeth on edge; the thought of *Rod's* pampering her was something else again.

She was engulfed by kids and cats the minute she walked in the door; the overwhelming sense of having come *home* brought tears to her eyes and a burst of joy to her heart like she'd never felt before. Rod planted her on a padded redwood chaise out on the deck with a glass of juice as the kids blathered to her about this, that and the next thing for a solid half hour. Then they vanished back into their own worlds, leaving behind the relative silence of a thousand birds chirping their hearts out.

Rod eased himself into an Adirondack chair beside her, his forehead creased. One day, she was going to figure out how someone could look that dignified in jeans and a T-shirt, but for now, she was content to just feast her eyes on him. The frown deepened.

"What?" she encouraged, and he smiled.

"I didn't tell you," he said after a moment, a rose-scented

breeze teasing his hair. "But…I looked at the diner. The day you ran away."

She went still. "Really?"

"Uh-huh. And I decided…" He looked at her. "No."

"Rod—"

He folded his hand around hers. "Hush, woman. Hear me out. This might sound odd, but *knowing* I could take a stab at this, if I wanted to, is enough. Knowing you and the kids would support me…" He paused. "But it's not right. Not now, not for us. Yes, I'd thought, for about ten minutes, perhaps this might be a fitting tribute to my mother. But starting a new business, especially a restaurant, would be hell on the family."

"Rod." She tried to keep the irritation out of her voice. Sort of. "You don't have to sacrifice anything for anyone anymore. Do you hear me? Do what *you* want to do, dammit!"

"What do you think I'm doing? I'm the one who doesn't want to miss all the stuff I missed out on when Hannah and Schuy were little. Trust me—I'm not sacrificing anything. And there's more. I'm giving up the consultancy. You—and everyone else—were right about that. *Too,*" he added with a smile. "I finally realized I'm burned out on marketing products I don't even like. Hate it, actually. So I'm winding down, should have all the loose ends tied up by Christmas."

All she could do was stare at him, her mouth open.

"Well, look at that—I've succeeded in rendering you speechless. However, just so you don't think that means I'm going to sit around all day, I've finally agreed to do something Arlen's been after me to do for years."

"What's that?"

"I've accepted an appointment to serve on the board of his Domestic Abuse Foundation. Going to head up their new national campaign, aimed at getting kids to talk to someone when they think there's abuse going on in their family. To help them realize it's not a stigma to come from an abusive home, just something that needs to be healed."

She looked out over the garden, taking this in. "Your mother would be proud."

Rod was quiet for a moment, then said, "Yeah, I think maybe she would be, even though at the time she refused to acknowledge the problem. But *I* will be, and that's what counts. Time I let other people know that keeping the peace isn't necessarily the best thing. And maybe I'll scout around for a teaching position, who knows?" He stretched, then folded his hands behind his head, grinning up to the sky. "For the first time in my life, I feel as though I really *can* do anything I want." He looked over to Nancy, and the grin softened, as did the expression in his eyes. "Thanks to a certain someone who kept hitting me upside the head."

She grinned back, holding up her juice in a mock toast. "That's what I'm here for," she said, and he nodded, sighed, leaned his head back on the chair, his eyes closed. From inside the house, Hannah called Schuyler a dweeb. At the top of her lungs. Rod chuckled.

"Life is good," he said, settling his hands over his stomach.

A little foot prodded Nancy's bladder. "Yeah," she said. "Ain't it just?"

Epilogue

Schuyler and I can't believe it's been a year since the twins were born, but here we are, helping Nancy and Elizabeth hang like a gazillion balloons out in the garden for their first birthday party. Not that the babies are gonna know from birthdays, but Dad says to humor Nancy, since she's waited so long for this moment. Uh-huh. Like we can't see how much fun he's having, too. I think he's going to dress up like a clown or something, which would be real dorky if anyone other than Dad was doing it.

Since he quit that job, he's around a lot more, which could be a pain. But most of the time, it's pretty cool. I mean, he smiles like *all* the time now. Well, except when he's mad. You should've seen him when I came home with my hair cut all short and stuff. Actually, maybe not. It wasn't pretty. The way Dad blew up at me, I mean, not the hair. The hair *rocks,* and it's a lot easier to take care of after a basketball game. But I have to admit, at that moment? I almost wished things were back the way they were when Dad held it all in. Almost. If having him go ballistic every once in a while is the price we all have to pay to see him happy most of the time—to hear him say he loves us—we'll deal with it. Besides, Nancy's real good at calming him down. Not that she looked any too thrilled with the hair, either, but she didn't say anything. Just shook her head and walked away.

But back to the twins. We got a boy and a girl, in case you're wondering. Quinn and Kelsey. Quinn's got curly dark hair, just like Nancy's, and Kelsey's bald with blue eyes. I have to admit, they're *real* cute. Since Nancy couldn't nurse them both exclusively, we all took turns giving them bottles, which was actually kinda fun. I could've lived without changing diapers, but oh, well. Both babies are walking now, so the cats are like *never* around.

Let's see…what else? Oh! Schuyler won the state science fair last year, and like all these colleges are already sniffing around, do you believe it? Jeez—he just turned fifteen last month. Our basketball team totally blew away the competition last year, and the coach is so cool. And don't tell anyone, but I've got a boyfriend. Yeah. A senior. Ryan's real quiet, and sweet. I mean, he brings me flowers and stuff, which is really neat. Kinda reminds me of Dad, in a way.

Schuy and I see Mom from time to time, whenever she's in town. She's still married to what's-his-face, believe it or not, but they travel a lot, so she's not around much. Just as well. I guess this is one of those things-work-out-for-the-best deals.

Oh, Lord—Dad and Nancy are making kissy-face with each other again. Actually, as long as they restrain themselves when my friends are around, I don't mind. It's kind of neat to walk into the kitchen and find them just standing there, hugging each other. Or laughing together. Or see them cuddling on the sofa watching TV after the babies are in bed. Makes me feel, I don't know…peaceful. Like, no matter what happens, things'll always work out, you know?

And we do things together now. All six of us. Even went to Disney World last summer, just like a real family.

Huh. I guess that's what we are. A real family. Not just a

bunch of people moving in and out of each others' lives, but something complete and whole and maybe not perfect, but close enough. Man, I never thought it would happen to me, but whaddya know? It did.

Cool.

* * * * *

Be sure to watch for Karen Templeton's next romance set in Spruce Lake, coming only to Silhouette Intimate Moments in late 2000.

If you enjoyed what you just read,
then we've got an offer you can't resist!

Take 2 bestselling
love stories FREE!

Plus get a FREE surprise gift!

Clip this page and mail it to Silhouette Reader Service™

IN U.S.A.	IN CANADA
3010 Walden Ave.	P.O. Box 609
P.O. Box 1867	Fort Erie, Ontario
Buffalo, N.Y. 14240-1867	L2A 5X3

YES! Please send me 2 free Silhouette Intimate Moments® novels and my free surprise gift. Then send me 6 brand-new novels every month, which I will receive months before they're available in stores. In the U.S.A., bill me at the bargain price of $3.80 plus 25¢ delivery per book and applicable sales tax, if any*. In Canada, bill me at the bargain price of $4.21 plus 25¢ delivery per book and applicable taxes**. That's the complete price and a savings of at least 10% off the cover prices—what a great deal! I understand that accepting the 2 free books and gift places me under no obligation ever to buy any books. I can always return a shipment and cancel at any time. Even if I never buy another book from Silhouette, the 2 free books and gift are mine to keep forever. So why not take us up on our invitation. You'll be glad you did!

245 SEN C226
345 SEN C227

Name	(PLEASE PRINT)	
Address	Apt.#	
City	State/Prov.	Zip/Postal Code

* Terms and prices subject to change without notice. Sales tax applicable in N.Y.
** Canadian residents will be charged applicable provincial taxes and GST.
  All orders subject to approval. Offer limited to one per household.
  ® are registered trademarks of Harlequin Enterprises Limited.

INMOM00   ©1998 Harlequin Enterprises Limited

Look Who's Celebrating Our 20th Anniversary:

Celebrate
20
YEARS

"Working with Silhouette has always been a privilege—I've known the nicest people, and I've been delighted by the way the books have grown and changed with time. I've had the opportunity to take chances...and I'm grateful for the books I've done with the company. Bravo! And onward, Silhouette, to the new millennium."

—*New York Times* bestselling author
Heather Graham Pozzessere

"Twenty years of laughter and love... It's not hard to imagine Silhouette Books celebrating twenty years of quality publishing, but it is hard to imagine a publishing world without it. Congratulations..."

—International bestselling author
Emilie Richards

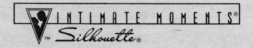

INTIMATE MOMENTS®
Silhouette®

SILHOUETTE'S 20TH ANNIVERSARY CONTEST
OFFICIAL RULES
NO PURCHASE NECESSARY TO ENTER

1. To enter, follow directions published in the offer to which you are responding. Contest begins 1/1/00 and ends on 8/24/00 (the "Promotion Period"). Method of entry may vary. Mailed entries must be postmarked by 8/24/00, and received by 8/31/00.

2. During the Promotion Period, the Contest may be presented via the Internet. Entry via the Internet may be restricted to residents of certain geographic areas that are disclosed on the Web site. To enter via the Internet, if you are a resident of a geographic area in which Internet entry is permissible, follow the directions displayed on-line, including typing your essay of 100 words or fewer telling us "Where In The World Your Love Will Come Alive." On-line entries must be received by 11:59 p.m. Eastern Standard time on 8/24/00. Limit one e-mail entry per person, household and e-mail address per day, per presentation. If you are a resident of a geographic area in which entry via the Internet is permissible, you may, in lieu of submitting an entry on-line, enter by mail, by hand-printing your name, address, telephone number and contest number/name on an 8"x 11" plain piece of paper and telling us in 100 words or fewer "Where In The World Your Love Will Come Alive," and mailing it via first-class mail to: Silhouette 20th Anniversary Contest, (in the U.S.) P.O. Box 9069, Buffalo, NY 14269-9069; (In Canada) P.O. Box 637, Fort Erie, Ontario, Canada L2A 5X3. Limit one 8"x 11" mailed entry per person, household and e-mail address per day. On-line and/or 8"x 11" mailed entries received from persons residing in geographic areas in which Internet entry is not permissible will be disqualified. No liability is assumed for lost, late, incomplete, inaccurate, nondelivered or misdirected mail, or misdirected e-mail, for technical, hardware or software failures of any kind, lost or unavailable network connection, or failed, incomplete, garbled or delayed computer transmission or any human error which may occur in the receipt or processing of the entries in the contest.

3. Essays will be judged by a panel of members of the Silhouette editorial and marketing staff based on the following criteria:

   Sincerity (believability, credibility)—50%

   Originality (freshness, creativity)—30%

   Aptness (appropriateness to contest ideas)—20%

   Purchase or acceptance of a product offer does not improve your chances of winning. In the event of a tie, duplicate prizes will be awarded.

4. All entries become the property of Harlequin Enterprises Ltd., and will not be returned. Winner will be determined no later than 10/31/00 and will be notified by mail. Grand Prize winner will be required to sign and return Affidavit of Eligibility within 15 days of receipt of notification. Noncompliance within the time period may result in disqualification and an alternative winner may be selected. All municipal, provincial, federal, state and local laws and regulations apply. Contest open only to residents of the U.S. and Canada who are 18 years of age or older, and is void wherever prohibited by law. Internet entry is restricted solely to residents of those geographical areas in which Internet entry is permissible. Employees of Torstar Corp., their affiliates, agents and members of their immediate families are not eligible. Taxes on the prizes are the sole responsibility of winners. Entry and acceptance of any prize offered constitutes permission to use winner's name, photograph or other likeness for the purposes of advertising, trade and promotion on behalf of Torstar Corp. without further compensation to the winner, unless prohibited by law. Torstar Corp and D.L. Blair, Inc., their parents, affiliates and subsidiaries, are not responsible for errors in printing or electronic presentation of contest or entries. In the event of printing or other errors which may result in unintended prize values or duplication of prizes, all affected contest materials or entries shall be null and void. If for any reason the Internet portion of the contest is not capable of running as planned, including infection by computer virus, bugs, tampering, unauthorized intervention, fraud, technical failures, or any other causes beyond the control of Torstar Corp. which corrupt or affect the administration, secrecy, fairness, integrity or proper conduct of the contest, Torstar Corp. reserves the right, at its sole discretion, to disqualify any individual who tampers with the entry process and to cancel, terminate, modify or suspend the contest or the Internet portion thereof. In the event of a dispute regarding an on-line entry, the entry will be deemed submitted by the authorized holder of the e-mail account submitted at the time of entry. Authorized account holder is defined as the natural person who is assigned to an e-mail address by an Internet access provider, on-line service provider or other organization that is responsible for arranging e-mail address for the domain associated with the submitted e-mail address.

5. Prizes: Grand Prize—a $10,000 vacation to anywhere in the world. Travelers (at least one must be 18 years of age or older) or parent or guardian if one traveler is a minor, must sign and return a Release of Liability prior to departure. Travel must be completed by December 31, 2001, and is subject to space and accommodations availability. Two hundred (200) Second Prizes—a two-book limited edition autographed collector set from one of the Silhouette Anniversary authors: Nora Roberts, Diana Palmer, Linda Howard or Annette Broadrick (value $10.00 each set). All prizes are valued in U.S. dollars.

6. For a list of winners (available after 10/31/00), send a self-addressed, stamped envelope to: Harlequin Silhouette 20th Anniversary Winners, P.O. Box 4200, Blair, NE 68009-4200.

Contest sponsored by Torstar Corp., P.O. Box 9042, Buffalo, NY 14269-9042.

ENTER FOR
A CHANCE TO WIN*
Silhouette's 20th Anniversary Contest

Tell Us Where in the World
You Would Like *Your* Love To Come Alive...
And We'll Send the Lucky Winner There!

Silhouette wants to take you wherever
your happy ending can come true.

Here's how to enter: Tell us, in 100 words or less,
where you want to go to make your love come alive!

In addition to the grand prize, there will be 200
runner-up prizes, collector's-edition book sets
autographed by one of the Silhouette anniversary
authors: **Nora Roberts, Diana Palmer,
Linda Howard** or **Annette Broadrick**.

DON'T MISS YOUR CHANCE TO WIN!
ENTER NOW! No Purchase Necessary

Silhouette®
Where love comes alive™

Visit Silhouette at www.eHarlequin.com to enter, starting this summer.

Name:

Address:

City: _____ State/Province:

Zip/Postal Code:

Mail to Harlequin Books: **In the U.S.**: P.O. Box 9069, Buffalo, NY,
14269-9069; **In Canada**: P.O. Box 637, Fort Erie, Ontario, L4A 5X3